C000060512

E. M. Kkoulla

Wrath of Olympus

Ships of Britannia

Book 1

Copyright © 2020 E.M. Kkoulla

All rights reserved, including the right to reproduce this book, or portions thereof in any form. No part of this text may be reproduced, transmitted, downloaded, decompiled, reverse engineered, or stored, in any form or introduced into any information storage and retrieval system, in any form or by any means, whether electronic or mechanical without the express written permission of the author.

This is a work of fiction. Names and characters are the product of the author's imagination and any resemblance to actual persons, living or dead, is entirely coincidental.

The views expressed in this work are solely those of the author and do not necessarily reflect the views of the publisher, and the publisher hereby disclaims any responsibility for them.

ISBN: 9798566666396

PublishNation
www.publishnation.co.uk

*For Jane, who's been with Maia and me
every step of the way.*

Place names with their modern equivalents.

Londin, abbreviated form of Londinium, - London

Portus – Portsmouth

Noviomagus – Chichester

Isca – Exeter

Dumnovaria – Dorchester

Isles of Sillina – Isles of Scilly

Hibernia- Ireland

Caledonia / Pictland – Scotland

New Colonias – South Eastern USA

New Roma - Florida

New Eboracum – Petersburg, Virginia, USA

Vinland – North-Eastern USA

Neapolis – Naples

The Northern Alliance – Scandinavia and Iceland, plus parts of Northern Germany and the Baltic States

I

It was only the ninth hour of the morning and her mistress was already in a foul mood. Maia could hear the sound of objects hitting the walls of the bedchamber and knew that Marcia Blandina wouldn't be satisfied with simply destroying her surroundings.

She glanced over at the cook. Chloe was arranging her mistress' breakfast on a tray and studiously avoiding eye contact. Another, louder crash from upstairs caused both women to raise their heads.

"You'd better take this now," Chloe said. The look of dull suffering on her face spoke volumes and Maia knew that hers held the same expression. The chains that bound the cook's ankles clinked as she turned to offer the tray and the large bruise up the left side of her face came into view. It had faded over the past fortnight, but still stood out as a yellow mass against her pale skin. Their mistress didn't take kindly to her slaves answering back and Chloe had learned the hard way. Maia had only been there a week and was still learning. As an indentured servant, supplied via the Foundling Home in Portus, she was worth less than a cook and far easier to replace.

"I wish you could just poison her and have done," she said. Chloe cringed.

"The Adepts would find out and then I'd end up in the arena as the opening act, along with the rest of the murderers."

She was right. The scientist-healers had their own methods of determining causes of death and something as obvious as poison would be picked up on immediately. That would mean certain torture and death, possibly for all of them.

"Pity." Maia lifted the tray and made her way out through the service area to the backstairs. She wished that they had a dumb waiter installed so that the food could just be sent up, but no such luck. Marcia Blandina liked her servants to be visible, all the better to see the fear in their eyes.

1

The noise had stopped for now, replaced by a heavy silence that didn't bode well. Maia reached the top of the stairs and shoved open the door that led into the main part of the house. The dirty, cracked plaster and bare wooden boards immediately gave way to smooth, decorated walls and an expensive rug ran down the centre of the landing. Maia balanced the tray on one hip and walked down the floor to the side. Stepping on the carpet was expressly forbidden and would earn her a beating at the very least.

She winced as the tray caught her arm. It was still sore where her mistress had jabbed her with a hairpin two days previously.

The door was partially open, but there was no sign of Flora, Blandina's personal slave. The woman would probably be in hiding and doubtless sporting several new bruises. The Gods alone knew what minor infraction had enraged her mistress this time; nothing that would have been of any consequence to a sane person. Maia wished she were a million miles away, but, like the others, she had no choice.

She pushed the door open a crack, to try and give herself some warning. Blandina was lying on a couch examining her face in a mirror, turning it this way and that as she searched for new wrinkles. She turned as the door opened, her jewelled earrings winking in the light and arched her skilfully painted brows.

"Put it down and clear that mess up."

Maia scuttled over, placing the tray on a small inlaid table and trying to keep as far away as possible. She picked up a metal basin and ewer, together with another tray and a lamp which were now marred by large dents. Blandina hadn't thrown any of her glass vials full of expensive perfumes, she noticed. She was wondering whether to take them away, or replace them in their positions, when Blandina noticed her momentary dither.

"Give them to Xander," she snapped. "I want new ones by tonight."

She started to pick at the assortment of dishes. Maia balanced the damaged objects carefully and started for the door as fast as she could.

"Wait."

The command froze her in her tracks.

"You were talking to that boy. The one that delivers the fish."

There was no use in denying it. The woman was quieter than a cat when she wanted to be and her chief delight was spying on her household.

"Yes, mistress."

"What did you say to him?"

"He only said that he'd not seen me before, mistress. I told him I'm new here."

"Hmm. Fetch my hairbrush."

Maia was forced to put down her load down. She tried to be careful but the basin slipped from her fingers and clattered on the floor with a ringing that seemed to last forever.

"Ah! My ears! You stupid girl!" Blandina screamed at her. Her face showed no distress; quite the opposite. Her eyes danced with evil glee at the thought that it was time to mete out punishment. "You're not only small and ugly, but witless and incompetent too! I'll have to beat some sense into you, you good-for-nothing chit!"

She snatched a supple wooden cane from the side of the couch. Maia could only watch in horror as her mistress leapt up and began whipping it across her unprotected shoulders. She tried to stay silent, but the stinging pain made her yelp and raise her arms to protect herself. The cane clanged off the jug she was still holding until Blandina dropped the weapon and twisted Maia's wrist until she let the jug fall. Maia couldn't stop her scream, receiving a back handed blow in return that knocked her to the ground in a heap. Blandina's fine leather slippers filled her vision and a sudden blow to her side told her she'd been kicked. She scrabbled across the floor, dragging at the rug in her haste to get out of range and gasping for breath.

"Tell Flora I want to see her now," Blandina said conversationally, watching her squirm with avid eyes.

Maia dragged herself to her feet and took off at a run.

"And don't you dare tread on the rug!"

The screech followed her down the landing.

Maia's upper body hurt all over and she had a sharp pain in her ribs. She hoped they weren't broken as there was no chance that Blandina would let her be seen by an Adept. On the surface, at least, this was the respectable house of a wealthy widow, not the home of a woman who wasn't fit to keep a dog. She wished for the umpteenth time that her last placement had lasted longer. The work had been hard, non-stop from morning until night, but at least there hadn't been abuse. Her master had died and the household broken up. It was her bad luck to end up here, just as it had been her bad luck to be abandoned as a baby.

If she'd had the energy, she would have railed at her fate but it could have been worse. She could have been born a slave, bearing the mark that singled her out as property to be bought and sold on the open market like an animal. So much for the Great and Mighty Roman Empire, she thought bitterly. It hadn't done anything for the likes of her and Chloe. Thus it was in Britannia, for over twelve hundred years.

She made her way back to the kitchen, cradling her side as best she could. Xander, the gardener-cum-handyman was talking in low tones to Chloe as she entered. Both started in horror at her appearance.

"You're bleeding," he said to her. Chloe wrung out a rag and began to dab gently at her face. Maia hadn't realised that she had a cut on her cheek. She must have been caught by one of Blandina's rings. It was hard to distinguish one hurt from another when she had so many.

"So, she's started on you now," Xander said, angrily. "I swear, one day I'm going to give her a taste of her own medicine!"

Chloe's eyes widened in alarm. "Shush! She'll hear you! There's nothing we can do."

"Taurus, from the bakers, told me that word was she poisoned her husband for his money," he continued, ignoring her. "I believe him. The Adepts don't know everything."

"You can't prove that," Chloe said wearily. "Wasn't he old?"

"So what? They said it was a stroke. Evil magic, more like. She probably got the Daughters of Hecate to put a curse on him."

"You mustn't say that," Chloe insisted.

"Why? What will she do? Sell me?"

"No, she'll chain you in the cellar, then beat and starve you," Chloe told him. "I've been here longer than you and I know things."

Xander frowned.

"What do you mean?"

"You think she works alone? You've seen the Cyclops. Who do you think she gets to do her dirty work?"

They both stared at her dumbly. The Cyclops guarded the door, a great brute of a man with one eye, hence his nickname. He rarely spoke and Maia avoided him as much as possible. She hated the way he leered at her whenever they met.

"Believe me," Chloe went on. "You've only been here a month. I've lasted two years and I think it's only because she likes my cooking. People disappear round here. Take the two girls before you, Maia. Blandina told us they ran away."

She lowered her voice to a whisper.

"I think she murdered them."

Maia felt her stomach lurch. She'd seen the look on her mistress' face. It would be so easy for her to lose control and go too far. Suddenly, she remembered her errand.

"Oh no! I was supposed to tell Flora the mistress wants her."

All three of them cocked their heads, listening instinctively for any signs of displeasure from above.

"I'll get her," Xander offered. "It's a pity we can't all go armoured, like one of the old legionaries. That'd make her think twice about raising a hand to us. I swear, she has less conscience than a harpy!"

He left to find the maid and Maia didn't envy Flora. She'd only been bought two months ago.

They would all be lucky if they lasted the year.

*

Several days later, Maia was on her hands and knees scrubbing the mosaic floor in the entrance hall when she felt that she was being watched.

She gave no sign that she'd noticed, trying to catch a glimpse of her surroundings without making it obvious. It was probably that Cyclops, leaning on the doorframe and watching her work. Well, she wouldn't give him the satisfaction of letting him see how much he frightened her. She worked hard, applying herself to the dirtier spots, trying to finish as soon as she could, so that she wouldn't have to be anywhere he might be. It was her worst nightmare that he would have the chance to get her alone.

5

Finally, she could stand the suspense no longer and straightened up for a good look. If it was the Cyclops, she could always throw the bucket at him and leg it.

To her surprise, there was nobody there. A shiver ran down her spine. Perhaps the place was haunted?

As she worked, she reviewed her options. Blandina hadn't summoned her for a while, perhaps to allow time for her injuries to heal before she inflicted new ones. The woman must know that questions would be asked if she ran through too many girls, though she wouldn't put it past old Varus, the Overseer of the Home, to turn a blind eye, as long as it benefitted his pocket. He made a pretty penny selling their indentures to the highest bidders. Now there was another hypocrite who prided himself on being a pillar of the local community.

A pox on them all, she thought fiercely. Perhaps she could approach the local polismen?

As if they'd believe her. It would be Blandina's word against hers, so that option was out unless she could somehow find where the bodies were buried, but that was impossible. She still had over two and a half years of her servitude left to run and the end seemed a very long time away.

The slaves were in an even worse position. Theirs was a life sentence, with little chance of escape.

Feet entered her line of vision. Flora.

"She wants to see you in the morning room," the girl told her. Maia stared at her, noting that her face was unmarked. Unlike her, Flora attended her mistress when her friends came to call, so Blandina made sure that the marks didn't show, though the girl's red-rimmed eyes told another story.

"Is she in a mood?" Maia asked as she hauled herself to her feet. The floor would have to do for now.

"When isn't she?" Flora replied, her northern vowels rough. "I pray daily that the Gods will strike her down, but what can you do?"

They exchanged a look of sympathy.

"Perhaps one will hear you," Maia said. Flora's mouth twisted.

"Why should they hear us? We're not really Roman, are we, for all that many of us have Roman names? There's no God of slaves to help us. At least you're free born."

She was right, of course. It was no wonder that some resorted to older, darker ways, conjuring ancient spirits in the night. If she'd known of any, she would have seriously considered it.

"Yes, free born. For all the good it's doing me," she replied. "I'd better go."

She hurried to the kitchen to dispose of the dirty water, before setting off to face her mistress.

*

Blandina's morning room as she called it, because it faced the east, had previously been her husband's office but there was little evidence of the man now. Only a few shelves remained, where he would have kept his account books. Everything else had been stripped out and replaced with items that suited his widow. Maia had the impression that she enjoyed occupying the space that had previously been off limits to her. She screwed up her courage and crept through the door, taking up her position just inside. Blandina was standing in the middle of the room holding a small silver box in one hand.

Maia lowered her head, peering through her lashes. It wouldn't do to take her eyes off the woman for an instant.

"My pearl and ruby earrings are missing," Blandina announced. "They were in this box and now they're gone."

Maia said nothing.

"Flora says she put them in here."

Maia remained silent. She'd not been asked a question and she had no intention of answering unless she had to.

Blandina stepped forward.

"I think they've been stolen," she said slowly, her eyes fixed on Maia. "Now, who's new to the household and might have a liking for pretty things?"

"It wasn't me, ma'am," Maia replied firmly.

"Really? It wasn't you? So, if I ordered your bed to be searched, nothing would be found, would it?"

7

"Nothing I put there, ma'am," Maia answered, warning bells clanging in her mind. It was clear that her mistress was looking for an excuse. What better reason to beat a servant, or worse, than to prove that she was guilty of stealing?

"You deny it?" Blandina said, lightly.

"I do, ma'am. I've never seen that box before and I have no idea where you keep your earrings."

"You filthy liar!"

The sudden scream made Maia jump.

"You stole them and now you have the nerve to be insolent! You deserve everything you're going to get!"

Before Maia could react, Blandina tossed the box to one side and covered the distance between them in three strides. She yanked on Maia's hair, forcing her head back and making her cry out in pain.

Maia tried to twist away, but her scalp felt like it was on fire. Blandina's face was flushed with rage, her eyes wide and showing the whites all around. All she needed was a nest of serpents for hair and she would have doubled for Medusa. Then her hands shot to Maia's throat, crushing it in strong fingers and cutting off her air as the taller woman began slowly and surely to throttle her.

Maia's lungs burned as she felt her vision tunnelling into blackness. She was going to die and be disposed of like the others, shoved into an unmarked hole in the dead of night by a grinning Cyclops. She clawed at the other woman's face, but her arms weren't long enough to reach and she could feel herself growing weaker.

Abruptly, the pressure ceased. Maia gratefully dragged in a huge, painful breath, her lungs heaving as she tried to suck in as much oxygen as possible. What had happened?

Blandina was hurtling away from her, doubled over at the waist, for all the world as if someone had pulled her off Maia and was dragging her backwards. Faster and faster across the room she sped, her feet lifting off the floor as something unseen forced her towards the glass-paned doors that led to the central courtyard. Her scream rose to a howl as she crashed through them, shards of wood and glass tearing into her skin.

Maia, still coughing, ran after her. The woman skidded across the gravel path, before landing in an ungainly heap at the base of one of the statues that adorned the walkway. Her head lifted in bewilderment and she raised an arm as if pleading for help.

As Maia stared, a violent gust of wind erupted into the courtyard, ripping at bushes and scattering flower petals. Blandina turned her head at a loud crack, but it was too late. Ancient mortar failed as a statue toppled majestically from its plinth and crushed the prostrate woman.

Maia was rooted to the spot, unable to take her eyes off the scene. The statue lay in broken pieces, but the damage was done.

The scream came out of nowhere. For a confused moment, Maia wondered how her mistress could still make a noise before realising that it was coming from behind her. She swung round. Flora's mouth was open wide as she took in the scene and her eyes met Maia's, filled with fear. Maia tried to speak, but broke off in a bout of coughing. Her throat was so sore she could barely swallow.

"You," Flora whimpered, her eyes like saucers. "You killed her!"

Maia shook her head frantically. "No, it was-"

Flora just screamed even louder. All the commotion would bring others and soon she would have to try and explain the inexplicable. Then it would be a lingering death in the arena for her.

She snapped herself out of her stupor. The strange wind had vanished as suddenly as it came, leaving only the ruined garden as evidence of its passing, but she couldn't rely on that defence. There was only one option.

She ran.

There was no way that she could get out the front, not with the Cyclops lying in wait, so she shot to the kitchens. Chloe had been alerted by the noise and she was grateful that Xander wasn't around.

"What's happened?" the cook asked. "Who's screaming?"

"Blandina's dead," she said, grabbing a loaf of bread and some cheese from the pantry. Chloe watched her in bewilderment. On the way out, she snatched her cloak, her other set of clothes and a blanket from the cubby hole she slept in, wrapping the lot in the coarse material. She owned nothing else of value and time was what mattered now.

She ignored Chloe's stammered questions. She'd find out what happened soon enough and it was more important to save her own skin.

The back door, used for deliveries and the household's comings and goings was, by some miracle, unlocked for once. She thanked whichever Gods were listening that she didn't have to shin up a tree and over the wall as she'd feared and dashed out into the lane that ran at the rear of the property. It was deserted, so she hurried as fast as she could, before forcing herself to slow and adjust her bundle. Nothing alerted people more than someone running.

Fortunately, the day was cool enough to warrant her cloak and it had even started to drizzle, so she pulled up the hood and made her way into Portus proper, just another servant girl out on an errand for her mistress.

Now she had to find somewhere to hide.

*

"You're sure nothing's been moved?"

The young Mage fixed the polis sergeant with a piercing glance. The man stared back at him stolidly.

"No, sir. It's as we found it."

Jackdaw nodded, looking around at the mess. The plants and hedges lay shredded on the torn ground, their roots exposed, whilst pots and ornaments lay smashed in pieces. Even the carefully trained fruit trees had been ripped from the walls. It was if a mad bull had been on a rampage.

To his left, the City Prefect was in earnest conversation with two other polismen who were busy taking notes. This was a high profile death. The woman was rich and had important friends throughout the city so the pressure would be on to provide answers as quickly as possible. If it wasn't for the rest of the damage, it might have been written off as an unlucky accident, but the total devastation spoke of something else that wasn't as easy to explain away. He sidled over to where his friend and colleague, Scabious, was examining the body, gently moving the chunks of statuary to one side as he worked.

"Find anything?"

The Adept glanced up. "She's definitely dead."

Jackdaw rolled his eyes. "Why do you always have to say that? I would have thought it was obvious."

"Not necessarily," Scabious sniffed. "There are many states that mimic death."

"Yes, but then you wouldn't be able to examine a corpse."

Scabious grinned. "True. I prefer my patients to lie still and not wince every time I approach them with a sharp instrument. That's not to say they can't tell me all about themselves nonetheless." He grinned happily.

Jackdaw peered over Scabious' shoulder.

"Crushed?"

"And there's extensive damage from being chucked through the doors, then dragged along the path. Nasty. Mercury here finished her off nicely. What about you?"

Scabious rocked back on his heels and looked expectantly at his friend. They made a good team, investigating crimes for the Portus Polis, which suited both of them. Jackdaw regarded the statue's arm, broken off at the shoulder but still holding its caduceus. The wand was bloodied where it had come into contact with Marcia Blandina's head.

"I suspect it's more a matter for the Priests," Jackdaw said, sourly. He hated it when he had to give up his authority on a case. "Getting smashed on the head by a God is more in their line of work."

"You can't sense any Potentia, then?"

Jackdaw made a face. "Human Potentia and Divine Potentia are largely differentiated by degree. If it's human Potentia, then there was a lot of it and we need to find the person responsible as soon as possible. If it was Divine, then we're back to needing a Priest. I've not heard of anyone coming forward to claim responsibility."

"True," Scabious admitted. "If this had been Divine vengeance there would have been a parade of happy clerics outside, all trumpeting the glory of their deity."

11

"That would guarantee a steady flow of offerings," Jackdaw agreed. "Instead – nothing.

That's weird."

"Weird's the word," Scabious said cheerfully. "My report will be simpler, though I'll need a better look at her. The witness says she was pulled backwards by an unseen power. If it was something material that seized her, there should be marks of some sort. If not, being immaterial, it's out of my sphere."

"Great," Jackdaw muttered.

"I still recommend dumping it on the temples. Unless you can sense a trace of magical Potentia?"

Jackdaw shook his head. "It wasn't a Mage, if that's what you mean. I'm hoping it wasn't a rogue. They'd have to be pretty powerful to do this." He sighed. "There's no sense in speculating, though the Prefect won't be happy if we can't wrap this up nicely with a big bow on it, just for him."

They both glanced over at Placidianus. The two men he'd been talking to hurried off purposefully, leaving his gaze to fall upon them. He made a beeline for the pair, his expression hopeful.

"You can talk to him," Jackdaw muttered. Scabious started to frown, then thought better of it as his superior approached.

"Well, gentlemen?" Placidianus began without preamble. His hair was thinning, Jackdaw noticed, despite the artfully teased locks. He'd be as bald as Caesar before too long. The Prefect fancied himself as a man about town, though Jackdaw thought he looked more like a horse with indigestion.

"I'll need to take a closer look at her back at the station, sir," Scabious said.

Placidianus gave his usual sniff. "Is that really necessary? Her friends would rather this was cleared up quickly."

"I need to determine what did this," Scabious explained patiently. "It's looking like a deity could have been involved, though the only witness seems to think it was as a result of human Potentia."

Placidianus sniffed again. "Ah, the slave girl. Yes, well, she's hardly in any fit state to give rational testimony. Jackdaw, what do you think?"

"It wasn't a Mage," Jackdaw replied. "My bet would be a deity of some sort – a very angry one by the looks of things."

"Then we should inform the Priests and hand things over to them."

"Sir?" It was the sergeant, emerging from the house. He was usually unflappable, but something had got him rattled.

"Yes, Grumio?"

"We've arrested the slaves. Some of them are showing signs of mistreatment. The cook was shackled and covered with bruises and the maid too." He lowered his voice. "There might have been some funny business going on."

Jackdaw and Scabious exchanged glances. This was going to be anything but a clear-cut case.

"Do we have all the staff?" Placidianus asked.

"All but one. There was a girl from the Foundling Home but she ran off. The maid says that the victim was throttling her when all this happened. She made a habit of it, apparently. There might be other bodies hidden somewhere. She also mentioned that the doorkeeper might know more than he's saying."

Placidianus sighed and raised his eyes to the skies.

"Ye Gods! I take it nobody suspected?"

Grumio shook his head.

"Right. Get a description of this girl. We'll make finding her a priority. Take the slaves down to the station and have them questioned under magical compunction immediately. Jackdaw, I'll leave that to you. Keep the cordon up and send to the Temple of Mercury to see if they can shed any light on this. Scabious, can we move the body?"

The Adept rose and brushed the dirt from his robe, his dark eyes troubled.

"Yes, sir. I've learned all I can here."

"Very well. Grumio, I'll put you in charge of the hunt for the girl. Carry on, gentlemen."

They nodded respectfully and watched as the Prefect made a hasty exit. It was going to be a very long day. Grumio ambled off to shout at some juniors to move the corpse, whilst Scabious deftly packed his instruments away in their case.

"I'll send a message to the temple," Jackdaw said, glumly. "I've got the feeling that we've just uncovered a big can of worms. I hate questioning under compunction."

"Got to be done," Scabious told him, not without sympathy. "Now you know why I prefer working with the dead."

He looked down at the battered corpse.

"Right, ma'am. Let's get you moved so we can have a proper conversation."

"And that's not creepy at all," Jackdaw commented sourly.

*

The landlord of The Anchor was a bald man with a bushy beard and a skin weathered like old oak from a life at sea. He looked Maia up and down.

"I could do with the help," he said after a time, "but the work's hard. You might do better up the street at Mistress Vera's place. She's never short of custom."

Maia knew what he meant and shook her head vigorously. She tried to keep the desperation out of her eyes, but after three days hiding in an abandoned shed, she was starving and this was the sixth place she'd tried. He nodded slowly.

"All right then. I can't pay you much, but you can sleep in the attic if you want."

Seeing her hopeful expression, he softened slightly.

"You can start straight away. There are floors to scrub, pots to wash and latrines to swill. I hope you're good at ducking as well; we have fights here on a regular basis."

"I'll manage."

"Right then."

He smiled, showing blackened stumps. "My name's Casca and I own the place. I was at sea for over twenty-five years before I settled down and I served on some damn fine Ships."

For a few seconds he was far away, back out in the oceans of his past.

"Now I serve ale and bore folks with old stories." He looked around. "Max? Max! Oh, here he is." An amiable round-faced youth appeared from the yard at the back. "This here's..., what's your name, girl?"

"Dilys," she supplied quickly.

"Dilys. Show her where to stay, will you? There's a good lad. Max is my pot boy," he explained. "Well, off you go upstairs and dump your stuff, then I'll see you back here. There's always plenty to do."

"Thank you, Casca."

She followed Max with a growing sense of relief. Now all she had to do was to keep her head down, work hard and see what life had in store for her.

At least it wouldn't include Blandina.

She was safer in Portus. It was the only place she knew and she would be one more anonymous girl in the mass of locals, sailors and transient visitors that frequented the busy south coast harbour. She hadn't seen anything to show that she was a wanted fugitive. Perhaps Flora had kept her mouth shut, or hadn't been believed but, whatever the cause, she was grateful she'd escaped with her life. She still had a ring of bruises around her neck from the woman's fingers and had had to rip off the hem of her cloak to use as a makeshift scarf to hide them.

Casca was right. The work was hard, backbreaking and smelly. There were frequent calls to clean up spills and the aftermath of too much drink but she bore it all with good grace, ever mindful that it was an improvement on a hastily dug hole in the ground.

She wasn't sorry that Blandina was dead – the woman had got what she deserved. What she didn't understand was how it had happened. Flora had blamed her, but she knew that she hadn't done anything. She'd been too busy trying to breathe. She ran over every detail in her memory, seeing her mistress flying through the air. Had there been faint, transparent arms circling her waist from behind, or had she imagined it? The mind could play tricks, especially after witnessing something so traumatic.

She was no nearer understanding it now, even after several days had passed.

Over the next fortnight, Maia quickly got into her new routine. The Anchor was usually full, having a good reputation for its ale and catering to sailors on shore leave as well as a few locals. A few upstairs rooms were rented out as a side line, mostly to travelling businessmen. When it was quieter, Casca liked to share a drink or two with some old comrades as they swapped stories of life at sea.

Maia would move nearer to listen while she scrubbed the stools, tables or floor, enjoying the tales of sandy beaches under bright blue skies, near misses with huge krakens and orcas above the endless deeps, or nights when they thought the Ship would be wrecked for sure. Former officers were remembered and toasts drunk to Ships they'd served on, the latter remembered with respect and affection. There were hair-raising tales of ghosts, curses and angry deities too. If they were all true, she reflected, then the ocean was a scary place indeed, inhabited by great beasts and the Mer-people who followed Neptune and his wife, Amphitrite. No wonder sailors needed their Ships to protect them from the terrors that lurked far from land.

Then there were the songs. All it would take was for someone to turn up with a drum or a whistle and the music would start, rough sea-shanties that had everyone stamping and clapping along to the beat. She even learned a few, though some were definitely unfit for delicate ears. She just laughed with the rest, swapping jokes and banter, until she felt that she'd come to be seen as part of the furniture. It suited her and Casca and Max kept an eye open to make sure that she wasn't bothered by customers overstepping the mark. The other barmaid, Cara, gave as good as she got and was happy to show her the ropes.

After a while, it started to feel like home and the unhappiness of the past slowly but surely started to fade.

*

A few days later, Maia was upstairs at The Anchor finishing her daily clean of the guest rooms, when she heard the conversation. Her mind was on the list of chores to be done, so at first, she took little notice until a name caught her attention.

"Marcia Blandina, yes. I remember her late husband. Can't say I ever met her."

Maia paused. The men's voices were coming from one of the rooms and she crept closer to listen.

"It's a bad business, Dog. I heard they dug up at least six bodies." That was the thin-faced, dark-haired man they called

Milo. The other would be his friend, Caniculus. They were regular visitors and rumour said they were both Agents of the Crown.

"No! Are they sure she did it?"

"That's what they're saying at the polis offices. It was a big hulking slave that disposed of the remains for her. Jackdaw put him under and got the grisly details out of him."

"He'll be for the arena, then."

"Possibly, or sent to the lead mines and worked to death."

"Too good for him. Pity his mistress wasn't found out earlier."

The voices grew louder as they emerged and Maia began to mop the corridor, keeping her head down. The two men ignored her as they passed, still speculating on the fate of someone who could only be the Cyclops.

Down in the bar, Cara was holding forth to some regulars, all agog with the news.

"And they say that the Gods struck her down themselves," she was saying with relish. "Ripped her apart, they did. They must have sent something nasty to deal with her."

"Serves her right," one old sailor said, to a chorus of agreement. He took a swig of ale. "There is some justice after all."

"Just goes to show, you never know what's happening in these places," Cara said. "I hope the ghosts of her victims were waiting for her."

Maia hoped so too. It was some consolation that they'd been found and would be put to rest with the proper rites. Perhaps that was why she'd always felt watched? At least Chloe, Xander and the others would have the chance of a better life now.

She had been the lucky one, after all.

*

The Anchor was busy this evening. Several new vessels had come in with the tide and their crews were making the most of their precious shore leave. The main bar of the tavern was crowded with sailors, all determined to get drunk as quickly as possible and the noise was deafening. A babble of different tongues hit her from all sides as she weaved her way through the throng, collecting pots to take to the kitchen and wash. Casca was busy pouring drinks as fast as he could, his hands gripping multiple pots as he emptied the large kegs lined up at the back of the bar. His bald head gleamed with sweat, but he was grinning through his huge bushy beard. Business was good.

Maia managed to duck under an outstretched arm, wishing that its owner had gone to the baths first, when shouts alerted her. Two men were facing off against each other and she knew that there'd be a fight. This wasn't unusual by any means and Casca kept a stout club behind the bar as a precaution. He wasn't averse to cracking heads if needed.

The noise died down as the other customers stopped so watch so she could hear what the argument was about.

"Your Captain is a braggart and a fool!"

The speaker, a tall, rangy Northman with fair, braided hair half way down his back, was jeering in the face of a swarthy man dressed in the uniform of His Majesty's Navy. There were several Ships in Portus, so she couldn't tell which one he belonged to.

"What would you know of good Captains, you barbarian scum?" the navy man bellowed. His mates grabbed him, whispering urgently in his ear. The treaty with the Northern Alliance was only a couple of years old and they clearly didn't want any trouble.

The Northerner smiled, white teeth flashing in the smoky gloom.

"Your Ships, now. Why do you use women, instead of great and powerful spirits like us? I tell you, they aren't fit to haul garbage!"

Sneering at an officer was one thing, but no sailor would stand by and allow his Ship to be insulted.

Maia heard the sudden indrawn breaths, before the Northman's head was snapped back by the first blow. Blood streamed from his nose and he staggered back into his friends, who charged forwards, yelling. The bar instantly erupted into a boiling mass of punches and kicks. Maia fled to safety as stools and tables were overturned and bodies piled up on top of each other, gouging and biting. She reckoned that the Northmen would come off worse; they were outnumbered in a foreign port and old grudges ran deep.

Casca appeared at her side.

"Trust those Northern savages to start a big fight! I've sent Max to fetch the polismen. They can break it up."

He winced as a stool missed one man's head and shattered against the wall.

"Jupiter blast them! I'm going to claim damages for this!"

They'd have to spend time banging the dents out of the metal pots, but some would be unusable after the pounding they were getting. As for the furniture, well it was a good job that there wasn't a lot of it. The Anchor specialised in ale, not food.

Strident whistles and shouts heralded the arrival of a squad of Portus' finest peacekeepers. They were well used to this, wading in with relish and emphasising their points with a few taps from their short cudgels. At last, they managed to get the warring parties separated. Men lay groaning on the floor, blood streaming from cuts and gashes and there appeared to be a few broken noses and other bones. The walking wounded soon had all the fight knocked out of them and were lined up against the wall, holding various parts of their anatomy. The tall Northman who'd started it all was unconscious on the floor, but didn't appear to be dead. He'd be missing any coin and valuables he'd had on him for sure – Casca had gone to look him over, together with anyone else who was past resisting.

"All right, Casca?"

The polis sergeant strolled over to where the landlord was just straightening up and pulling his hand out of his pocket. He was an older man, sporting an impressive set of mustachios and had a face like a belligerent bulldog.

"Sergeant Grumio." Casca nodded to the prone barbarian. "He started it. Made a very rude remark about the lads' Ship."

Grumio sucked his teeth. "Bloody idiot. Deserves all he got. I'll tell the Prefect."

He prodded the unconscious man with the toe of his boot. "The Adepts can take him. The higher-ups will let him go, more's the pity. Politics, you know. Did he throw the first punch?"

"Didn't notice," Casca said, his face innocent.

Grumio raised his eyebrows. "Right. No-one saw anything in the heat of the moment." He pulled out a battered notebook and made a few jottings before glancing round. "Not too much to sort out, I hope?"

"I've just hired some extra help," Casca replied, indicating Maia with a jerk of his head. "She's scrawny, but a good worker."

19

Grumio's eyes flickered over to her, then away again. "Right. Well, that's all for now. We might need statements later. Or we might not. Either way, we can't have a load of hairy foreign barbarians causing chaos and insulting our Ships, can we?"

"Too right, Sergeant," Casca agreed. Maia noticed some coins discreetly changing hands. The sergeant took a last look at the dismal scene and exited. Two Adepts' apprentices appeared and hastily carted the Northman away on a stretcher. He was still out cold, but would be tended to. The other injuries were mostly minor and would get seen to at the local hospitium, or a friend might patch them up if they'd already spent all their money.

Maia sighed and went to fetch a broom, hot water and cloths.

*

As soon as most of the debris was cleared, Casca left her and Cara to finish off and re-opened the bar. Patrons weren't long in reappearing. Many of them were ones who'd been in earlier, as shown by their split lips and black eyes. They all seemed quite happy, but there were no more Northmen. Maia hoped that they'd learned their lesson and would stay away in future.

"That barbarian was lucky," Casca told her. "Nobody insults our ladies like that. Even ordinary vessels are well-regarded, but crews will kill to defend a Ship's honour."

She scrubbed at the bleached boards, but the bloodstains were stubborn. It was always hard to get the worst of them out but after a while they would fade, to be replaced by others soon enough.

She retrieved a metal pot from where it had rolled against the wall and straightened up, stretching her back to get the kinks out of it. Turning, she almost bumped into Flora. Maia stood frozen, staring at her in shock and disbelief, until the maid nodded.

"Yes, it's her."

A man stepped out from one side, wearing the robes of a Mage. Before Maia could react, he spoke a word that pierced her like an arrow and she fell into oblivion.

II

She could hear a man's voice in the darkness. He sounded old, his words half-whispered as if there was no strength in him. Confused, she fought to remember where she was and what had happened. Slowly, the memory came back to her. There'd been a fight, she was clearing up and then...Flora.

The shock brought her back to her senses and she realised that she was sitting up in a hard chair. Had she fainted? She'd never fainted before.

"Ah, you're back with us at last."

It was the old man. She opened her eyes. They felt gritty, like she'd been asleep for a long time. When she tried to move, she couldn't and she could see that she was tied to the chair. The room was quite dark, with stone walls and a damp atmosphere.

"You must be wondering where you are."

She focused on him. The oldest man she'd ever seen was sitting opposite her. His Mage's robes were drawn around his sparse frame, out of which poked a head that was as wrinkled and seamed as an ancient tortoise. Thin wisps of white hair stood out from his pink scalp like a nimbus and gnarled, liver-spotted hands lay clasped in his lap. She looked into a pair of clouded blue eyes.

A circle of chalked lines surrounded her chair, with strange symbols inscribed around the edge. She stared at them blankly.

"So, we know that you are Maia Abella, approximately fifteen years old, raised in the Foundling Home here in Portus and lately indentured to one Marcia Blandina. Deceased."

His tone was light and unthreatening, but the hair stood up on the back of her head nonetheless. She remained silent, watching him.

"My name is Raven and, as you have no doubt surmised, I am a Mage. I would like you to tell me how Marcia Blandina came to meet her end."

Maia swallowed. This was it. She was doomed.

"I didn't kill her," she croaked through a dry throat. Raven raised one eyebrow.

"We have a witness who insists that you did."

It had to be Flora. There'd been no-one else around.

"She's mistaken." She lifted her chin defiantly and glared at her accuser.

"Very well," Raven said, after a moment had passed. "What happened, then?"

Maia balked. What should she say? She had the feeling that this Mage would know whether she was telling the truth or not. She decided to be honest.

"Something dragged her into the garden, like a big wind and dropped a statue on her. That's what I saw."

"Something? Did you see what it was?"

She shook her head dumbly.

"And what was Marcia Blandina doing at the time?"

A brief hope flared in Maia. Had Flora seen her being attacked?

"She accused me of stealing her earrings. When I denied it, she tried to strangle me."

He nodded, slowly.

Surely the others would have corroborated her story. They would have found Chloe bruised and in chains and Flora's body would bear marks as well. Not to mention the victims that were unearthed.

"She was a vile harpy and deserved her fate!" she said, vehemently.

"So, you were defending yourself?" he asked.

What could he mean? She frowned at him, not understanding.

"No. She was choking me to death. I tried but I couldn't."

The Mage cocked his head on one side, like his avian namesake.

"So, you're saying that it was her or you?"

"I thought I was going to die. One second, I was about to black out, the next she was flying backwards through the window. I don't know any more than that."

She heard the resignation in her voice and so did he.

"Then why did you run?"

"Flora started screaming and I knew nobody would believe me," she said dully. She felt cold and tired and her arms ached from the straps. If only she could sink into the ground and vanish! She would have struggled, but the straps were too tight.

Raven was silent for a few moments.

"I believe you," he said eventually. "You didn't mean for her to die. The question now is, did you act unconsciously, or was there an outside agency involved? Tell me, did you feel different when it happened?"

"I don't know what you mean."

"Has anything like this happened before? Have objects moved around you, or appeared out of nowhere? Can you see things, or people, that others can't? Do you hear strange voices in the air?"

She nearly laughed in his face. He was asking if she had Potentia.

"Do I look like I've Divine blood?" she said sarcastically.

"I don't know," he said, calmly. "Do you?"

So, he couldn't see her. She'd thought he might be blind.

"I'm small, thin and ugly," she told him, bitterly. "I'm nothing special. Even my own parents didn't want me. My only advantage is that I'm free born and so entitled to starve on the streets whenever I want. So, no. No Divine blood that I'm aware of."

If she'd had the strength she would have laughed in his face. The idea that she was descended from the Gods was ludicrous.

"I think you're too hard on yourself, Maia," he whispered.

"Thank you. Now, any chance I can get back to work? I'm sure that there's a pile of pots that needs washing."

"Why? Do you enjoy washing pots?" he asked.

"It's what I'm good at," she answered boldly.

"I'm sure you are. However, that may not be the only choice open to you now."

Maia rolled her eyes in frustration.

"Am I going to be charged with murder? Or do I have to sit here listening to your riddles all day?"

To her surprise, he laughed briefly.

"No, not at all. I just think you could be more gainfully employed. As we know nothing of your origins, it's entirely possible that you could possess some Potentia of which you are currently unaware. Your desperate plight could have allowed it to surface. It's clear that the woman was about to add you to her list of victims until something, or someone, intervened."

"Maybe the Fates had had enough of her?" Maia offered.

"She was a very evil woman," he said. "However, the Fates don't crush people with statues, or not overtly anyway. I am attempting to determine the author of her death."

"It wasn't me."

He was silent for a few moments and she shuddered as she felt his Potentia wash over her. The circle around her chair flared briefly. He raised his eyebrows.

"Interesting. Well, I think it's time for you to stop being treated like a criminal. I don't believe you're a danger at the moment, so we've no need for all of this."

Maia felt the great knot inside her start to relax. She wouldn't be charged and thrown in the arena after all. The straps holding her arms loosened and slithered away. She rubbed at her wrists, conscious of the red marks where she'd pulled against her bonds.

"I'm sorry that we had to put you in here," Raven said, "but we weren't sure what would happen when you woke up. You could have hurt someone else, or worse."

"Now you know I don't have any Potentia," she said. She hadn't killed Blandina, she knew that much. If she'd been able, she would have done it as soon as the woman had begun to torment her. The old Mage must be mistaken

"That remains to be seen. It's true that I can detect nothing at the moment, which is why I've released you. There will have to be further tests."

She fell silent, watching him. Maybe if they thought she could be a threat, they might treat her better? This could work to her advantage if she played the game carefully.

"You must have questions," Raven continued.

She thought quickly.

"Can I go back to The Anchor now?" A job was a job and she'd felt safe there.

Raven's eyebrows shot up.

"Good Gods, no! We can't take the risk of releasing you into the community. I don't think that you understand how dangerous

24

it could be. You'll have to be placed somewhere the authorities can keep an eye on you."

The knot in her stomach returned. She would be imprisoned until it was plain that she had no Potentia whatsoever, then she would be just kicked out to fend for herself.

She eyed the door. The Mage was old and wouldn't be able to stop her if she made a run for it.

"It's no use running. The door is locked until I say it isn't."

Could he read minds as well? She wasn't sure exactly what Mages could do, after all.

"Logical deduction," he told her. "You don't want to be kept against your will again, so escape must seem like the only option. Stick it out and, maybe, you'll be a lot better off in the long run. If not, you won't have lost anything."

She glared at him, but knew that she would have to go along with whatever was planned for her. She couldn't end up much worse off.

"Am I to be locked up?" she said.

"No, not at all. There are a number of establishments that admit young ladies and provide training for a future career. *If* you have the aptitude, you could end up as a Priestess, a midwife, or even in the Navy."

"I've had training," she told him. "In the Foundling Home. I can clean, sew and do some cooking, as well as lay fires."

He grinned at her, looking like Death himself and she shuddered. The chill of the room was seeping into her bones through her thin dress.

"I'm sure you're very good at it, but now is the time to learn new things. Come with me."

She followed the Mage out of the heavy oak door and saw that they were in a corridor. Raven moved fast for one so aged and she had to trot to keep up, his blindness seemingly no impediment. It led to offices which were filled with men in the uniform of the Portus Polis and she realised that she must have been in a cell. They stopped to stare at them both as they passed, which made her feel self-conscious and automatically guilty of something, until Raven led her through to another room, where there were couches and tables.

"Do sit down. I expect you're hungry and thirsty."

"Yes," she admitted.

"I've ordered food. There's a lavatory through that door where you can wash and relieve yourself."

He waved at a painted door opposite. She wasted no time in using the facilities and washing her face and hands. Her hair was a mess, even though she tried to comb it through with her fingers, but at least she looked better than she had. It wasn't as if she'd been able to use the public baths, as she'd been too afraid that someone would see her and recognise her. She stared at her reflection in the spotted mirror above the basin. Maia Abella, pale and thin, with grey eyes and mousy hair, who always faded into the background like a good servant should.

Nobody had ever given her a second glance, until now.

She returned to the room to find that the table was covered with plates. The Mage had helped himself to a chicken leg and gestured for her to start. It was more food than she'd seen in a long time and certainly more than she'd ever been offered before. She dived in with enthusiasm, worried that it might be taken away before she'd had a chance to do it justice.

Raven watched with approval. She still didn't trust him, though.

When she'd finally had enough, she sat back, enjoying the sensation of a full stomach. The ancient Mage had been silent through her meal but when she finished, he began again.

"Do you have any preference for your placement?"

She shook her head, before remembering that he wouldn't be able to see her. Or could he?

"No."

"I understand."

He seemed to be about to say more, when there was a knock on the door.

"Come in."

The door opened and a clerk, dressed in a naval uniform, entered. He saluted the Mage.

"Master Mage Raven. My name is Pollio and I bring you a message from the Admiralty. Captain Berwyn sends his regards and asks that you bring the potential candidate to the offices immediately."

Maia narrowed her eyes and glared at the man. What potential candidate? Her suspicions were confirmed when Raven nodded.

"Please give Captain Berwyn my compliments and tell him that we will be with him shortly."

The clerk saluted once more and exited, leaving Maia fuming.

"My apologies. It seems that the decision has already been made. The Navy have got in first."

"What was he talking about?" she demanded. "I take it he meant me?"

"He did. I was thinking that you could be apprenticed to a temple but now you're going to be evaluated as a potential Ship."

A Ship? But she'd need Potentia for that.

"I'm not suitable," she insisted. She had to make him realise what he was asking of her. She would be found out and exposed as a fraud. Her hope of pretending, until she could talk her way out of it, was fading rapidly.

"Hmm. I'm afraid I must agree with you," he said apologetically, "but the Navy is desperate these days. Come on now, we don't want to keep the Captain waiting."

Maia rolled her eyes in frustration. How on earth was she going to get out of this one? It seemed that she had only exchanged one peril for another. She quietly sent a prayer to any God who might be listening that they come to her aid, or even to confess their involvement in Blandina's death. That would let her off the hook in more ways than one.

She clutched the tiny hope like a warm coal as she followed the Master Mage once more out of the polis offices and out into the street. The fight had begun just after noon and she was shocked to see that darkness had already fallen. She must have been knocked out for longer than she had thought. The streets were emptier and the smell of tar and fish was strong, overlaid with rotting seaweed. The tide would be turning soon, carrying vessels out of the harbour mouth and away into the open sea of the Britannic Ocean. She could always tell, as if the moon pulled and pushed at her too as the sea rose and fell away, but there was no moon tonight. The land and the water had merged into darkness.

*

They didn't go too far before Maia could see the familiar outline of a tall and imposing building looming over its fellows. The Admiralty Headquarters in Portus was all fancy portico and statues of Neptune ruling the waves, with Britannia and the Roman Eagle offering tribute. She had seen it before, standing to admire the painted images and the eagle's gilded wings and watching the officials coming and going up its broad entrance steps. She expected to be ushered round the side to some unimportant little door, but no, up the steps they went, past the towering columns and in through the huge entrance doors which swung open to admit them. She wondered that Raven still moved confidently, despite his blindness. He must have another way of seeing that only Mages knew about.

The guards inside snapped to attention as Raven appeared and they crossed the atrium, their footsteps loud in the cavernous space. There were few people around, presumably because of the late hour and she took the opportunity to glance around. The floor was made of fine marble, with colourful inset mosaics depicting creatures of the sea. More reddish marble columns lined the walls on either side with corridors leading to the rest of the building and the whole area was lit with wall and ceiling lamps that burned with a steady glow. It was all very impressive, especially after the smoky tavern and dingy holes she had been forced to live in lately.

Directly facing them was a grand staircase flanked with two life-sized statues. After a second, she realised that they were figureheads, finely painted and lifelike, each holding an object, or tutela, that represented their vessels. One held a gilded and bejewelled ribbon, with another in her elaborately sculpted coiffure. The other had a little bird, its curved wings spread as if taking flight from her hand. Their faces were beautiful but stern, their draperies falling to conceal their feet. Raven came to a halt before them and waited. The one on the left suddenly turned her head and spoke.

"Master Mage, greetings! You may proceed. Third door on the right."

Maia couldn't help but stare. What she had taken for statues were actual Ships. The lettering on the speaker's sash proclaimed her to be the *Diadem*, whilst the other was the *Swiftsure*. Maia swallowed. She wondered why they were here and not on their vessels, but didn't dare ask.

"Thank you, ma'am."

The *Swiftsure* peered at Maia.

"Caught a little fish have you, Raven?" She grinned at the Master Mage. Her voice was old, despite the youthfulness of her looks and her little bird fluttered in her hand as if about to take flight.

"Possibly, ma'am," Raven replied.

Both Ships were now examining Maia. She felt small and dirty under the intensity of their gaze and impulsively dropped a quick curtsey. Civility cost nothing, as her old teacher used to say. Although the Ships' scrutiny didn't abate, she sensed a slight approval on their wooden faces.

They were admitted by a clerk, who showed them into a room panelled with old, dark oak. The same lamps burned on the wall as in the atrium and Maia marvelled at the light they gave off without any sign of smoke. Surely there had to be magic involved. Large paintings adorned the walls, showing scenes from naval history. She would have liked to study them further, but a gentle push between her shoulder blades urged her on into the room. Facing her, a large table or counter jutted out about four feet directly from the panelling, above which were two heavily curtained windows. Maia thought it strange that it was clearly designed for no-one to sit at, unless they wanted to have their backs to the room. Instead, two men were sitting to the left on separate chairs, whilst the clerk who had answered the door returned to a small desk to the right which had books, pens and an inkwell.

She could tell that one of the men was a Captain by his insignia and earring. He would be this Berwyn then. He regarded her haughtily down his long nose. He didn't seem impressed, but then again, why would he? Her clothes were already starting to tatter and her shoes had holes where the leather was gaping and worn. Her lank, tangled hair and pale eyes didn't make much of an impression on anyone either. Lately that had been to her advantage – nobody was interested in some nondescript little waif.

The other man was a Priest. His robes were plain, but she saw that he was wearing an amulet shaped like a caduceus and she had to repress a shudder. The last time she had seen one of those was when it had smashed Blandina's head. Raven moved to a third, empty chair, leaving her standing alone.

She fought the urge to fidget as the Captain scanned her, assessing every detail carefully. His expression didn't change as he beckoned her forward.

"What is your name?"

"Maia Abella, sir," she replied, clasping her hands before her so they wouldn't tremble.

"Age?"

"About fifteen, sir."

"Hmm. So you're the one that got away. Well, Master Mage, have you had time to form an opinion? Oh, and thank you for bringing her here so promptly." The Captain turned to his ancient companion who was sitting, head cocked and listening intently.

"My opinion," he said drily, "is that you should introduce ourselves and Nestor should fetch Miss Maia a chair before she falls down."

Maia noted that the Captain had the grace to look abashed and 'civility costs nothing' flashed through her mind again. She cast the old Mage a look of gratitude, before remembering that he mightn't be able to see it. Nestor hurried to do as he was bid and Maia seated herself, glad to get the weight off her feet at last.

"I am Captain Berwyn and this is Nuntius, a Priest of Mercury."

The Priest, a young, sharp-featured man with dark curly hair smiled at her.

"You must be wondering why you have been brought here," the Captain continued. "I think we should convene this meeting without further delay. Ladies, if you would join us?"

Ladies? Maia started to turn to look at the door to see who would enter, but movement to the front caught her eye. What she had taken for a table was beginning to ripple, vast eddies surging through the wood and twisting the grain as, slowly and majestically, two heads emerged; Ships travelling through the substance of the building as fish through the sea, their essence reforming using the great slab of ancient oak as their medium.

Higher and higher they rose, features becoming clear and colours emerging with more clarity and detail until she could see their shoulders, then their torsos, proudly displaying their names on their identifying sashes. They were the *Diadem* and the *Swiftsure*, the two she had seen in the atrium.

All three men stood, Captain Berwyn saluting, arm across chest and the Ships did likewise. Maia stood and curtseyed as she had before. A naughty little thought made her wonder if their arms ever ached from all this saluting.

Ships and men regarded each other for a moment before the tension in the room broke, everyone resumed their seats and an air of business took over. Maia felt the focus switch back to her and tried not to cringe under so much scrutiny. She noticed that the Ships didn't blink at all and remained unnaturally still between movements.

"Firstly, we must establish whether our efforts will be profitable." Captain Berwyn began. "Master Mage, what do you sense?"

The ancient rose and approached Maia, stopping about a foot in front of her. He raised his arms, fingers spread and spoke a word that she couldn't quite make out. There was a strange silence as the room seemed to gather its breath and the air became thick and heavy. Maia was suddenly conscious of tiny splinters of time falling in slow motion, as if through a huge hourglass. She felt dizzy, suspended on the edge of a high cliff, held up only by the pressure of an unseen wind as it swirled and gusted about her in an icy gale that seemed to rush past her. Then she was back in the room, shuddering like a frightened horse with the sound of harsh breathing in her ears. At first, she didn't realise that it was coming from her.

Raven still stood before her, his arms now down by his sides. She stared at his ravaged face, knowing with total certainty that his next words could swing her life into a new direction, an uncharted ocean. To her surprise, he frowned.

"I'm not entirely sure. I sense a faint connection, but that's all. I don't think she has any personal Potentia."

Captain Berwyn was unimpressed.

"What do you mean? Either she has Potentia or she doesn't and, if she doesn't, then we're all wasting our time."

Maia could only gape, concentrating on bringing her breathing under control and calming her racing heart after the touch of Raven's magic.

By the time she had collected herself and gathered what was left of her scattered wits, the Master Mage was seated and the clerk was at her elbow. His florid face was creased with concern as he proffered a glass of brandy.

"Here, take this. You look like you need it."

Maia took the glass with shaky hands. A sip of the fiery liquid made her cough, but she welcomed the warmth that ran down to her stomach.

"Perhaps I may be of assistance?" the Priest said. Everyone looked at him expectantly. "You're sensing something, but you're not sure what, Master Mage. Am I correct?"

"You are," Raven said cautiously.

Nuntius nodded. "I am permitted to tell you that she should be accepted for training at the Naval Academy, even though she exhibits no Potentia. I can say no more, save that the God has spoken."

Both the Captain and Raven looked surprised and, although the Ships were silent, Maia sensed that they were talking amongst themselves, despite there being no outward sign.

"But if she has no Potentia -" Berwyn began, only to be silenced by Nuntius' upraised hand.

"This is most irregular," he muttered. "How will she cope if she has nothing to draw on?"

"The God was very clear," Nuntius insisted.

"Well, we can't argue with Mercury," Raven said. He was still frowning, as if trying to work out what he was missing.

"Erm, no, not at all," the Captain blustered.

Nuntius seemed amused by his discomfiture and flashed her a wink while the Captain was gathering his thoughts.

The two Ships looked at each other. They seemed as surprised as everybody else.

"This must be confusing for you, Maia," Raven said. "We'd better explain. You know that we Mages are always on the lookout for those who have been, for whatever reason, gifted with some Divine Potentia." She nodded. "There are many applications of this, whether it be as a Priest, Mage, Adept or sundry other lesser roles, usually in the service of His Majesty's Government. Lately it has been harder to find young people with the sort of Potentia that is needed for the more, shall we say, demanding jobs. The blood of the Gods is thinning, so there are fewer and fewer candidates. This situation won't change unless Jupiter wills it, thus it is that when a possible recruit comes to our attention, we make haste to seek them out and do all we can to test them as quickly as possible."

Maia listened to him in disbelief.

"It seems that, despite testing negative, you're to be accepted as a candidate for the Service," he continued, glancing at the young Priest. "We need Ships now more than ever as the Empire expands and Britannia's influence grows. I know that great strides have been made in navigation and propulsion, but nothing beats the skill and Potentia of a living Ship, as these ladies and the Captain here can attest. They are currently awaiting brand new vessels," he added, "which is why they are temporarily land bound."

"We can't force you into this," the Captain said, "but surely you must agree that it's a better alternative to your previous situation? For one thing, the investigation into any part you might have played in your former mistress' death will be closed and no blame attached to you."

"I didn't kill her. I have no Potentia," she insisted. "I don't know what did it."

"Then you have nothing to fear," Berwyn told her.

Maia felt her world tilt. She couldn't see that she had any option but to take the offer. She took another sip of the sharp spirit to cover her confusion but how could they expect her to do the job if she didn't have the necessary requirements? Nuntius said the God Mercury had spoken and it had been a statue of him that had finally dispatched her mistress. Did that mean that he was involved? There were too many questions without answers. She plucked up her courage and turned to the Priest.

"Please, sir. Does this mean that Mercury killed Marcia Blandina?"

She'd asked the question everyone wanted the answer to.

"He did not," the Priest said. She had the feeling that he was choosing his words carefully, "but it was a form of Divine intervention nonetheless."

She looked at him hopefully, feeling a great wave of relief wash over her but he shook his head, refusing to be drawn. Raven and the Captain looked as puzzled as she did.

"So, you'll inform Prefect Placidianus of this?" Raven asked Nuntius, who nodded.

"I shall, though I fear that the investigation is not yet over. There is more to be uncovered."

It had to be more missing servants, Maia thought in horror. But if it hadn't been Mercury, then who had saved her?

"And I'm sure that the Prefect and his men are the best ones to sort that out," the Captain said hastily. "Now, Miss Abella, we need some more information. Do you know ought of your parents?"

She shook her head. "No, sir. I was called after the month when they took me in and they gave me Abella at the Home as they were back to the beginning of the alphabet. That's how they pick names, see." The boy after her had been Beric. Captain Berwyn looked disappointed.

"Perhaps something will come to light," he remarked. "You have no mark, so presumably you are free-born."

He nodded at Nestor, who scribbled a note. "It would help us if we knew something of your origins. In the meantime, I am happy to say that His Majesty's Navy is going to make you an offer of contract."

Maia felt her eyes widen, though he could hardly have refused her after Mercury's endorsement. Very few girls were chosen for the Navy. Priestesses and midwives were much more common but there were few other professions open to them.

A contract! It was certainly a better prospect than a life drudging at The Anchor, but she sensed that there would be different sacrifices to make, even if she was somewhat unclear about what would be expected of her. Ships weren't entirely human after all. She listened carefully as the Captain continued.

"You should understand that there are no guarantees that you will become a Ship. There will be years of study and some do fail but, after the proper training and if you apply yourself diligently, you too could serve."

Her eyes moved automatically to the two Ships. The *Swiftsure*'s wooden face was smiling.

"They that seek to overturn this one will come to much grief, methinks!" the Ship said gleefully. Captain Berwyn's face assumed a polite expression, but she thought the Master Mage stiffened slightly.

"As always, ma'am, you speak your mind. Thank you," the Captain said.

"Aye. Have a care for angry Gods!" She cackled at her own joke and *Diadem* rolled her eyes. Again, there was a ripple of unspoken communication moving round the room like an invisible current.

"I think it's decided, then," Raven said. "Nestor, please could you pass the contract?"

The clerk, who had stopped with his pen mid-air and mouth open, snapped his mouth shut, picked up a piece of vellum and hurried over to Maia.

"Can you read Latin?" he asked. She hesitated.

"Not much." A lot of the words were unfamiliar but fortunately Nestor was sympathetic.

"This is a standard contract committing you to a period of three years' initial training at the Naval Academy here in Portus." He glanced at her to make sure that she understood. Maia stared at the elaborate lettering, full of flourishes. The first word, whereas, was much bigger than the rest. The King's name was picked out in red, as was the date and her name. Maia didn't feel like wading through it and, really, what choice did she have? One person was already dead and though she wasn't sorry about what had happened to them, she had been terrified that she would get the blame. Now she was exonerated, she had to do something with her life.

Maybe she'd get a new pair of shoes and some decent clothes. A silly thought, but she couldn't help it. They wouldn't keep her in rags and she'd be safe and well-fed. If it didn't work out, they might find her another job. She took the clerk's pen and signed her name carefully in the place he indicated.

"Do you have a favoured God?" he asked. "We can add the name to your oath of service."

Maia shot him a look of surprise and Nuntius snorted loudly. Nestor blushed.

"Yes, of course. By Mercury, then."

Nestor took the contract, returned to his desk and began to add the relevant clauses. "With your permission, Miss Abella, I'll add the separate Neptune oath as well."

"Better had," the Captain said, crisply. "It'll cover her later, should she stay."

Directive from the God or not, he clearly wasn't convinced that she would succeed and she had to agree with him. She was beginning to feel really tired now. One step at a time, she decided. This morning she'd been elbow deep in filthy water with little hope of anything better and now she was in a warm room with a full stomach. It had to be an improvement.

*

The well-worn brass plaque on the flaky stone architrave confirmed that he had come to the right place. An iron chain hung beside it and his eyes followed it up to where it disappeared into the wall. His sharp tug set it jangling and he could hear the noise of the bell sounding within being answered by light rapid footsteps. There was a brief scuffling on the other side of the door as a key rattled in the lock and a bolt drawn back.

He adopted his most pleasant expression and tipped his hat to the young woman who peered out at him.

"Sorry to keep you waiting, sir," she said, "but all this rain's made the lock stiff."

He gave her his best smile. "Please, dear lady, do not worry yourself. My name is Milo and I'm here to see the Overseer. He should be expecting me."

Milo was not his real name – few knew that and those that did were very high up in the service of the state.

A note had been sent earlier, bearing the authority of the Collegium of Mages. The man would be probably be wetting himself wondering what it was about, as Milo knew from bitter experience what could happen behind the doors of institutions.

He'd asked around as a precaution, but apart from the usual petty skimming and expense fiddling this place seemed no worse than most and a lot better than some, though there had been a whiff of scandal lately.

"Oh yes, sir," the maid replied. "Please come this way." The girl showed him through into an atrium which led to a corridor lined with coat pegs, such as might be found in any school. Milo noted with approval that the hanging clothes didn't look too shabby. She then turned left to enter a room and he was glad to see that a fire was already laid, as the day had turned cold. The girl took a box of vestas from the mantel and struck one, applying it to the heaped kindling until a merry flame caught and danced, crackling in the stillness. She carefully added some coals until it was giving off heat.

"If you'd like to take a seat, sir, I'll tell Master Varus you're here." She curtsied and scuttled off and Milo took the opportunity to warm himself at the fireside. A low noise in the background had to be children at their lessons, he thought, repeating the teacher's words by rote. At least they were learning to read, write and count – even the girls would be taught some reading and writing skills, as well as how to perform domestic duties. Memory beckoned, but he thrust it away and settled patiently into a chair to wait. Patience was a necessity in his line of work.

It wasn't long before heavier footsteps outside heralded the arrival of a short, plump man in a thick woollen coat. His round face was flushed and his cap slightly askew, which confirmed Milo's suspicions as to the effects of the message. He broke into an ingratiating smile as his beady eyes lit on his visitor.

Milo disliked him instantly.

"My dear sir, welcome to the Home for Foundlings and Orphans. I am Arfon Varus, the Overseer. All the little darlings are in my charge, so they are. I stand ready to assist the Collegium in any way, yes, I do, of course. Pray, sir, would you care for some refreshments? Letty! Bring us some wine and cakes!"

Milo managed to get a word in. "Most kind, sir, but I don't want to keep you from your duties for too long."

"Not at all, Master, not at all. I am only too happy to help with anything that is required, only too happy indeed." He paused, looking at Milo expectantly.

"I am Agent Milo. My master simply needs some information about one of your former pupils." Varus' fixed smile didn't change. "I take it that you keep proper records?"

Varus was all too eager to agree. "Oh yes, Agent Milo. All proper and correct. Everything about each little treasure entrusted to us. Now, which of them is it?"

"Maia Abella. She left your charge and went into service about two years ago. You placed her again recently."

The Overseer's smile faded. They both knew where she had been placed and what the outcome had been. Milo knew the Overseer had already been questioned at the Polis Offices, but there was no proof that he'd known what was going on. The one-eyed slave was another matter. The questioning under compunction had led them to the bodies and the man was going to be executed at the start of the next Games. It was just a pity his mistress couldn't meet the same fate. Varus had wriggled out of it due to his connections and, being free, couldn't be compelled. The very least he'd done was to turn a blind eye for money.

"Oh, yes. Maia Abella. Quiet little thing. Biddable enough and a good worker, but nothing out of the ordinary as I recall. No family that we knew of – no token left for later, like some. I have a good memory for these things, I do. Been here near on thirty years." He cast a worried glance at Milo. "That's all that springs to mind I'm afraid."

Milo fixed him with a sharp eye. "That's a pity. My master was wanting information."

Varus shrugged. "I'm sorry, but she came to us anonymously, as most of them do."

"Is there anyone else who might know more?"

"Alas, no. She was naught but a babe."

Letty returned with the cakes, but Milo declined. "Some wine, then?" Varus offered.

He accepted a cup of thin wine, warmed with spices. If there was better, it would be in the Overseer's private quarters. He wouldn't want to appear too affluent before guests.

"I sincerely regret I can't be more helpful," Varus insisted. "Please give your master my compliments. If anything does turn up, I shall be sure to send the information to him immediately. May I ask his name?"

"Master Mage Raven," replied Milo and sat back to enjoy the sudden coughing fit as Varus choked on his cake. His master's reputation was often useful, though he usually wielded it more subtly. If there was anything else to be found out, Varus surely now had an urgent incentive to discover it. The thought that he'd come to the senior Mage's attention would be enough to give him a few nightmares too.

He rose, brushing aside the other's protestations of loyalty and immediate action.

"I'm sure the Master Mage can rely on you, sir," he said through gritted teeth. "I shall be lodging at the sign of The Anchor should you remember anything further."

As he left, he took the time to wonder what some unremarkable little foundling had done to come to the Master Mage's attention. He filed the case away in his memory with the others, all neatly labelled. After all, one never knew when it might be of relevance later. Some cases might prove useful to remember, while others could grow teeth and return with a vengeance.

He shrugged and went to give his report to Raven.

III

It was all arranged. As soon as she signed the contract, the atmosphere in the room relaxed and Captain Berwyn even came over and shook her hand.

"I wish you good fortune and a long and happy career," he said.

Nuntius was even more forthcoming. He clasped her hand in both of his and gazed at her earnestly. His eyes were very dark and penetrating.

"May the Gods smile on you, Maia Abella. Work hard, obey your superiors and don't waste this opportunity to make something of yourself."

"Thank you, sir," she replied. "I'll do my best and I'll thank the God properly as soon as I can."

He winked at her. "I know he'll appreciate that."

A little shiver ran through her as she met his eyes, but it had been a long day and she dismissed it as fatigue. Obviously, magical sleep wasn't like real sleep and lately she'd not had enough of the latter.

"Good fortune to you, child," the *Diadem* said, then she and her sister Ship sank down into the wood once more. The Captain and Nuntius also left, along with Nestor, leaving her alone with the Mage.

"It's time to get you settled in, young lady," Raven said. He rose from his chair, smoothing his robes. She was getting used to his shrivelled appearance now, though she was still wary. He hadn't been the Mage who had bespelled her in The Anchor; that had been a younger man from the glimpse she'd got of him.

"What happens now?"

"Now, you come with me and I'll take you to the Academy. You'll meet Matrona. She'll make sure that you have all you need."

She knew that the Academy was just across the harbour from the Admiralty offices, with a good view of the sea. She hoped that she wouldn't be expected to walk.

"We'll take a ferry," he said.

She trotted after him once more as they made their way out of the building and down to the quayside. The spring night was chilly and she shivered in her thin dress, hugging herself to keep warm though the wind had dropped and the night was unusually still. It was the ferryman who saw her distress and found a blanket to wrap around her bony shoulders.

"Eh, lass, you've not much meat on them bones and what you 'ave ain't enough to keep a sparrow warm!"

He shot the Master Mage a disgusted look as they settled into the boat.

Raven, who seemed preoccupied, waved a hand in her direction and she felt the air around her grow perceptibly warmer. She wished he'd done it earlier as her feet felt like ice and her fingers were numb. Perhaps high-and-mighty Mages were above such trivialities as feeling the cold?

They were the only passengers and the water was calm. Stars peeped through the covering of cloud as the ferryman bent his back to the oars and rowed them out into the harbour. The masts of moored vessels made it seem as if they were moving through a forest of tall, shadowy trees, with spars and rigging instead of leaves and branches. Their lights reflected prettily as they rocked at anchor. Nearer to the shore were merchantmen and galleys from all over the Empire, filled with the wares from four different continents. Some had even crossed the ocean from New Roma, or from the far-flung lands of Africa and Chin. She'd served their crews often enough. Anchored out to sea, she spotted the bulks of the great naval vessels, many of them Ships in between assignments. The great dockyards were even further away and she wondered if that was where the *Diadem* and the *Swiftsure* were being rebuilt. Did they like being on land or would they rather be back with their vessels and crews?

There were so many questions and she wondered just what she'd signed up to.

"Can you see the Northern Ships?"

The ferryman's voice broke the stillness. Maia peered about until she spotted the sleek vessels with the strangely carved prows. There were three of them, moored together for company in a strange port. Figures moved about their decks, on watch in the night.

"Who'd 'ave thought we'd come to an arrangement with that lot?" the ferryman said. He didn't sound like he approved. "Still, it's better for business, as long as they keep to the terms. I wouldn't trust 'em as far as I could throw 'em." He spat expertly over the side to emphasise his point.

"I've seen some of their crew," Maia told him. "They got beaten up in a fight. They started it," she added.

"Hah, sounds about right," the man said. The oars dipped rhythmically, in and out, leaving little whirlpools in the smooth surface. "They love nothing better. They don't 'ave Ships like we do, you know."

"I've heard."

"Aye. They use animal spirits, savage things from their 'omeland. Wolves an' bears an' such. T'ain't civilised, if you ask me."

Maia was feeling warmer now and tried to make out which animals controlled these vessels. It was dark and the carvings were stylised, but she thought that one was definitely a wolf. She could see its gaping jaws outlined against the light that hung from its bow. It certainly looked savage enough, with its jagged teeth and staring eyes.

"Nearly there," the ferryman told her.

Sure enough, they had drawn up to stone steps leading up to the quay. The ferryman expertly shipped the oars before tying the little boat to a great iron ring set into the wall.

Raven seemed to wake up, handing over some coin as the ferryman touched his forelock respectfully, while raising his eyebrows at Maia to show his true opinion of Mages and their ways. Some of the new-fangled gas lamps lit the stairway, so she could see where they were going. She handed back the blanket with a word of thanks and the boatman nodded.

"Gods keep you, miss."

"And you, sir," she replied. Perhaps she'd see him again if she was ever allowed out of this place.

"Goodnight," Raven said, his whispery voice sliding through the darkness. She wondered what time it was, though her body was telling her it was very late indeed. There was no sign of the dawn yet and she couldn't stop a huge yawn as she climbed the steps. She was hoping that it wouldn't be too long before she could get some sleep.

"We're expected," Raven said briskly. He didn't seem affected by the late hour and Maia wondered if he slept at all. She trailed after him, along the cobbled frontage until they came to a small side door away from the main entrance. Raven knocked gently and it was opened immediately by a tall man, shrouded in a cloak and carrying a lantern.

"Hello, Basil."

"Master Mage." Basil bobbed his head. "Matrona got your message."

He stood aside to let them enter and Maia felt herself under scrutiny. She wasn't cold anymore; whatever spell the Mage had cast was still doing its job, but it didn't stop the leaden sense of fatigue that was steadily overtaking her.

They passed the doorkeeper's cubby hole and went down a long corridor into the bowels of the building. Two other gates stood in their way, which Raven opened and locked behind them with a muttered word. Maia observed the security with dismay. This place would be hard to break out of.

At last, the corridor opened out into a vestibule paved with black and white tiles. An ornate chandelier hung from the ceiling, casting a soft glow on to the statues that lined the walls, five on each side. Maia saw that they were all Ships, their painted faces staring blankly, but another glance told her that these were stone, not wood. She took in some of their names; *Augusta, Victoria, Imperatrix*. Their stern expressions sent a shiver down her spine.

She only had a moment to stare before a set of double doors slid back and an older woman entered. Her gown was white under a navy-blue coat, clearly some kind of uniform and her curly grey-brown hair was tucked up under a cap of the same colours. She made a beeline for the Master Mage.

"Welcome, Raven. So, you have brought us a new candidate."

A pair of dark eyes turned to Maia and her brow creased with concern.

"You poor child! You must be frozen and exhausted, especially crossing the harbour at this time of night! My name is Helena Quintilla but everyone calls me Matrona, as that's my job description. I'll be in charge of your welfare while you're here with us. Heavens, you look about ready to drop."

She pursed her lips at the Master Mage who seemed oblivious to her censure.

"Ma'am." Maia curtseyed.

"I'll show you to your bed and in the morning we'll see about getting you fitted for some clothes."

Her tone told Maia what she thought of the shabby ones she was wearing.

"And decent footwear," Matrona added. Maia was too tired to smile.

"I think that's my job done with," Raven said. "Believe me, she's warm enough."

I am now, Maia thought crossly.

"Glad to hear it," Matrona said briskly. "Come along, Maia."

"Goodbye," Maia said to the ancient Mage.

His clouded eyes met hers for a moment. "Goodbye, Miss Maia. Good fortune!"

Matrona led her through the doors and on to the start of her new life.

*

"Nothing at all?" The Master Mage frowned. Over the many years of their acquaintance, Milo had got used to the way those milky eyes seemed to look right through him, focusing instead on a point somewhere behind his head. The Collegium office was dark but he could still feel Raven's blind stare boring deep.

"Not much, sir." He'd questioned some of the staff before he left, but had only got a little more information, none of it particularly helpful. "One of the teachers remembered her arrival at a few days old, wrapped in a bit of blanket. No tokens or notes to leave a clue and no indication that anyone would be returning to claim her."

Raven tutted in annoyance. "What did he say?"

"Quiet and biddable. Learned quickly. Pleasant enough."

"So, nothing of note." The Mage paused, thinking. "No name, no token, no unusual traits, almost as if…" he trailed off. "Did he want to know why you were enquiring after her?"

"He was too worried to ask. I got the feeling that he was glad it wasn't something else."

Raven nodded absently. "Hardly surprising. Ah well. That's that. Never mind. It seems that some things may never be known, save by the Gods. At least we know she didn't kill Marcia Blandina. Thank you for your efforts, Milo."

The agent left quietly, leaving the old Mage sitting alone and thinking of things that could have been secretly and deliberately hidden. And why.

*

Maia awoke to the luxury of a comfortable bed and clean bedlinen. For a second, she wondered where she was, before the memories flooded back. She could tell that it was late in the day as the light had an afternoon feel to it.

The room was sparsely furnished, but clean. There were a couple of chairs, a wardrobe and a small table in the corner, next to another door that was painted in blue and green to match the wall. The cheerful colours made a change from grey, crumbling plaster or bare brick. She looked around for her clothes, before remembering that Matrona had taken them away with her. Her shoes had been replaced by soft slippers but she hesitated to use them while her feet were so dirty. She hoped that she hadn't messed up the crisp, white bedsheets.

The door opened a crack and a face appeared. The woman was wearing a navy-blue dress and a white cap, similar to the one Matrona had had, but with a narrower blue stripe across the front. Strands of curly ginger hair were escaping across her forehead, matching the liberal sprinkle of freckles across her nose. Her eyes widened when she saw that Maia was awake.

"Hello, miss. Are you ready to get up now?"

Maia sat up in the bed and rubbed her eyes.

"Yes, I think so."

The woman bustled into the room. "My name's Branwen, miss. I'm to be your servant. I'll just get your bath ready."

Maia watched in astonishment as the maid went through the painted door. Soon she heard the sounds of water splashing into a tub. She was to have a servant? Somehow, she'd thought that she would be expected to work for her keep, as she'd always done. The thought that someone was going to wait on her felt wrong, somehow. Branwen was about ten years older than she, but looked much better fed and clothed and she wasn't wearing a slave collar.

She climbed out of bed and padded over to the bathroom. Steam was rising from an enormous porcelain bath tub and Branwen was adding some perfumed oils. The maid smiled at her as she entered.

"There you are, miss. It'll be ready in a minute."

Maia's gaze went to the latrine in the corner and she wasted no time in relieving herself while Branwen busied herself making sure that the water was at the correct temperature. She watched the woman carefully for any signs of hostility, but couldn't detect any.

"All done!" Branwen pushed up the taps, which were shaped like leaping dolphins and the flow of water ceased. Maia saw that the water was faintly pink and smelt of roses.

"I'll fetch you a robe, miss."

"Er, yes, please," Maia said. She hoped that she wouldn't have to wear her old, shapeless servant's dress. Maybe they'd been able to get some of the stains out, though she feared that it was only the dirt that was holding it together. She'd been saving up what few coins Casca had given her for a new one, but there was no way of getting her money now. She was ashamed that she'd have to put it back on in this place.

"All right. Take as long as you want, then I'll bring you some food. What would you like, miss?"

Maia had to stifle a laugh. She'd never had a choice before and some of the things she'd been forced to eat would have choked a pig.

"Anything you've got is fine," she said lamely. She had the horrible feeling that Branwen would be laughing behind her back, but she couldn't help that. Instead, the woman's earnest expression didn't change.

"I'll find you something nice, miss," she promised. "Don't let the water get cold!"

"Oh, no. Thank you."

Branwen bobbed a curtsey and left, closing the door behind her. Maia realised that her mouth was hanging open and hastily stripped off the nightgown that she'd been given.

The water felt just right on her skin as she climbed into the tub and lowered herself into the perfumed water. The warmth was soothing, though she noticed a film of dirt rising to the surface. She was too dirty for a proper bath, she thought, or maybe they didn't have a bath house here? The thought of food made her stomach rumble in anticipation, so she quickly took a cloth and began to scrub. A bar of soap helped to get most of the dirt out but she took her time in washing and rinsing her hair. She'd have to ask if she could borrow a comb as she'd literally arrived with nothing and, despite rubbing it with cloths, it had turned into a tangled mess over the past few days. She'd left it loose to hide her face for as long as she could, though it hadn't fooled Flora.

It must have been that polis sergeant, she decided. He'd given no sign that he'd recognised her, or perhaps it was her very plainness and the fact that she'd just been taken on that alerted him. It wasn't as if she had any distinguishing features.

She hoped that Casca wasn't too put out by her arrest. He was a decent sort and had been prepared to give her a chance. Perhaps she could get word to him that she was all right? Maia stared down at her wrinkled hands and chipped nails, feeling the hard callouses soften in the warm water. Nobody could ever mistake her for a lady, no matter how many servants she acquired.

A soft knock at the door told her of Branwen's return. She scooped up a large towel from a rail, holding it out for Maia to step into, then helped her to dry herself, rubbing efficiently. This was followed by a silky dressing gown and the slippers. Maia looked at the scum floating on the bath water, but Branwen merely pulled a lever and the tub began to drain, the gurgling water taking the filth along with it.

"If you don't mind, miss, I'll just need to take some measurements for your uniform. You get three sets. The tailors should have them finished by tomorrow."

Maia stood obediently while Branwen used a tape measure, jotting down the numbers on a little piece of paper. She'd clearly done this before.

"What sort of uniform is it?" she asked.

"Oh, it's white, with a navy-blue jacket like the one Matrona wears." Branwen checked her numbers and nodded to herself, satisfied. "I've set the table out here," she said. "Matrona will be along shortly to see you."

The woman was certainly eager to please. Maia still felt uneasy, but brightened at the plates of sliced bread, meats and cheeses that covered the table."

"I got you some cake too, miss," Branwen said, "as it's the afternoon."

"Thank you, Branwen."

And if she didn't eat it, Branwen would, on the way back to the kitchens. Maia knew all the tricks, though she'd never had much opportunity to steal cake.

She set to with a will. Sure enough, a smiling Matrona appeared a few minutes later. She dismissed Branwen, who left without a word, before pulling up the other chair.

"No, no, carry on eating," she told Maia, who'd started to rise. "You need to get some food into you. You look half-starved. I take it that your life hasn't been easy."

Maia shook her head.

"Raven told me some of your story. You must be wondering what you're doing here."

Maia nodded, her mouth full of cake.

"Well. Let me see. You know that this is the Naval Academy, where boys are trained to be officers?"

Maia swallowed. "Yes, ma'am."

"Oh, do call me Matrona. Everybody does. Prospective Ship candidates from all over Britannia and our Colonias in New Roma and elsewhere are schooled here too. You won't see much of the boys as you have separate lessons and your own areas. You will have your own room, like the other girls and you can choose which furnishings you would like. Everyone has their own taste, after all. You'll be meeting the others shortly. I felt it was a bit much on your first day here."

Matrona looked at her expectantly and Maia realised that she was supposed to say something.

"Most kind ma...Matrona."

The woman beamed. "Excellent! I must say that you look better for a good long sleep and a nice hot bath. We do have a proper bathing suite here that we can use at certain times, but I felt you might like to have one to yourself for now."

She was both kind and diplomatic. Maia watched her, waiting for the rest. So far, she'd seen plenty of carrot and no sign of a stick, but she was sure that there was one lurking somewhere. She put on her most attentive expression and helped herself to some creamy cheese and bread. Matrona watched her approvingly.

"All I'll say for now is that if you work hard, you will reap the rewards. I won't pretend that it will be easy, but it will be fulfilling. Good behaviour brings special privileges."

And bad behaviour brings punishment. Maia understood that only too well, but Matrona didn't elaborate.

"I thought that you'd like to choose some things for your stay here. Just mark off the items you like in the books and I'll have them brought.

"May I have a comb?" she asked.

"Oh, my goodness, yes. There should be a bag of essentials for you in the bathroom – wait a moment."

She returned in a few seconds, carrying a striped cloth bag.

"Here you are. I knew there was one."

Maia looked inside. There were wash cloths, a toothbrush, various little flasks and a comb and brush set. Including the robe, slippers and nightgown, it was more than she'd ever had in her life. She touched each object with wondering fingers, scarcely daring to believe that they were hers. Matrona saw her expression.

"I'm glad you're here," she said. "We get girls from all over, you know. Even slaves."

She nodded at Maia's surprise.

"Oh yes. Potentia comes in all shapes, sizes and circumstance of birth. It's amazing how many important men pass on their Divine blood through their slaves." She snorted. "Or maybe not. They can't benefit from their father's wealth, not in the ordinary sense, but they're special all the same and many come here to be trained."

Maia fought hard to hide a sudden stab of panic. Matrona must surely know that she didn't have a drop of Divine blood in her veins and no Divine blood meant no Potentia. And no Potentia meant that she would fail, regardless of what Nuntius had said.

She clutched the little bag, wondering if they'd let her keep it when she was thrown out in disgrace.

Matrona misunderstood her sudden panic.

"Oh it's all yours!" she told Maia with a laugh. "Don't worry. There's plenty more where this came from. Now, I suggest you rest and I'll send Branwen in with the catalogues for you to choose from. Do you like this room?"

Maia looked around and nodded.

"The colours are nice."

"The view over the garden is good too," Matrona assured her, adding "you haven't looked out yet, have you?"

"No. This will be fine, honest."

"Good. That's settled then. Remember, just mark off anything you want."

"Branwen isn't a slave, is she?" Maia asked.

"No, she's a paid servant. I prefer them to slaves. She's a capable woman and I hope that you'll get along."

Something in Matrona's tone piqued Maia's interest, but she didn't comment.

"I'm sure we shall. It's just strange to be waited on when it's always been me doing the running around."

"Oh, I know, believe me. You'll get used to it before too long."

So Matrona was from humble origins too. Maybe she'd even been a slave herself. Many freedwomen did very well in great households and business.

Maia eyed the rest of the food.

"Help yourself and just ask if you want any more. Branwen will keep you company and tomorrow you can meet the other girls. We currently have two, so we're doing well at the moment. It's been difficult to find candidates lately, as you may have heard, then three come along in two years. Astounding!"

Maia smiled weakly.

"Well, I must attend to my duties. I'll see you in the morning."

"Thank you," Maia said. She liked Matrona and, so far, she'd been shown nothing but kindness.

True to her word, Branwen appeared with leather bound books containing everything from fancy furniture to soft furnishings, curtains and even statues and paintings. Maia was quite bewildered by the choice, though she had admired some of the nicer things Blandina had displayed in her house. These weren't quite to that standard but she reckoned they weren't far off it.

A little voice at the back of her mind warned her that the Navy wouldn't be this generous if they didn't expect a lot in return. A gilded cage was still a cage and she would be expected to sing for her supper.

That thought echoed in her mind as she picked out what she fancied, aided by Branwen's eager suggestions. The maid seemed to be enjoying it more than she was and, as the light in the room faded, all she wanted to do was to crawl back into the luxurious bed.

As she settled down to sleep, she wondered what she would look like in her new uniform.

*

The next morning, Branwen ran her another bath then brought the sets of uniforms in for her approval. Maia picked up each garment, admiring each piece and loving the fact that nobody else had worn them. All she'd had before were clothes that had been handed down several times, frayed around the edges and threadbare. The only decent item of clothing had been the coats that were worn outside as they could be seen by the public and old Varus, the penny-pinching skinflint, wanted no criticism.

Even the underclothes were good quality. She looked up to see Branwen grinning at her.

"Well, miss, are you actually going to put them on? You don't want to be late on your first day, do you?"

She dressed hastily and allowed Branwen to pin up her hair so that it at least looked neat. The little cap with its stripe was pinned on top and, while she couldn't say she looked pretty, she did look smart. Branwen nodded in approval.

"That's much better!" she said. "I'll show you to the mess room. The others should be there, but I'll bet that Tullia's late again. She takes ages to get ready."

Maia hadn't asked about the other girls, but she did now.

"There are two," Branwen informed her. "Briseis Apollonia has been here for just over two years. Her father was a Priest of Apollo somewhere on the New Continent."

A Priest! That would explain where she got her Potentia from. Maia's insides quailed at the thought of being surrounded by grand and important girls.

"The other one's Tullia Albana. Her father's an Admiral – one of the important ones, so he's very keen on her becoming a Ship."

Maia knew that they would ask about her parentage and she wondered briefly if she should make something up. Her father could be someone important too. She was still debating whether to say that he was a Priest or a rich merchant when they arrived at the mess room.

"This is where you'll eat your meals," Branwen explained.

Maia squared her shoulders and went in. There was only one girl there already, her head bent over a book, but she looked up to see who the new arrival was. She was pretty, Maia noticed with a pang of envy, her dark curly hair cascading down her back and large lustrous eyes set in an oval face. Her skin was light brown without the trace of a blemish, as if the sun had kissed it in childhood. On seeing Maia, her face lit up into a smile, showing even teeth like little pearls.

"Hello! You must be Maia Abella. I'm Briseis Apollonia. Pleased to meet you."

Maia took the offered hand politely. Briseis had an accent that she associated with the sailors that crossed the ocean from the New World.

"Likewise," she said, shyly.

"Come and have breakfast. I was waiting for you, or Tullia, whoever came first. I'm not surprised it's you. Tullia's usually late."

Branwen waggled her eyebrows at Maia in an 'I told you so' look. Maia took one of the two empty chairs and helped herself to a plate of food, while Briseis did the same.

"So, how do you like the uniform?" Briseis asked her. Maia was relieved that she was friendly.

"It's very nice," she said, cautiously.

"I think so too, but Tullia's always complaining that it's not fashionable and makes her look dowdy."

Maia was beginning to think that this Tullia was a little madam, but it wasn't fair to judge someone she hadn't met yet.

"Have you come far?"

"No. I'm from Portus."

Briseis sighed. "Lucky you. I never get to see my family, though they send me messages. My parents and brother are back home in New Eboracum. Yours will be able to visit you here."

This was it. Should she lie? No, it wasn't a good idea to make something up. She'd get found out sooner or later.

"I don't have any family. I was a foundling."

She stared at her plate, expecting the inevitable sneer.

"Oh, I'm sorry." Briseis was full of genuine sympathy. "Still, you're here now and all Ships are sisters, so we can be your family."

Maia felt her eyes unexpectedly filling with tears. Briseis was immediately distraught.

"Oh no! You've been here five minutes and I've upset you! What a silly goose I am!"

The image made Maia smile. "It's not your fault," she said quickly. "I don't usually cry. It's just that the last few weeks have been a bit trying."

Briseis patted her shoulder awkwardly.

"Please tell me if there's anything I can help with and don't think I'm some rich girl. My mother was a temple slave until I was born and my father freed us both and married her, so I was only a slave for a week. My brother was born free. He's training to be a Priest too. Father says we're descended from Apollo somewhere in the distant past."

Maia remembered what Matrona had said about slaves frequently being admitted.

"I was trained to be a servant," she said. "I've more in common with Branwen than anyone else."

"That's going to change," Briseis said. "You'll learn a lot, if you apply yourself. Oh – here she comes!"

53

A loud voice echoed outside in the corridor.

"…don't forget to bring it back with you. The new one, not that tatty old thing!"

Briseis rolled her eyes and whispered, "I swear she makes Hilda's life a misery, but she's not a bad person."

The door opened and Tullia Albana breezed in on a cloud of perfume. Maia's nose wrinkled as she caught a gust. The girl was wearing the uniform but had added a scarf of blue silk over the top, fastened with an expensive-looking gold brooch and her chestnut hair was piled high in the latest fashion. Her eyes raked across Maia appraisingly, but she stopped and held out a hand.

"Greetings! I am Tullia Albana, daughter of Admiral Lucius Albanus Dio."

Maia stood and took the hand, noting the fancy gold bangles and gold-painted nails. Tullia had expensive taste to go along with her cut-glass vowels.

"Maia Abella," she said simply.

Tullia hesitated, then smiled brightly.

"I take it Briseis has introduced herself? Good. It's nice to see a new face."

She peered at several dishes before selecting some fruit and bread then applying a liberal amount of honey.

"I was just telling Maia that she'll learn a lot here," Briseis said.

"Oh yes," Tullia agreed between dainty mouthfuls. "We're constantly being crammed with information. Let me see. There's history, geography of course, some philosophy, but not much because they don't want us to think for ourselves, and the lore of the ocean. Plus, religious studies, etiquette, world politics, literature, both prose and poetry…"

She broke off to laugh at the look on Maia's face. "And that's not counting all the practical subjects like seamanship, weather and navigation. Some of those will have to wait until we're partnered with our training Ship, of course. Briseis is closer to that than I am. I've only been here a year."

She sighed dramatically. "A whole year of wearing an unflattering uniform, no parties and the only members of the opposite sex being ancient tutors. I swear I can't stand much more!"

"Oh Tullia!" Briseis said, reprovingly.

"What? It's true! I don't want to be here. I should be getting ready to marry some rich aristocrat who'll shower me with gifts, not slaving away at boring…*stuff*!"

"Then why are you here?" Maia asked curiously. Tullia made a face.

"Father, why else? He's determined to have a Ship in the family. I pointed out that there is one already, the *Diadem*. She's my umpteenth great aunt apparently, but no, he wants another one to further his ambition. My two sisters don't have a lick of Potentia between them and I have two brothers in the Navy, so I'm expendable!"

Maia was slightly embarrassed by Tullia's outburst, though from Briseis' expression she'd heard it all before.

"Just say you don't want to be a Ship," she said. "Surely your father can't force you?"

"Hah! I've no choice in the matter. I'm hoping I fail at something, then they'll have to let me go."

"That's unlikely," Briseis said. "I was supposed to be a Priestess, but the Navy stepped in and overruled my father. I hadn't actually been contacted by the God yet and my Potentia manifested physically so they claimed precedence."

"Don't you want to be a Ship either?" Maia said, hoping that nobody would ask about her Potentia.

"Oh, I don't mind," Briseis said. "I'm glad I can serve my country. My parents are proud of me anyway. It must be the will of the Gods."

For the first time in her life, Maia was glad that she had no familial pressure on her. When she failed, nobody else would suffer.

They were just finishing, when a bell rang three times. Maia looked around.

"What's that?"

"Lesson time," Tullia said glumly. "We're all starting with history this morning. I swear, I can't remember what happened yesterday, never mind hundreds of years ago. It's so *boring*!"

Maia followed the others out. It felt strange to leave the table without having to clear up.

The three girls went to another room that was set up as a classroom. Maia was instantly reminded of her childhood in the Home, but there they'd all crowded on to benches and shared slates. Here, they had a desk each, equipped with slates, tablets and a selection of writing implements, chalk, pens and styli. The walls were lined with books and a large board was attached to the wall at the front.

Tullia sighed again and threw herself down on a chair. Maia took the desk nearest the door and together they waited for the tutor.

To her surprise, Matrona came in.

"Good morning, girls!"

Maia copied the others as they rose and saluted in the Roman fashion. Matrona returned the salute and waited until they had re-seated themselves.

"So, I hope you've all become acquainted over breakfast?"

They nodded obediently.

"Excellent! Today we'll start with some history and you can help Maia as you know all the answers, don't you, Tullia?"

"Yes, Matrona," Tullia said, without enthusiasm.

"Let's start at the beginning. Maia, I don't know how much you know already, so why don't you tell me something you've learned in the past?"

Maia was suddenly conscious of being put on the spot.

"Erm. The Romans came from Italia a long time ago and made Britannia part of their Empire?"

She hoped that Matrona didn't want dates.

Tullia suppressed a snigger, but Matrona nodded encouragingly.

"Yes, that's right. Tullia, when was that?"

The smirk disappeared from Tullia's face as she tried to remember.

"Briseis?"

"796 F.R., Matrona," Briseis replied promptly.

"Correct. Seven hundred and ninety-six years from the Foundation of Roma. Maia, what year is it now?"

Maia had a moment of panic, then the date popped into her head. She'd seen it on a new coin. "2044, Matrona."

"It is indeed. And do you know which Emperor led the invasion of Britain?"

Tullia's hand shot up eagerly.

"Claudius!"

"Yes, though you mustn't interrupt, Tullia. Emperor Tiberius Claudius Drusus Nero Germanicus. Julius Caesar came some years before but didn't stay."

Even Maia had heard of Julius Caesar. He was stabbed, she remembered, lots of times. She'd seen a street play about it one Saturnalia but she didn't know much about this Claudius. She tried not to wriggle in her seat, though it was hard to be inconspicuous when there were only three pupils.

"And King Artorius Magnus went to Rome in…?"

Tullia looked blank and Maia had no idea. Briseis once again came to the rescue.

"1163, Matrona. He reformed the Britannic Legions, including Mages in their ranks for the first time and went to the aid of the two Emperors. He drove the barbarians back and, when one of the brothers died, installed Honorius on the Imperial Throne in 1164."

Matrona was clearly pleased with her, less so with Tullia. Maia listened with interest. She hadn't known the dates as it wasn't thought important for the girls in the Home to know all this. They'd spent more time learning how to get wine stains out of tablecloths and the finer points of ironing.

"Now, I'm going to make a start with Maia. Briseis, you can finish off your latest assignment and Tullia, I would like you to write me out a timeline, complete with notes, of all the Kings of Britannia, from Artorius Magnus to the present day."

Tullia opened her tablet and reached for a book from the pile on her desk. Her stylus was ragged at the end and, sure enough, it disappeared into her mouth as soon as Matrona's back was turned. She threw Maia a look of self-pity as she set to writing out her list. Briseis was already immersed in scribbling notes, her forehead creased in concentration. Maia watched as Matrona chose a book from a shelf and brought it over to her.

"This has most of the basics, Maia. Start at the beginning and work your way through. If there are any words you're not sure of, just ask."

Maia accepted the book and opened it at the first page. She was pleased to see that there were pictures, but her pleasure turned to horror as she saw that it was written in Classical Latin, not Britannic. Matrona picked up on her confusion immediately. "Ah. Silly me, I've picked up the wrong book. You can start on that one later, after a few more lessons. I'll get you another."

Maia already felt ignorant, now she felt worse, but grateful for Matrona's understanding. She knew some everyday Latin – most people did, as it had been assimilated over the years and it was the official language of the Empire, but she couldn't understand half the words in this book.

Matrona came back with a slimmer volume and Maia accepted it gratefully. This one was much simpler and she settled down to read, using her finger to follow each word.

Briseis was right. It would be harder work than she'd imagined.

IV

Several weeks later, all three candidates were sitting in the courtyard garden, enjoying the July sunshine. Maia was glad of the break from lessons; her eyes ached from all the reading, though Matrona was pleased with her progress. She absorbed the information quickly, each word engraving itself into her brain and she found that she could retrieve the information with ease when required.

Matrona was surprised and delighted.

"You have an eidetic memory, Maia! Didn't you know?"

Maia had no idea. She'd never heard the word before.

"It means that you can remember things when you've only seen them once," Matrona told her. "It's quite rare and will give you an advantage in your studies. You must learn to actively cultivate it."

Maia's spirits rose.

"Is it linked to Potentia?" she asked, carefully. Matrona thought about it.

"To be honest. I'm not sure. It could be another aspect but then again there are some people who have it without having Divine blood."

She felt her hopes subside. Still, it was a useful thing to have and certainly something that Tullia didn't possess. She imagined her mind was like a library. If she needed to look inside a book she'd read, all she had to do was find the proper shelf, mentally pull it out and find the right page. Still, she'd have given it up for just a smidgen of Potentia. Perhaps it would help her to find work when she was forced to leave.

Tullia's voice snapped her out of her musings.

"It's all right for you two!" she complained. "I can't remember anything and I've got a test tomorrow!"

She threw the book she was holding on to her couch and stood, stretching her back.

"All this stress is giving me wrinkles. Look!"

She thrust her face at Briseis, who shook her head.

"I can't see any."

"Well, I can. It's not fair!"

"You won't have to worry when you're a Ship," Briseis said.

Tullia looked at her in horror.

"And made of wood! Stuck on board a vessel, rarely coming to land, following orders day in, day out for hundreds of years!" She burst into tears. Maia and Briseis exchanged glances and Maia thought that she'd never seen any girl as unsuited to being a Ship as Tullia. She should be adorning her father's house, hosting entertainments and parties and waiting for a husband, not stuck in rigorous training for a life of obedience and self-sacrifice. Maia had seen older versions of her, flocking to Blandina's house to visit and gossip. Tullia was fashionable, non-academic and desperately unhappy. It wasn't a recipe for a successful Ship. Why couldn't Matrona see that?

"Oh look, now my face is all blotchy! I'm going inside," Tullia wailed. "Hilda! Hilda?"

Her voice faded into the distance as she set off to find her unlucky servant.

"Poor Tullia," Briseis said. "I wish they'd just let her go."

"Perhaps we could talk to Matrona?" Maia suggested, but Briseis only smiled sadly.

"Tullia's father outranks Matrona and he's one of the Admirals who has the final say. Do you really think that he'll admit that his daughter has failed?"

Maia had never met an Admiral, only Captain Berwyn and he'd been scary enough. She told Briseis.

"Oh, you met Camillus Berwyn? He's a senior Captain – well, Commodore now, I believe. He's been with the *Diadem* for several years. She's a Royal Ship, you know."

"I saw her at the Admiralty Offices, with the *Swiftsure*," Maia said. "What's a Royal Ship?"

"Oh, each Sovereign can, if they want, designate a special Ship as Royal. There are usually ten of them, but there hasn't been another one made for a hundred years or more. Did you read that book on famous Ships I gave you?"

Maia looked guilty. "Not yet," she admitted. "I'm still ploughing through the Odyssey. I finished the Iliad and then I'll start on the Aeneid. It's on the list."

"Well, if you fancy a break from all those manly heroes, Gods and monsters, start on that. I think it should interest you. It begins with the *Argo* and finishes with the *Imperatrix*. She's one of the younger ones and used to be Admiral Albanus' before he moved to land duties. The oldest is the *Augusta*. She's the Flagship."

Maia remembered the statues in the vestibule and the two Ships she had seen, stern, proud and unchanging over the centuries. She felt guilty for being relieved that she'd never have to be transformed into one of them but Briseis didn't seem worried about it. Perhaps she thought that it was the will of Apollo?

Mercury had definitely done her a favour, getting her somewhere she was well-treated. Perhaps one of her unknown parents had petitioned him on her behalf? She had no illusions that he actually meant for her to go through the whole process. She dismissed the thought as she would surely be released from the Navy long before it was time to give up her human form.

She caught Briseis with an undecided look on her face.

"Come on. What aren't you telling me?" she demanded.

"I'm going to be leaving in the next couple of weeks," the older girl told her. "I've learned all the theory, including sailing a dinghy in the harbour, so now it's time to put everything into practice on a Ship."

Outwardly, she was her usual serene self, but Maia saw the anxiety lurking in her brown eyes.

"You'll be fine," Maia assured her, though the thought of being left alone with the mercurial Tullia wasn't an appealing one. "You've worked hard and you're a brilliant student. It'll be exciting! Do you know which Ship you're going to?"

"She's called the *Blossom*," Briseis said, "and she's been training Ships on and off for the last twenty years, so she'll be used to having a novice aboard. Matrona told me that she was born on the New Continent too, so I hope we'll have something in common."

"What happens?" Maia asked her, curious to learn something of the process.

"Well, I'll be taught aboard the Ship and get a duplicate earring, so that I can sort of piggy-back on *Blossom* and learn directly."

"You keep your body then?"

"Oh yes. We only give them up when we're initiated but nobody knows how that happens. It's a Ship Mystery and never talked about."

Maia took a few seconds to digest this information.

"Do you think Matrona knows?"

"I don't know. It's probably only Ships and Matrona hasn't been one. I get the feeling that she's some kind of Priestess but I've never had the nerve to ask her outright."

Maia had heard of Mysteries. There were lots of different sorts, for Mages, Adepts, temples and even some trades. Their knowledge was kept close and never shared with outsiders.

"Do you think we can come and see you off?" she asked, hopefully.

"I'd like it if you could," Briseis said. She looked so forlorn that Maia gave her a hug. She'd never trusted many people in her life, but Briseis was one of them and they'd become close. It was heart-wrenching to think that she might never see her again, even if she'd known that this day would come. She could even end up on her own when Tullia went too, unless another candidate was admitted.

She opened her mouth to change the subject to something more cheerful, when an almighty crash sounded from inside the building, followed by a scream. Both girls leapt up. A running figure appeared in the colonnade and Maia saw that it was Sylvia, Briseis' maid, who was normally as unflappable as her mistress. The girl's pale face was even paler than usual.

"Miss Briseis! It's Miss Tullia, she's using Potentia on Hilda!"

Briseis' face set and she hurried after Sylvia, with Maia in hot pursuit. The screaming started again as they got to Tullia's door and Briseis dodged to avoid a vase, which shattered against the wall. Maia had thought that it was Hilda who was making the noise, but it was Tullia, red-faced and throwing a tantrum of epic proportions. Another vase splintered, followed by vials, cushions and ornaments in quick succession. Hilda was trying to placate the furious girl to no avail, her arms raised in defence.

Briseis didn't hesitate. She strode into the room.

"Tullia! Stop this now!"

When the girl showed no signs of hearing her, Briseis marched in and slapped her, hard.

All the levitated objects fell to the floor immediately, leaving Tullia clutching her cheek.

"What on earth?"

Matrona appeared in the doorway, surveying the scene. Maia was shocked as she gazed around at the devastation. It looked like a whirlwind had entered the room and ripped everything to shreds. Even the furniture was broken in pieces and the bed overturned. The bed linen and curtains looked like a wild beast had savaged them with claws and teeth.

"Girls, leave us," Matrona said quietly.

The sudden silence was broken only by Tullia's sobs.

The four of them left quietly.

"Come to my room," Briseis whispered. "Sylvia, where's Branwen?"

"Ironing," Sylvia whispered back. Hilda, a large boned girl whose mother came from the wilds of Northern Germania, was unshaken.

"I swear, that's the last time she's doing that to me," she said, fiercely. "I'm putting in a formal complaint this time."

"I don't think you'll have to," Briseis said. "She's overstepped the mark today. We aren't supposed to use our Potentia for any reason, unless it's to prevent loss of life," she told Maia, "and certainly not to throw a full-blown tantrum like a spoilt toddler!" She sighed. "The silly girl!"

Maia and Hilda followed Briseis to her room, leaving Sylvia to find Branwen and tell her the tale.

"She could have seriously hurt you," Briseis said to Hilda. "She shouldn't have lost control like that. What set her off?"

The maid spread her hands and shrugged. "She couldn't find an earring, probably because she never puts them away properly when I'm not there. I have to find them and put them on the stand. She just went crazy."

Maia shuddered. She had her own memories of madness and missing earrings. It was an unpleasant coincidence.

"What will happen to her?" she asked.

Briseis bit her lip.

"Matrona will decide on her punishment. It'll fit the crime, believe me. This isn't the first time that Tullia has broken the rules. I don't think she was ever denied anything in her life before she came here."

All three girls shared a moment of sympathy. Their lives had been quite different. Tullia would have been brought up in luxury by slaves who had to obey her every word, her parents being largely absent.

"Hilda, you're bleeding!"

A thin trickle of red was running down her arm above her elbow. Hilda twisted to look at it.

"Hellfire!" she swore in her mother tongue.

Briseis fetched a cloth and cleaned her up. It was only a small cut but it went deep.

Sylvia knocked on the door.

"Matrona wants to see Hilda, miss."

Hilda exited, holding the cloth to her arm, her face like thunder.

"Sylvia, could you fetch us something to drink, please?" Briseis asked her maid.

"Of course, miss."

The girl disappeared, shutting the door after her.

Briseis threw herself onto a couch. Maia sat next to her.

"This might be for the best," the older girl said. "They have to see that she can't go on like this. Her control is getting worse the more upset and stressed she's getting."

Maia had a mental image of Tullia being sent home in disgrace. It wasn't a pleasant thought.

"She's stuck between Scylla and Charybdis," she said. She wondered what she would do if she was in a similar position, stuck between two evils. She'd already planned three ways of escaping in the first week, mostly involving going over the wall and running as fast as she could. Where she would go after that, she had no idea, though she thought she could disguise herself as a boy and stow away on board a vessel if she had to. Somehow, she didn't think that this plan would appeal to Tullia.

Sylvia brought them a tray and some of Maia's favourite honey cakes, but she'd barely had time to take a bite before they were both summoned to Matrona's office. To get there, they had to pass beneath the stony gazes of the ten Ships in the vestibule and she felt more daunted than ever.

Matrona was seated behind her desk as they knocked and entered. She looked upset but resigned.

"Hilda told me what happened. Briseis, I commend you on your quick thinking. I personally believe that you will make an excellent Ship and be a credit to the Service. You're more than ready to be partnered with the *Blossom*. Maia, though you've only been here a short time, you've also showed yourself to be a hard worker and a fast learner and I'm pleased that you've followed Briseis' good example."

She paused. "I'm afraid that the next thing I have to tell you isn't as pleasant. Tullia is to be punished by the removal of all her privileges. She has to learn to control her Potentia, or she will be a danger to herself and everybody else. To that end, I've ordered that she and Hilda will swap places for the next month."

Maia couldn't believe her ears. An Admiral's daughter demoted to a servant! Tullia wouldn't know where to start.

"Hilda will have Tullia's room and I've told her to go ahead and order new furnishings. Tullia will take on Hilda's tasks and wait on her hand and foot, just as Hilda has faithfully served her during her time here."

Maia had to force herself not to laugh. It was poetic justice indeed! She didn't think that Hilda would be vindictive; she wouldn't have to be. Every order would drive home the message that being an aristocratic candidate of Divine blood didn't mean that you could treat people like dirt. Well, here at the Academy, anyway. Even when her sentence was up, she'd still be surrounded by Hilda's choices until she could replace them with her own, if she was allowed to. That would rub salt in the wound all right.

Maia did feel sorry for her. There was no real harm in Tullia and she couldn't help her high-ranking birth. If anything, she had it worse than Maia and was being forced into a life that had absolutely no appeal to her.

"Matrona, Tullia's really unhappy here," she said tentatively. "She doesn't want to be a Ship. That's why she's behaving like this."

Matrona clasped her hands in front of her.

"I'm glad you're trying to help her," she said softly, "but her course is set, whether she desires it or not. Sometimes we have no choice as to where our fate leads us and the sooner she accepts that, the better it will be for her."

Maia bowed her head, but inside she was seething. Everyone might as well just give up in that case, she thought. How could anything change if nobody argued back, or devised new ways of doing things? She'd seen the men working on the new engines that were changing factories and transport in the cities, clever men - and some women no doubt, in the background as usual – all trying to change the way things were done. Meanwhile, Tullia would have to take her punishment and hope that the weeks passed quickly.

"Hilda will be at liberty to walk in the gardens and relax while you are having your lessons," Matrona continued. "Tullia will have to catch up on her work, as well as doing all the household chores and obeying Hilda. I hope that this will help her to understand what service really means. It is at the heart of what a Ship does, serving the Gods, the Empire and her Country. Captains order, Ships obey."

Briseis nodded fervently.

"Indeed, Matrona."

Matrona smiled at her. "You have four more days here, Briseis, before you begin the final stage of your training."

"Are Maia and Tullia permitted to see me off?"

"Maia is," Matrona replied. "I know you'll miss her, but it's good to have a friend you trained with in the Service. I pray that you will both be sister Ships together."

"Thank you, Matrona."

Maia felt like crying. She'd be losing a friend and disappointing Matrona too. Escape was looking more and more like the only option. She needed to talk to Tullia, soon.

*

Maia didn't see much of Tullia for the next few days. She caught glimpses of her retreating down the corridor and wondered how she was doing, having to cope with unfamiliar jobs like laundry and cleaning. Hilda was mostly in her new room, or sitting in the garden enjoying her unexpected holiday in the sunshine. She wore a variety of different outfits as, not being a candidate, she wasn't required to wear the uniform, or her usual navy-blue maid's dress. Maia finally caught up with Tullia outside the classroom after lessons were finished.

"Tullia! How are you?"

The girl's face was pale and her eyes had dark circles underneath them.

"I'll live," she said, sullenly. "It's just so hard doing everything. Why do I have to study as well? It's just so demeaning!"

"It's not long," Maia said. "You'll be back to normal soon."

"They're making me wash clothes!" she hissed. "Me!"

Maia saw that her hands, unused to the work, looked red and raw.

"You need to rub in some cream." She'd used lanolin from untreated fleeces, or oil when she could steal a little. "Come to my room and I'll give you some."

"I can't right now. I've got to take these dirty clothes to the laundry."

"Later, then."

"All right. If I can get away. I'm not supposed to bother you."

"If anyone says anything, say I have a job for you," Maia told her. Tullia nodded.

"I wish my Potentia could grow me some wings. I'd be out of here for good."

Maia gave her a sympathetic look. A noise in the corridor put them both on alert and Tullia hurried off with her heavy basket before she could be reprimanded for wasting time. It was truly an awful punishment for her, though Maia reflected that she'd have given her eyeteeth for a job like this one only a few months ago. This was easy compared to swilling out the latrines at The Anchor.

Matrona's voice startled her out of her reverie. She was coming down the corridor, accompanied by a tall, well-built man in a very fancy uniform. His face was square and clean-shaven, with sharp brown eyes that looked familiar.

"Ah, Maia, there you are. Admiral, this is our newest candidate, Maia Abella."

Maia curtsied. She had an idea as to this man was and her heart went out to Tullia.

"Admiral Lucius Albanus Dio," he said. His smile didn't reach his eyes and she distrusted him immediately. "Just finishing lessons, then?"

"Yes, sir."

"And what are you reading today?"

"The Aeneid, Strabo's Geography, the latest edition of course and Famous Britannic Ships."

He nodded. "Excellent. I hope you are making good progress?"

"Oh, she is, sir," Matrona assured him hastily.

"Well, I'm sure we'll meet again, young lady, and I look forward to working with you in the future," the Admiral said. "In the meantime, I'll not keep you from your studies."

Maia bobbed again and started back to her room. So that was Tullia's father. Had Matrona summoned him, or was it a routine visit? Maybe she'd find out later but in the meantime a pang of conscience re-directed her to the laundry. It wasn't fair for Tullia not to know that her father was here.

A great gust of moist steam enveloped her as she opened the laundry room door. She peered through the vapour and spied Tullia labouring over a huge copper full of boiling water, beating at the dirty cloth with a paddle. The expression on her face would have curdled milk at twenty paces.

"Tullia," she called softly. The girl looked around, then saw Maia in the doorway, beckoning frantically.

She dumped the paddle on the floor and came over, brushing damp hair back under her cap with reddened hands.

"What is it?" she said, crossly.

"I thought you should know. Your father's here."

The look of horror on Tullia's face told Maia all she needed to know.

"He can't see me like this!" she hissed.

"I'm so sorry-" Maia began.

"No! You don't understand. He'll see this as an insult to the family!"

"He'll blame Matrona?"

68

"He'll blame me! Just when I thought things couldn't get any worse. Oh, Gods above, what can I do?"

Her eyes darted from side to side like a trapped animal. Maia looked at the washing.

"Perhaps I can take over while you tidy yourself up?"

"That won't help!" Tullia snapped. "I'll only get into worse trouble because I'm not where I'm supposed to be! He won't come here anyway. I'll be sent for."

Maia genuinely felt sorry for her, so overlooked her rudeness.

"Well, I didn't want you to have a nasty surprise, that's all."

Tullia's moist eyes met her own.

"Thank you," she managed, turning back to her drudgery.

*

All too soon, it was time to say goodbye to Briseis. The latter had spent her last day excused from lessons, whilst she and Sylvia packed her new sea chest with her clothes and belongings. She would be rowed out to the *Blossom* that evening, so that the Ship could sail with the tide in the early hours. Maia had only had half a mind on her lessons that day, pretending to listen whilst Master Sulianus, who had to be seventy if he was a day, droned on about the Great Barbarian Wars almost a thousand years ago. She tried to show interest but the old man could make anything seem boring and as dry as dust.

"So, what happened when Artorius met Alaricus, the leader of the Barbarians?"

Maia jerked to attention. He'd asked her a question and now she didn't have Briseis to supply all the answers. She replayed the lecture in her head.

"Artorius was successful in paying off Alaricus to retreat to the East, where he died shortly after."

"Correct. Battles are sometimes won with carrots as well as sticks," Sulianus said. He sucked at his teeth and adjusted his spectacles. "It's a pity we can't just bribe everyone and have done with it, but there we are. It's not always possible, alas! If Alaricus hadn't died or had refused to take payment, Roma herself could have been sacked. Who knows? The Two Emperors certainly couldn't have coped on their own. I refer you to my

69

book. Read chapters eight and nine by tomorrow and yes, there will be a test."

He glanced over at the wall clock.

"Our time is up for today. I'll see you in the morning."

"Yes, Master," Maia replied, with ill-concealed impatience. "May I go? I would like to see Briseis before she leaves."

His watery blue eyes widened. "My goodness, is it that time already? It doesn't seem a minute since she started here. I swear that time's going faster every day. Do give her my regards."

"I will," Maia promised, grabbing her books and hurrying off before he could start to talk about something else.

Briseis already had her cloak on and was sitting on her bed, staring at nothing, when Maia knocked on the partially-open door.

"Come in, Maia. I'm just about ready."

Maia joined her on the bed.

"How are you feeling?"

"Nervous," Briseis admitted. "Matrona says that *Blossom* is very kind and she must have a lot of patience to train us up, but it's still scary."

"What have I told you?" Maia insisted. "You'll be fine. And don't forget to let us know how you're doing. You must have some time to yourself."

"I expect so. Oh, before I go, I've a present for you."

She reached inside her cloak and took out a small box, tied with a white silk ribbon.

Maia took it, pulled at the bow and lifted the lid. Inside was a string of exquisite tiny seed pearls, separated with little blue gemstones. She couldn't hide her pleasure.

"Oh, Briseis. They're beautiful!"

"I know you don't have any jewellery and I saw these. They seem appropriate somehow, though I'm not sure why."

Maia picked the necklace up and ran it through her fingers, enjoying the smooth feel of it.

"I'll wear it every day," she promised her friend.

Briseis laughed. "Then you'll remember me."

"Of course, I'll remember you!" Maia said, indignantly. "I made something for you too but they're back in my room. Don't go anywhere yet!"

She jumped up and shot along the corridor to fetch the embroidered handkerchiefs she'd sewn for her friend. She hadn't thought to order anything from the catalogues, wanting to put her skills to good use instead. She was just coming out of her room when she nearly bumped into Tullia.

"Has she gone yet?" the girl said quickly.

"No."

Tullia's face creased in misery. She looked different with her hair in a plain bun and no make-up.

"Matrona won't let me come and wave her off. Now that isn't fair."

Maia agreed with her.

"Tell her I'll be in touch when I can. And wish her good fortune!"

"I will," Maia told her. Tullia nodded and held up a pair of shoes.

"I've got to clean these. I can't believe it's only been four days. I won't last the week!"

"You'll get used to it," Maia told her. She wanted to add, *I did*, but that would have been unfair. She'd known nothing else. She debated whether or not to mention the Admiral's visit.

"My father said he'd met you," Tullia said suddenly as if she had plucked the thought straight from Maia's head. "What did he say to you?"

"He commended me on my studies and said he was looking forward to working with me," Maia said carefully. "I hope he wasn't too hard on you."

Tullia looked at the floor.

"He was angry," she said. "Understandably so, I suppose. It was my fault, after all. He said I'd brought my degradation on myself and he was right. I can't leave. He made that abundantly clear, though he promised..." She broke off and her face cleared for a moment, remembering something happier. "He said I'll be honoured as a Ship. He has great plans for me."

"I'll help you as much as I can," Maia said. "Failing that, we'll cut our hair off, dress as boys and make a run for it."

Tullia smiled. "That's a happy thought, but we wouldn't get very far. You do know that we're being watched? Matrona won't have been the one to tell him about this." She gestured to her

71

maid's uniform. "He's got a spy, probably that Hilda. Watch what you say and do around her."

Maia was surprised, but couldn't believe that anyone would be interested in her. It must just be his disobedient daughter that he was keeping an eye on.

"What will you do?" she asked.

Tullia shrugged. "There are worse things in the world and as a Ship I'll count for something. I'll also have my father's support and patronage. You could too, you know."

"What do you mean?"

Tullia's face took on a sly, knowing expression.

"He's a senior Admiral and has an eye on a promotion. Admiral Pendragon would rather be at sea with his beloved *Augusta* than spend time at Court, so that leaves the way open for father to get into the good graces of the Prince. He says that the old King won't last much longer."

Maia had been right about the man's ambition and an Admiral at Court was often worth two at sea. She decided to play along.

"Yes. But how could that help me?"

Tullia rolled her eyes. "Really, Maia, you're so naïve. My father will help you to get a superior vessel. You don't want to end up on a little sixth-rate, do you? The King has a nominal say but it's really the Admirals who decide. He just adds his Royal seal. My father can be a very influential friend and he has plans for the Navy."

"Plans?" Maia asked innocently. An alarm bell was ringing frantically in her head but it wouldn't do to antagonise Tullia.

The girl pressed her lips together.

"I can't say," she said at last, "but it will be so exciting! You'd do well to be on our side. Think about it!"

"I certainly will," Maia assured her. She wasn't sure what Tullia was talking about but she didn't like the idea of getting mixed up in politics one little bit.

"I must go. It's almost time for Briseis to be leaving."

"Yes, go! Tell her I hope I'll see her at her installation. They might let us attend that," Tullia said quickly. She gave the dirty shoes a look of disgust. "These are Hilda's. I'm thinking of hiding pins in the lining."

"It's not worth it," Maia said.

"Just wait until I get my privileges back!" Tullia sniffed.

Maia said goodbye and returned to Briseis to tell her what Tullia had said. Briseis was dismayed but not surprised.

"Her father has his eye on a political career," she said, "and he'll use anything and anybody to further his cause. Even his own family. I'd watch yourself if I were you, Maia. Be pleasant but don't commit yourself to anything."

It was good advice. "What sort of vessel do you want?" she asked her friend.

"Whatever they give me," Briseis said, with a laugh. "We can't all be great warships and smaller Ships are just as valuable. I just want a nice new vessel and a good Captain and crew to call my own."

"I hope you get the best of them all," Maia said fervently.

She gave her the handkerchiefs and watched as Briseis admired the monograms inside the delicate ring of flowers.

"They're lovely! You do exquisite work."

"I always liked sewing," Maia said, "though we didn't get much chance to embroider. They're for you to wave, not to cry into, mind!"

Briseis smiled.

"I'll write and tell you all about *Blossom*, as you'll be meeting her too. I'd better be going. Matrona will be waiting…"

"…and time and tide wait for no man. Or woman!" Maia finished.

They left the room arm in arm.

.

V

"I have a special treat for you, girls!" Matrona announced one morning. Briseis had been gone three months and both Maia and Tullia had hardly stopped working since.

They both looked at Matrona expectantly.

"You're being permitted to witness the *Diadem*'s installation and launch."

Tullia brightened up immediately. "Will there be entertainments?"

"Oh yes. The city is making a big thing of it. The King's uncle, the Lord High Admiral Pendragon will be officiating. You may even get to meet him, though I should warn you that there's always a lot of interest in potential Ships. Security will be high as large crowds are expected."

"Will the King be there?" Maia asked.

"I don't know," Matrona said. "His Majesty is very frail and can't travel far. The young Prince might be but the rumours are that he prefers to go hunting."

"I don't blame him for preferring to hunt," Tullia giggled. "I would too."

Matrona sighed. "What a surprise, Tullia. Princes have their duties too and launching Ships is one of them. He may turn up."

"I hope he does. He's supposed to be very handsome. Do we have to wear our uniforms?"

"Yes," Matrona said, firmly. Tullia pulled a face.

"How is he going to notice me if I have to wear this?" she grumbled.

"You'll be noticed anyway. We're candidates," Maia said.

Tullia had bounced back from her stint at the other end of the social spectrum. She was still served by Hilda and their relationship had settled into an uneasy truce, though she kept complaining that her hands were rough and sore. Maia noticed that the old callouses on her own hands had mostly disappeared and her nails had grown out, though they'd never look like a lady's hands.

"I'll have to spend more time on my hair and make-up," Tullia decided. "There's no rule saying that I can't wear jewellery too. I notice that you've got a new necklace." She leaned over and peered at Maia's pearls. "Small, but pretty."

"They were a present," Maia said. She didn't know if Briseis had given Tullia anything so didn't want to mention where she'd got them.

"Ooh! Have you an admirer?" Tullia teased.

"Hardly," Maia snorted.

"I wish I had a handsome admirer," Tullia sighed. "Perhaps the Prince will notice me and rescue me from bondage, like in the old stories."

That would probably be the only reason that her father would release her from her contract, Maia reasoned, but there was little to no chance of that happening.

"I expect he'll marry a Gallic princess," she said and was rewarded by a scowl.

"I'd make an excellent Queen," Tullia said, drawing herself up, haughtily.

Maia grinned. "Well, you never know."

"True."

Tullia's mood improved over the next few days, though she was reprimanded for not paying attention to her lessons. Master Sulianus was patient, but even he found Tullia's inability to remember even the simplest facts frustrating.

"Ships must be cultured and knowledgeable," he upbraided her for the umpteenth time. "We are not like the Northern Alliance, relying on brute spirits who roar and squeal like wild beasts. You will be representing the values of the Empire at all times and to do that you must be civilised!"

"Yes, Master Sulianus," Tullia said sweetly, but as soon as the old man turned his back, she stuck out her tongue and smirked.

"How do the Northerners control their spirit Ships, Master?" Maia asked, genuinely interested. Tullia rolled her eyes.

"An excellent question, Maia," Sulianus said approvingly, shooting a reproachful glance at Tullia. "It is thought that they bind the essence of a beast to their vessels, probably using some ancient barbaric rite. Thus, they have Wolf Ships, Bear Ships,

Boar Ships and possibly even Dragon Ships, though they're probably things they call firewyrms, not proper dragons. It remains unknown as to how they communicate with their Captains and crews but there are rumours of a blood link.

"Sounds about right," Tulia said. "All they're interested in is fighting and killing. Father says that they're fierce warriors. Look what happened on the New Continent."

"What happened?" Maia asked.

Tullia gave her a superior glance. "Oh, don't you know? They tried to extend Vinland further south a few years back and nearly overran the Colonias. The New Roma Legions beat them back, but only just and only with the help of the natives. Isn't that right, Master?"

"It is," Sulianus agreed. "I pray to the Gods that the current truce holds. They're a dangerous enemy and we've enough on our Eastern borders without worrying about the North too."

Maia remembered the tattooed Northman who'd been in The Anchor and the Ships she'd seen in the harbour. They had looked fierce.

"Some of them are tall and handsome, though," Tulia giggled and Sulianus shot her an exasperated look.

"If we may return to our lesson?" He began to write a verse of Latin on the board, the chalk squeaking loudly.

Tullia pulled a face, while Maia sighed and reached for her Latin dictionary.

*

Matrona stood in the vestibule and inspected both girls. She'd already sent Tullia back to her room to scrub off some of her make-up, an order that was received with ill grace, but Maia had passed muster. She was excited at the thought of leaving the Academy, even for a brief time and couldn't wait to see the outside world again.

"We'll be escorted by marines at all times," Matrona informed them "and we're going to be part of the procession. The Navy wants it known that there are candidates waiting in the wings to take up new vessels; remember, this isn't just a public holiday, but also a chance to promote the might of the Royal

Navy. Keep your cloaks fastened. It is October after all and it will be chilly. I'll be with you too, so ask me if you want to know anything. Remember your posture and wave at the crowds."

"Like this," Tullia said to Maia, demonstrating a regal wave of the hand. Maia wanted to laugh but managed to keep her face straight.

"We'll have our own vehicle," Matrona said, "just behind the *Diadem*."

"Will she be in a carriage?" Maia asked, wondering if wooden Ships could sit down.

"No, she'll be given a specially decorated cart," Matrona said. "Now, enough questions. We're going by land today so we can join the procession at the beginning, before we head for the Admiralty Offices."

Maia felt her insides lurch with excitement. She hadn't imagined that she would be part of the procession.

Matrona hustled them out of the Academy building and into a scene of organised chaos. There were several carriages lined up waiting, pulled by horses in naval livery. There were even two of the new mobile steam engines, idling while they waited and attended by uniformed Artificers. She stared at them curiously until a poke from Tullia directed her to one of the carriages. Other carriages were filled with boys from the Academy, laughing and chattering amongst themselves. They were probably as glad of the holiday as she was.

Matrona settled herself in opposite them and the carriage set off, rattling over the cobblestones. Maia squinted across the harbour, happy to see Portus again though she couldn't make out much in the misty morning light. Tullia pulled out a little silver mirror and began to inspect her make up.

"Oh, I do hope the Prince is here," she said, fluttering her eyelashes at her reflection.

"He might be," Matrona said. "Stop fussing."

Tullia gave her a wide-eyed look of innocence.

"Will we be staying in the carriage?" she asked.

"No. The Navy has organised a tableau with both of you as the centrepiece," Matrona said.

Tullia squealed with delight. "Ooh! Everyone will be able to see us!"

Maia's heart sank. She'd seen tableaux like these before and she didn't want to be the focus of everyone's attention. She cast her eyes in mute appeal at Matrona and the woman smiled sympathetically.

"I hope the wind doesn't ruin my hair," Tullia pouted. "It's not going to rain is it, Matrona?"

"No, the weather will be fine and you won't be cold."

Maia remembered the warming spell Raven had cast and wondered if that was why.

"I don't like to be stared at," Maia said.

"Don't worry, Maia. Everyone will be looking at me," Tullia said, confidently. "I should be the focus as I'm senior."

"You'll be together," Matrona told her, reprovingly.

"Yes, but everyone will still be looking at me." Tullia grinned at Maia, daring her to reply, but Maia refused to be drawn, looking out of the window instead.

They were coming into Portus proper now, entering the sprawl of factories, workshops and tenements that made up the suburbs. Most of the local business catered for the naval or sea trade and she could make out the great long buildings of the rope works and the naval warehouses, guarded by the high perimeter wall to her right. The streets were fairly empty; the few people about were all clearly in a hurry to be elsewhere and the air was clearer as even the factories had closed for the day of celebration.

The cavalcade began to make its way up to the starting point above the city. From there, Matrona explained, it would follow a prescribed route down towards the Forum and the Admiralty Offices, where there would be speeches, presentations and the *Diadem* would be brought forth in all her splendour. Maia was strangely disappointed. She'd hoped that they would be part of the crowd for a while and at liberty to walk around. Part of her had even thought that she might find Casca and tell him of her good fortune, but it was obvious that they were to be shepherded about with no say in their movements.

Just like Ships.

She sighed. So much for a holiday. They were going to be shown like prize heifers. She set her jaw and watched the scenery instead, trying to ignore the wild urge to make a run for it as soon as the carriage stopped. It was easier to lose oneself in a crowd.

And how would you disguise your uniform? a snide little voice said in her head. *You'd be picked up immediately and then Matrona would think up a punishment for you. Do you want to spoil the fact that you're still in her good graces?*

She sighed again.

"Oh Maia, don't be a wet blanket," Tullia said, crossly. "It'll be fun!"

Maia resisted the urge to kick her, hard. The girl was becoming more irritating every day and it was only a matter of time before she lost her temper with her.

"If you like being paraded like a cow at the fair, I suppose it is!" she snapped.

"Matrona!" Tullia wailed. "Maia called me a cow!"

"No she didn't, Tullia. Control yourself and stop baiting her," Matrona ordered. "We're almost there."

Maia could hear the noise of a large number of people up ahead. They passed through a security gate in a high wooden fence and into an open space full of bustle and movement.

"Here we are. Right, girls, out we get and I'll show you to the tent where the refreshments are. We've got about an hour to get ready, so you can have a drink and a snack. Don't forget to use the latrine before we set off. You don't want to get caught short halfway through, do you?"

"No, Matrona," they both chorused. Maia groaned inwardly. It was going to be a long day.

*

It was worse than she'd imagined. No sooner had they got into the tent than they were surrounded by women, all talking at once. The man in charge was elaborately coiffed and expensively dressed. He was flitting about, talking in a loud voice with an Italian accent and gesturing, first at one thing then another. As soon as his eye lit upon the pair of them, his face adopted an expression of delight.

"Ah! Our candidates!" He clasped his hands before him. "Here you are! My name is Gallus and I will make you shine like radiant beams of light from heaven!"

He clapped his hands and the women fell back to give him room.

"This is Gallus, the stylist," Matrona said evenly. "He has orders to dress you for the tableau."

Gallus gave her an ingratiating smile.

"Honoured Madam, I shall take great care of your girls, the ornaments of our great Navy!"

Maia watched him with suspicion. He was named for a cockerel and he certainly strutted like one. It was probably a nickname. Tullia, however, was lapping up the flattery and gave the man an arch smile.

"Now, let me see," Gallus said, adopting an expression of deep thought. "The theme of the tableau is the paying of tribute to Neptune and his court, so...you will be worshippers in his train!"

He snapped his fingers and one of the women rushed over with lengths of material as he tutted over their uniforms. For a horrible moment, Maia thought he was going to tell them to take them off so he could drape them in wispy gauze. Fortunately, Matrona had the same thought.

"The uniforms stay on."

Gallus' face fell. "But Madam-"

"They are Naval candidates, not actresses," she reminded him, fixing him with a fierce glance.

He spread his hands and sighed, raising his eyes to heaven in mock chagrin.

"As you will, Madam. Do I have your permission to add to their *uniforms*?"

"Within reason."

Gallus looked as if he was about to object but thought better of it. The looming presence of Basil reinforced Matrona's words. The big man was standing to one side, arms folded and glaring.

"Well," he said at last, with a dramatic sigh. "You tie my hands but I will do what I can!"

In the end, he was forced to compromise, draping some sea-green and blue material around them like sashes, held in place with golden shell clasps. Tullia twisted this way and that, fingering the jewellery happily. Maia suffered herself to be dressed and adjusted whilst Gallus watched and tutted.

"Now, the faces!" he announced. "They must be visible from a distance, no? They cannot be," he waved a hand at Maia, "plain!"

Tullia smirked and Maia felt her cheeks go pink but before she could object, she was pushed into a chair and draped with a cloth. Then the women started on her face. Across the tent, Tullia was being similarly treated; she needn't have spent so much time on her make-up after all. Her face was coated with some cool substance, then powdered before colour began to be applied.

"Close your eyes, please, miss," one of the women said. Maia felt the soft touch of a brush sweep across her eyelids, while, in the background, Gallus was trying to convince Matrona of the merits of removing their caps.

"What ugly things! Impossible! They shall have beautiful tiaras instead."

"They are part of the uniform - "

"They make them look like washerwomen, not revered candidates!"

"It's naval regulations -"

"I say pah to naval regulations! I shall design a new uniform!"

Eventually, Matrona relented and the caps went, replaced by tiaras adorned with gold and silver sea shells. It was probably the washerwomen remark that had done it, Maia thought, as nobody could call any part of the uniform flattering. Tullia was admiring herself in her little mirror. When she turned to Maia, her face had been transformed. Blue and gold paint, together with little spangles, adorned her face and her lips so that she looked more like a temple statue than a human girl.

"Don't I look splendid?"

"You look different," Maia allowed. The unfamiliar cosmetics made her face feel stiff, as if she was wearing a mask.

"And you don't look like you at all," Tullia said. She angled her mirror so that Maia could see into it.

A stranger looked back at her. The paint made her face rounder somehow, with fuller lips and larger eyes. She could hardly believe that it was her. The one good thing was that nobody could possibly recognise her now.

"Ye Gods!" she said in disbelief.

"Splendid!" Gallus trilled. "Though it could have been better," he added, shooting a venomous look at Matrona, who deliberately ignored him.

They had to use straws to drink through and still had to have a touch-up afterwards. Maia was glad when it was time to go and followed Matrona and Tullia over to the long cart that held the tableau. It was built into steps, with an actor playing the part of Neptune seated on a throne at the top. She and Tullia were guided to lesser seats below him. She had to admit that she was impressed with the whole thing, though she would have still preferred to be watching it from the street. Neptune waved his trident at them as they ascended. He couldn't move at all, she saw, as he was wearing a huge fish tail that coiled sinuously, ending in huge iridescent flukes. His beard fell to his waist and was braided with golden shells.

"Hello, ladies!" he boomed.

"Hello!" Tullia called back cheekily. She bounced into her seat and Maia scrambled after her, feeling a little dizzy. After them came some children, dressed as Mer-people and carrying baskets of sweets to throw at the crowd. They giggled and chattered like a flock of magpies as they took their places, their eyes like saucers as they took everything in. While all this was going on, Gallus trotted around at the base, shouting orders that nobody was listening to.

"Smile, everybody!" he shrieked, which caused another ripple of giggles from the children. Neptune pointed his trident at him until Gallus turned away, converting it to a rude gesture at his retreating back.

A sudden lurch and they were off. Maia could see Matrona mouthing something at her but she couldn't make it out over the noise and the shouting as everyone got into position. She shrugged helplessly. Matrona threw up her arms and gave her a thumbs up instead.

"We're off!" Tullia squealed. Neptune beamed down benevolently and Maia wondered if he'd done this before, but conversation was impossible. The cart that would hold the *Diadem*'s Shipbody rumbled in front of them, made to look like a vessel. Maia admired the gold paint and banners that flew from the miniature masts. It even had little cannons to fire rose petals over the crowds in salute. Everything was ready to convey the Ship to her new vessel, which was resting on a special slipway in the harbour having been sailed manually from the dockyards. There was a string of carriages at the front, full of dignitaries and high-ranking officers but there was no sign of royalty as yet. Hadn't Matrona said something about the King's uncle?

Behind her cart, arranged in neatly regimented lines, was a whole company of marines with their naval standard borne proudly before them. After them came the pupils of the Academy marching in step with their tutors, all in their best dress uniforms. Far behind them were more carts and tableaux towering over the procession but Maia couldn't make them out. It would probably be the standard fare of scenes from mythology and history, trotted out once more to please the public.

As soon as they passed the gate there was a mighty roar of approval. The street was already lined with onlookers, many of whom would move with the procession so as not to miss any part of the action. Maia looked out at the sea of faces and waving flags and felt very exposed.

She glanced over at Tullia, who was sitting upright with a regal air and acknowledging the crowds with a gently waving hand. Maia copied her, pretending that she was just a moving statue, a fixture and part of the scenery. Soon, everything just blurred and she stopped focusing on any one particular thing or even thinking about anything in particular.

The children were more animated, screaming greetings at people in the crowd and throwing handfuls of sweets which were immediately snapped up by outstretched arms. Banners bearing the Imperial Eagle and the Great Dragon of Britannia were hung from almost every window, bringing swathes of colour and festivity to the city. Soon, she began to register familiar landmarks. Shops and taverns she recognised came into view as they passed, until she was gazing at the familiar frontage of the Foundling Home. It looked different from this height, but she spotted the children on the steps, surrounding the portly figure of Varus. She leaned over and shouted at her attendants, pointing to the group.

"Throw them sweets!"

The children were happy to oblige and Maia had the immense joy of watching the foundlings race to grab the treats, ripping off the wrappers and stuffing them into their mouths and pockets as fast as they could. Varus remonstrated with them in vain, until he realised that the crowd was cheering them on so he just let them get on with it. The little sea nymphs kept up the cascade of brightly coloured goodies until they were out of reach and Maia sat back, happy that she'd made a tiny difference. She'd had one of those sweets once and could still remember the sweet taste of rosewater and sugar on her tongue.

It was the least she could do for them and the startled look on old Varus' face had been priceless.

The streets were packed to bursting now, a mass of cheering and shouting humanity climbing lampposts and hanging out of windows for a better view. The children had replenished their baskets and were hurling more sweets and trinkets into the enthusiastic crowd. Maia looked ahead, spotting the open space of the Forum where they would halt.

The wind had risen a little, turning to a stiff breeze blowing off the land, but she didn't feel cold. It had to be a spell surrounding the participants as she noticed that many of the crowd were bundled up. It was less sheltered as they emerged into the Forum, the largest public space in Portus, dominated by civic offices and temples, the largest of which were dedicated to Jupiter and Neptune respectively. They dwarfed the other buildings, with their brightly painted and gilded statues glinting in the sunshine.

Eventually, the procession ground to a halt, snaking round the area so as to get everyone in and Maia could see how long it really was. People were getting out of carriages at the front and being taken up to a raised platform, to be greeted by men in official togas, some of which had purple stripes. They must be senators and the others were people of influence. She strained her eyes.

"Can you see the Prince?" Tullia shouted over to her. Maia shook her head. Would there be any way of telling if he was there? The other girl was half-standing, so as to get a better view.

"I don't think he's here," Neptune called down to her and her face fell in disappointment. "I can see Admiral Pendragon though. He's the one in the middle, look, Cardo is bowing to him."

"Who?" Maia asked him.

"Julius Epolonius Cardo. He owns half the factories in Portus, everything from tanning to cloth making. He's made a fortune."

"Isn't he the one who freed all his slaves?" Tullia said.

"Oh yes. He started a trend all right. Why bother with slaves when you can have workers who are beholden to you? Free 'em, house 'em, charge 'em for rent and subsidised food and get most of your money back. They might be freedmen and women, but their kids will be born free and that gives him an enormous popular vote and a huge client base. Plus, most of them haven't got the money to set up in competition, so he keeps skilled workers. Clever, eh?"

Maia had to admit that it was.

"It's totally insane," Tullia announced. "They could move elsewhere."

"Not when the other factories use slaves," Neptune grinned. "I should know. He freed me. I'm doing this for cash because I look the part. And I get the best view. Hail, Cardo!"

He gave a great laugh and raised his trident in salute. The portion of the crowd that was nearest answered him with a roar.

The world was truly beginning to change, Maia thought. She looked at Cardo with interest.

"Girls!" Matrona's voice cut through the racket. She was standing at the base of the float, beckoning to them. Maia was stiff after sitting in one position for so long, but she climbed down, helped by Basil's strong arms lifting her down the last few feet. Tullia followed, shaking out her skirts.

"That was fun!" the girl said.

Maia had enjoyed it more than she'd thought, but the show wasn't over yet. She was just sad that Briseis had missed it.

"You're going to be presented to the Lord High Admiral." Matrona checked that they were both presentable. "Wait until he speaks to you and don't forget to salute. If he asks you a question keep the answer short. Come on."

They made their way across the Forum towards the steps that led up to the platform. The marines guarding the approach saluted as they approached and Maia experienced a tiny thrill.

Matrona led them upwards until they came face to face with the most important people in Portus.

Admiral Pendragon was a man of medium height, with iron grey hair and the weather-beaten face of a true sailor. This Admiral didn't spend all his time in an office. They waited patiently to one side while he finished speaking to another man, a Captain by his earring and uniform. It was only when the latter turned that Maia recognised Camillus Berwyn and her heart sank. She'd hoped she wouldn't see him again, but here he was.

"Ah, Lady Helena," Captain Berwyn said, with a smile and Maia remembered that that was Matrona's name. "My lord, it gives me great pleasure to present Lady Helena Quintilla and our two latest candidates. As you know, we currently have three, but one is already training at sea."

The Admiral's dark eyes turned to them and both Maia and Tullia saluted. He returned the salute smartly.

"May I present Tullia Albana?" Pendragon raised an eyebrow.

"Ah, you must be Albanus' daughter."

"I have that honour, my lord," Tullia replied sweetly.

"You honour your family and your country," Pendragon replied formally, though Maia had the sudden impression that he didn't like Albanus much.

"And Maia Abella, from here in Portus," Berwyn continued.

"A local girl, excellent!" The Admiral's eyes crinkled at the corners and Maia smiled back. She liked this man. Even though he was the head of the whole Navy and Royal to boot, there was something approachable about him.

"I hope to be welcoming you both aboard your own vessels before too long," he told them.

"Thank you, my lord," they answered.

"They are a credit to you, Lady Helena," Pendragon said. "Now we'd better get on with getting the *Diadem* installed. Your Ship has waited long enough Berwyn and so have you. Enjoy the day, ladies!"

They saluted once more and made their way back to the cart.

"I suppose the Admiral's married?" Tullia said wistfully.

"He is and has an adult son, Prince Marcus," Matrona said briskly.

Tullia sighed.

It was time to get into position once more and Maia hoped that the relatively short trip to the harbour would pass quickly. She was beginning to tire and the spangles on her face were starting to irritate. She wanted nothing more than to scratch them off, but didn't dare.

They had scarcely got back into position when a fanfare of trumpets rang out, echoing off the surrounding buildings. A procession of Priests appeared from the Temples of Jupiter and Neptune, each leading a bull, garlanded for sacrifice. They made their way to a specially- erected altar in the centre of the Forum, where each animal was dispatched, the entrails read and the carcass taken away to be jointed, roasted and distributed to the crowds. Clouds of sweet-smelling incense rose to the heavens as choirs chanted hymns in praise of the Gods.

Pendragon supervised proceedings, approving the offerings which included silver for the Temples and gold to be cast into the deep to appease Neptune. The *Diadem* would pay her tribute on her first sea voyage.

To everyone's relief, all went well, each animal submitting meekly. Any trouble would mean that the Gods were angry and refused the sacrifice, though Maia noticed that the steam vehicles hadn't been brought into the Forum; there was no sense in tempting fate.

After a while, the main sacrifices were over and the doors of the Admiralty Offices swung open. Everyone craned to see. Standing there was the *Diadem* herself, framed by garlands and banners. A murmur of awe rose from the crowd as the Ship glided slowly out and walked down the steps. Her Captain was waiting for her at the bottom to escort her to her vehicle. They saluted each other and the miniature cannon fired canisters of rose petals into the air as the trumpets sounded once more. The crowd erupted into cheers as she took her place on the little vessel, standing proudly at the bow and acknowledging the crowds.

How many times had she done this, left one vessel only to get another new one, like a snake shedding its skin? Maia had read that she was three hundred and twenty years old, so she must have had a few. Her wooden features surveyed the crowd, before she fixed her eyes towards the sea and her new vessel. Her Captain moved to stand just behind her to her right as the cart began to move past the cheering crowds and towards the main street down to the harbour.

Maia caught Tullia watching the *Diadem*'s progress with a calculating expression on her face, as if she was only now seeing the value of the position she would hold, if she passed her initiation. Would she decide that it was worth doing after all? Maia wasn't entirely sure that she liked what she saw, but that would be between Tullia and the Gods. A cold shiver ran up her spine, like somebody had walked over her grave and she suddenly felt sick.

Too much excitement and not enough food. She called to one of the children to pass her up a sweet, make-up be damned. The sticky confection in its coating of fine sugar was what she needed and she started to feel better immediately. Tullia's gaze was fixed on the *Diadem* up ahead and didn't notice, so she took another, winking at the cherubic little boy with the blue curly wig, who grinned back. He'd lost his front tooth, she noticed with a sudden pang. A wave of sadness brought sudden tears to her eyes. There had been no little boys or girls of her own for the *Diadem*. She'd have her youngest crew members, boys training for a life at sea, but she would never be a mother, a lover or a wife.

She turned forward, seeing the rigid back of the Ship and wondered what her name had been, long ago, when she was human. Had she ever regretted her choice? Had she even had one?

They were closer to the crowd now. Men and women threw flowers on to the cart calling blessings, their faces full of hope at the sight of their Ship and their potential Ships-to-be. Priests blessed them and old sailors waved their caps as they passed. Every face was filled with hope and adoration, as if they were in the presence of the Gods themselves, or the next best thing. Maia waved back, feeling the pressure of their expectations and the responsibility that was slowly but surely settling on her shoulders. Britannia needed Ships, to protect her shores, to escort her trade goods, to serve her people near and far. And she had no Potentia.

She held back her tears and prayed that Mercury knew what he was doing.

*

It was the dull tolling of the bells that told them the bad news. Maia was having breakfast and trying to ignore Tullia's chatter when the sounds rang out across the city. The girls looked at each other in alarm.

"What is it?" Tullia said, her eyes wide.

Branwen appeared at the door looking agitated, then burst into tears.

"What's wrong?" Maia was on her feet in a second.

"Oh, miss. The King's dead."

"He was very old," Tullia said, unperturbed. "Does this mean that Prince Artorius is the King now? At least they won't have to change the name on everything."

Maia shot her an exasperated look and went to find Matrona.

"Yes, the old King is dead," Matrona said sadly, "and his grandson will inherit. It's such a shame that his father, Prince Julius, died in that hunting accident. He would have made a good King, instead of which we're left with a nineteen-year-old boy with little sense of duty."

She drew a sharp breath and Maia knew that she must be stressed to speak so unguardedly.

"Ignore that last statement, please, Maia. Gods save King Artorius the Tenth."

Maia dipped her head in acknowledgement. She knew that Master Sulianus was of the same opinion. Artorius the Younger was very different to his predecessor. Perhaps he would gain wisdom with age but, until then, the country would be largely in the hands of his advisors.

Like Albanus.

Maia supposed it was natural to look to the future and it had been clear for a while that the old King's life was drawing to a close.

"I'll have to sort out mourning dress for all of us," Matrona said, matter-of-factly. "Most of the official events will be in Londin, but it will be marked here in Portus too. There will be eulogies and services and all the rest. After that, there will be all the celebrations for the accession of the new King, which will lead to far more cheerful times, Gods willing. All in all, it means a lot of hard work so I must get on with it.

"Please let me know if I can help," Maia offered and was rewarded with a smile.

"That's kind of you. I will," Matrona said. For a second, she looked as though she was going to say something else but then she sighed and bent to write in the ledger on the desk.

Maia went to finish her breakfast, pondering on how this change would affect them all.

VI

The incessant rain had finally stopped and the watery March sun was peeping through the clouds, promising more warmth to come. Maia was sick of being stuck indoors, so she threw on her cloak and decided to take a turn in the garden. The winter had been mild and wet, which had left everyone out of sorts and she'd had to admit to herself that she'd been relieved when Tullia had left at last for her partnership training.

The benches were wet, so she settled for a stroll along the narrow paths between the immaculately trimmed bushes, admiring the daffodils and crocuses in the borders. Noise from the adjoining buildings told her that the boys had been let out to play and get some fresh air too.

She looked around the familiar scene. After nearly three years at the Academy she knew every brick and stone and was used to the confinement and demanding work. She had been out occasionally since that first time, usually to be paraded at another installation or important naval occasion but not as often as she would have liked. Her favourite lessons had been the practical ones, learning to sail the little dinghies in a protected spot in the harbour, followed by some more challenging sailing off the coast. She was grateful that she hadn't been seasick either, as she understood that it was a misery for those afflicted with the condition.

Matrona kept her company most evenings, the two of them reading or sewing by the fire until it was time for bed. Maia kept hoping that more candidates would be found but, as the weeks and months passed, it seemed more and more likely that she would stay on her own. She knew that the Navy was worried and wondered what Matrona would do, with no candidates to teach.

"Some will appear, sooner or later," she said, philosophically. "I was fortunate to have three at once, if only for a short time. Alas, the Divine blood is thinning but there isn't much we can do about that. The Navy's even sent scouts to Caledonia to see if there are any suitable girls up there. I'm expecting a painted savage on the doorstep any day now."

Maia laughed. "Really?"

"Oh yes. Don't think we've not had them before, but the tribes are understandably wary of sending their daughters down to the wicked Roman south."

A Pictish candidate! That would be something to see, though anybody would be welcome. She hadn't had the chance to be senior to anyone yet.

"Have you heard from Briseis, or *Patience* as I should call her now?" Matrona asked her.

Maia fished in a pocket and brought out a letter.

"Yes, she wrote to me a few days ago."

She'd kept in touch with Briseis and visited her aboard her vessel when she was in Portus. Her friend been given one of the new three-masted sloops and seemed quite content with her lot, patrolling the Britannic Ocean for smugglers and pirates. Maia had had a shock when she first saw her after her installation. The warm girl she had known was replaced by a stiff wooden copy, like Pygmalion's Galatea in reverse, turned from living flesh to a living statue. Her movements were strangely unnatural, though the woman inside the shell was still the Briseis she knew. Nonetheless, a gulf of experience had opened up between them as if they were each standing on either side of a chasm and shouting across at each other. Maia hoped that, if by some miracle she was ever installed, that gulf would disappear and they could be close once more.

She had long ceased to worry about her lack of Potentia. There had been no call to demonstrate her lack of it at any time and she excelled in her studies, thanks to her eagerness to learn and her unusual quirk of memory. She knew that Matrona was sending regular reports to the Navy and they didn't seem worried either. What would be, would be. She'd never sought to deceive them at any time, so if things didn't work out, they only had themselves to blame.

The only thing that bothered her were the presents. They'd started arriving soon after she'd met Admiral Albanus and it seemed that his daughter hadn't been joking when she'd tried to recruit Maia to her father's cause. They'd been tasteful and expensive and she hadn't known what to do.

She'd gone straight to Matrona.

"You can't send them back," she said, examining the little inlaid trinket box thoughtfully. "It seems that he wants your support when you get your vessel. It's not common but if he's making a play for seniority, a word in the right ears from a supportive Ship can make a difference, especially when you've a few miles under your keel."

"And here I was thinking that Ships don't get involved in politics."

"They don't, mostly," Matrona answered, her brow furrowed. "There's a lot of gossip, of course and chatter about Captains and such, but it's mostly internal." She thought for a moment. "Perhaps it's just because he sees you as a friend of his daughter. You did help her pass her examinations, you know. I don't think she could have done it otherwise."

It had quietly astounded both of them that Tullia had suddenly applied herself to her lessons and managed to scrape through the written tests.

"That must be it," Maia agreed, though a certain amount of disquiet remained, rumbling in the background.

"I'd send him a note of gratitude and leave it at that," Matrona advised and Maia complied. Since then she'd had other pretty things sent at Saturnalia, Beltane and midsummer and had replied with thanks.

The sun was a little stronger now, so she brushed off the raindrops and sat on a little wooden bench, enjoying the feeling of warmth on her face. It wouldn't be long before she was supposed to be following the others into the final part of her training aboard the *Blossom*. Tullia had been partnered with the Ship for several months, on and off and would soon be ready for her initiation. She'd been warned by Matrona not to question Briseis about it but it was obvious to Maia that the experience had changed her in more ways than one.

She shuddered a little and drew her cloak around her. She wasn't as bony as she had been when she'd arrived as a friendless little foundling and her looks had settled into a moderate plainness that she was happy to live with. Still, the time of reckoning was approaching rapidly. She tried not to think how horrible it was going to be, when she couldn't go any further. Perhaps there'd just be embarrassment all round when she couldn't link to the *Blossom*? She was preparing herself to stand up, shrug and say, "I told them I have no Potentia!" in a very loud voice.

After that, she didn't have a clue. Perhaps she could teach?

Her less-than-pleasant thoughts were interrupted by Branwen. They'd become friends over the years, so the maid didn't stand on ceremony.

"Aren't you cold out here? It's all wet." She wrinkled her nose at the soggy bench.

Maia grinned.

"This isn't wet, just a bit damp."

"Matrona has some news for you," Branwen said.

"What is it?"

"I'll let her tell you. All I'm saying is that some people get more than they deserve in life, for sure." She sniffed loudly and made a disapproving face but wouldn't answer any more questions. Maia guessed it was news of Tullia as Branwen couldn't stand her.

She stood and shook out her cloak. "I'd better go and find out then, hadn't I?"

Matrona was waiting for her in her office, a smile on her face.

"I'm pleased to tell you that Tullia passed her initiation." She seemed relieved and Maia immediately wondered what would have happened if she'd failed.

"That's good news."

"Yes. She's been assigned one of the new first-rates as well, because of her father's influence, no doubt. The Admiral is in the new King's inner circle, apparently."

Maia nodded, thinking that Albanus had been building up to this moment for who knew how many years. His pride wouldn't allow his daughter to have anything but the finest vessel available.

"I take it that she's been installed?"

"She has. Her vessel's in the Royal Dockyards near Londin, waiting to be launched. I believe the King will be doing the honours himself this time."

With his best friends by his side, no doubt. Maia was quietly pleased that she wouldn't be attending, though the launch of a brand-new Ship was always a cause for celebration. Would Tullia's self-centred nature have been altered by her trials, or would she still be the madam she'd always been? If she came to Portus, she knew for a certainty that there would be an invitation, if only so she could be well and truly put in her place. It was only the fact that Tullia thought she had Potentia that had caused her to be friendly at all.

"Talking of Ships, it's time for you to be partnered, Maia."

Maia had the sudden urge to confess all to Matrona but stopped herself just in time. She wanted her to be able to truthfully deny that she knew anything about Maia's circumstances and that would save her from any possible repercussions. She bit her tongue and kept her mouth shut. Matrona picked up on her startled expression.

"There's no need to worry. You've been an exemplary student."

Matrona sounded so proud that Maia wished that the earth would open up and swallow her before she was sent away in disgrace.

"Thank you, Matrona. Everybody's been very kind."

"So, you'll be starting tomorrow."

"Tomorrow!" Maia's head shot up in shock. "I'm not ready!"

"You're more than ready," Matrona assured her. "You don't really believe in your abilities, Maia. It's time to use them to their full capacity. Branwen has already started packing for you."

Maia felt sick. All the anxiety that she had kept firmly repressed was threatening to rise up and overwhelm her in a black tide of fear and despair. She made her way out of the office through sheer force of will and into the vestibule, only to meet the accusing gaze of ten Royal Ships. She imagined Tullia among them, pointing and laughing at her imminent failure. A sudden dizziness forced her to stop and lean against the wall for support.

Slowly, the light-headedness passed and she was able to stand up straight. She avoided looking at the statues as she hurried out for some fresh air, not wanting to see anybody else just then. She went straight to a little arbour in the garden, which was screened from the other buildings by a row of fruit trees, before collapsing on to the bench and bursting into tears. She rammed her coat into her mouth so as to muffle her sobs and stayed, curled around her pain, for what felt like an eternity.

*

The next morning, Maia, packed and ready, was summoned to Matrona's office after breakfast. She hadn't wanted to eat much but managed to force down some bread and honey. She was still feeling nervous when she knocked on the door and heard Matrona's voice bid her enter.

To her surprise, she wasn't alone. Sitting opposite her was a man in a Captain's uniform. She spotted the wooden earring that pierced his right earlobe and enabled him to communicate with his Ship at all times. He was in late middle-age, with iron grey hair tied back in a neat queue and calm brown eyes. As soon as she entered, he rose and bowed politely.

"Maia, this is Captain Gaius Plinius Tertius, of the *Blossom*. He's come to escort you to his Ship."

Maia saluted, feeling the tension in her stomach ease just a little. The Captain smiled warmly at her and she couldn't help liking him immediately. He was so different from Captain Berwyn, or Admiral Albanus for that matter and he seemed genuinely pleased to see her.

"Hello, Maia. I'm delighted that you're going to be completing your training aboard the *Blossom*."

"Honoured to meet you, sir," she replied.

"The Captain has just been visiting his wife ashore," Matrona explained.

"I have indeed," Plinius replied. "I get to see my family more than some. *Blossom* and I have been training candidates for the best part of twenty years, so we're usually confined to fairly local waters. Oh, and I go by the name of Plinius here, as my two older brothers, Primus and Secundus aren't here to confuse the issue," he said. "Our parents were very traditional and somewhat lacking in imagination."

She smiled dutifully at his little joke. Having family in Portus would be a bonus for him. Many Ships were at sea for months, or even years.

"I'm looking forward to working with you, sir," Maia replied, hoping that the welling doubt in her mind didn't make the statement seem forced.

"Don't worry," he said. "It's usual to be nervous, isn't that right, Matrona?"

"Oh yes. Well, it's time to fly the nest, my dear. I'll be kept informed of your progress and don't forget to write!"

She stood and clasped Maia's hands in her own.

"I won't forget how kind you've been to me," Maia told her.

"And you deserve only the best. Look after her, Captain."

"She's in good hands," Plinius told her, smiling. Maia had the feeling that they'd known each other a long time.

Soon, the Academy was behind her and they were boarding a Ship's boat to take them both out to the *Blossom*. It needed neither oarsmen nor steering; at this distance the *Blossom* could control both and would be guiding them in. Plinius pointed her out with pride.

"There she is, at her usual mooring. She can't wait to meet you!"

Maia gripped her cloak tighter against the cutting March wind and followed his pointing finger.

The *Blossom* was a trim two-masted sloop designed specifically to help candidates literally learn the ropes of vessel operations. They were able to get to grips with the practicalities under the guidance of an experienced Captain and Ship who had trained many others before her, including Briseis and Tullia.

Maia took long slow breaths as they approached the vessel that would be her home for the next six months, all being well. She concentrated on maintaining a calm state of mind as she had been taught whilst watching the coming and going of sailors lugging crates, barrels and casks on board from supply boats. Some were manoeuvring the cranes to lift bulkier items, provisions for the journey they would soon make. The Captain was quiet as they approached over the water and she sensed that he was communicating directly with his Ship. When candidates were partnered, they were able to communicate directly with either of them, though they could also be blocked when necessary. Eavesdropping was absolutely forbidden.

He gave her a cheerful smile as they approached the wooden flanks of the Ship, on the opposite side to the other boats. A rope sling with a wooden seat was sent down for Maia, whilst the Captain made for a ladder.

"It keeps me fit," he told her. Maia was glad she wouldn't have to climb in skirts.

She settled herself, holding tightly to the ropes, then felt herself lifted into the air, moving swiftly up the painted sides, past closed gun ports, higher and higher until she could see the deck. Plinius moved nimbly up the ladder, keeping pace with her until he reached the gap in the rail and stepped on to his vessel.

"Captain on deck!" A female voice rang out, along with a loud whistle and the sailors on board immediately stopped, stood to attention and saluted. Maia was swung over the rail and down, her feet touching the planks. The Captain stepped forward to take her hand as she steadied herself and looked around. The crew saluted her and she returned the salute as she had been taught, turning to include the quarterdeck where the Ship awaited them. For an instant she remembered being surprised at all the saluting as it was second nature to her now.

The *Blossom* was waiting for them. "Welcome aboard!" the Ship said.

Maia and the Captain made their way over to where she stood waiting to greet them, her gown falling to merge into the wood of the deck itself. As she drew nearer, Maia saw that *Blossom*'s Shipbody was part of the vessel, growing from the living wood that was the central Mystery of all Ships. She looked just like a skilfully carved statue until she smiled, teeth white against her dark skin. Her black hair was woven into a multitude of tiny plaits which were wound into an elaborate topknot adorned with exotic flowers and her brightly patterned gown was a riot of colour against the plain wooden planks at her feet. Her tutela was a large bouquet of the same beautiful flowers, which she raised in greeting as they approached. She seemed delighted to see Maia.

"Thank you, ma'am," Maia answered her. She'd been afraid that *Blossom* might have been like one of the haughty and terrifying Ships she had met on her first visit to the Headquarters.

Captain Plinius saluted his Ship smartly and she laughed at some secret comment.

"Of course I'm looking beautiful!" she said in her rich, deep voice. "Maia, come on up here and let me see you properly."

Maia walked over to her and *Blossom* stretched out her arms in welcome. Maia went to clasp hands, but instead found herself enfolded in a hug. The Ship's arms were more pliable and yielding than normal wood, but they still felt strange and not at all like human flesh.

"Stand next to me and I'll make the introductions," *Blossom* told her as several men trooped up. "This here's my Mage, Heron." Heron was tall and thin with a large nose, bushy hair and piercing green eyes. He examined her for a second, as all Mages seemed to do, like a habit they'd got into on meeting people for the first time, then bowed.

"Pleased to make your acquaintance, ma'am."

"And this is my senior lieutenant, Durus," *Blossom* continued. The young officer was a stocky, pugnacious young man with a firm chin who looked like he could hold his own in a fight. He bowed and said, "Marcus Laevinius. Honoured, ma'am."

The last man was clearly an Adept of Aesculapius, who saw to the mental and physical well-being of the crew, doctoring them up when necessary. He was introduced as Campion. Adepts took their names from plants, just as Britannic Mages were called after birds. He was a plump middle-aged man with sandy hair, a snub nose and watery blue eyes that fixed on her amiably.

"If you need anything chopping off, he's your man," Plinius remarked and they all laughed. It was clearly an old joke. *Blossom* rolled her eyes, but the Adept just grinned.

"We're a small crew," the Captain told her, "but we all get along and I hope that you'll enjoy your stay here. Now, shall we make a start and get you settled in?"

Maia found that she had a small cabin to herself in the stern, with a window of thick glass that let in light and reflected ripples on to the walls and ceiling. It was a little cramped, but cosy and she was pleased to see that it had a hanging captain's bed – a surprising luxury. She'd thought that she would have to get used to sleeping in a hammock like most of the crew. Her sea-chest was waiting for her, her initials proudly emblazoned in gold paint. It gave her a thrill of pride every time she saw it. She'd never had anything like it before, or any possessions to put into one. She knelt to unclasp it and raised the lid to reveal the beautiful blue velvet lining with its inset tray. When she had first been given the chest, she had spent a long time just touching it to reassure herself that it was truly hers. Now she gave it a quick pat before beginning to sort out her possessions, everything from clothing to a comb and hairbrush, as well as a couple of little luxuries she had treated herself to.

It was Briseis who had persuaded her to part with some of her coin and buy creams for her face and hands.

"They'll get chapped on board with the salt air and the wind," her friend had pointed out.

She picked up the little pots, as well as her beautiful pearl and gemstone necklace. The girl's voice echoed in her head as she placed them carefully in the tray. Part of her still felt guilty for spending the money, but having some things of her own cheered her. She decided to wear the necklace, so took it from its little box and clasped it around her neck, silently thanking Briseis for her generosity and advice. She would have to write her friend a note before they set sail, or maybe *Blossom* would relay her a message? She fingered the necklace. If, by some miracle, she passed the training and became a Ship, she wouldn't need any of it and it would all be put into storage. But that was for another day. She shook herself out of her reverie and continued to unpack.

Lessons were due to begin on the morrow. For now, she would be expected to familiarise herself with the Ship and her crew, so she ran through the latter in her head. As Captain Plinius had said, she wasn't large compared to some of the other, bigger Ships, with a small complement of marines and only thirty guns. She recalled the lesson Master Sulianus had given when, for once, even Tullia was interested in what he had to say.

"Now, we come to Ships and their counterparts, the so-called 'inanimates'," the old tutor had said. "The latter have no guiding intelligence, or anima, and need large crews to attend to every task on board, much like large versions of the dinghies you've been sailing in the harbour. If you make a mistake, you have only yourself to blame."

He stared over the tops of his spectacles at Tullia and Maia wondered if she'd nearly ended up sinking her boat.

"Officers are trained to sail inanimates before they are entrusted with the command and care of living Ships. They are taught how to take bearings, plot courses and deal with wind and weather, as you will be. They keep these skills sharp, should their Ship become incapacitated for any reason."

Maia wasn't sure how that could happen. Ships' vessels were their bodies; their control extended throughout, investing each part of the vessel with their Potentia and anima.

"Captains order and Ships obey. They relay orders and can move anywhere on the vessel. They aren't confined to the deck, though it is impolite to suddenly appear in a private space without asking first. Some sailors are more tolerant than others – you'll learn your Captain's and crew's preferences when you're installed, Gods willing."

He glared at Tullia, who was smirking again.

"Tullia. Cast the thought of surprising gentlemen in their cabins from your mind and tell me the purpose of the Captain's earring."

Tullia pouted.

"It helps them to communicate with their Ship and, er, it's made of the same wood as the Ship's body."

"It doesn't *help* them," Master Sulianus pointed out. "It is the sole reason that they are able to do so. Captains don't need Divine blood. The Potentia they possess resides in the wood, which is activated by the Potentia in the Ship."

Maia remembered the fear that had shot through her at his words. No Potentia, no activation and the earring would be useless.

So far so good. Yet...there were many things Maia was still curious about and she would be asking lots of questions. She gazed out of the leaded window at the blurry view of the harbour and the other vessels, wondering how many were Ships. Potentia or not, she was trapped here now; even if she could get off the vessel, there was no way of getting back to land. She had never learned to swim.

The sound of a bell made her jump. That told her it would soon be time for dinner in the officers' mess, adjacent to their day room. There was a partition which could be moved to make one great space, for people on board Ships had more room to move than the cramped and often filthy conditions that existed on inanimates. Maia wondered what the food was like. She'd not had to forage for scraps for a long time; not that anyone could call her overly fussy.

A quiet rap on her cabin door made her start.

"It's Durus, ma'am."

She got up and smoothed her skirts, touching her necklace for reassurance. The lieutenant was standing outside waiting to escort her into dinner and she was touched by the courtesy. He bowed politely, his eyes twinkling and she bobbed a curtsey in return.

"I hope you're hungry. The Captain keeps a fine table, especially in port."

"I have a good appetite," Maia admitted. The bread and honey had kept her going but she was ready for a more substantial meal.

The table in the mess was set with fine linen, china plates and silver cutlery. The Captain, Heron and Campion were already there, together with two men, one young, one older whom she hadn't met before. They all stood and bowed politely.

"Miss Abella, please sit by me," Captain Plinius said, indicating the empty chair to his right. Durus took the seat to his left, next to Heron and when they were both settled, he signalled to his servants who came forward to pour wine.

"Allow me to make further introductions," he began. "This is Apprentice Mage Robin, who has been with us for a while now and opposite him is our Priest, Cita, who is our link to the Gods. As you can see, he favours Neptune, but he insists that he's on speaking terms with many others as well."

The Priest, a portly old fellow with a completely bald head let out a bellow of laughter.

"You'd be surprised, my dear Captain!"

"No, I wouldn't," Plinius replied, drily. "I'll never forget you trying to chat up that nymph off the coast of Sillina. Much good it did you."

Cita leered. "And how do you know how much good it did me, my dear Captain? She was a sprightly one all right!"

There were a few sniggers round the table, then Cita remembered his manners.

"Honoured to meet you ma'am. You must excuse an old man. And may I say that no nymph could compare to you."

Maia smiled, a trifle ruefully. That flattery had gone well wide of its mark and she suspected that the glass of wine Cita was holding wasn't his first, second or third of the day. She fancied that the Captain shot him a quick look of annoyance. Still, she would have to get used again to the company of men and their bawdy talk and, after several months at sea, any woman could appear as lovely as Venus herself. The Gods knew, she'd heard enough of it at The Anchor. She'd heard of female sailors, but the Navy wouldn't accept them as they were thought to be trouble and the cause of disputes, though in her opinion that was more down to the men, as usual. Perhaps they should have all women crews?

"And now, a toast. To His Britannic Majesty King Artorius the Tenth. Long may he reign!"

"Vivat Rex," everyone chorused, obediently. The sherry was not too sweet, more like a dry sack but very palatable. The Ship's purser obviously knew his wines.

"To Miss Abella. May your stay on *Blossom* be a fruitful one!"

"I'm most grateful for this opportunity," Maia said sincerely. "You're all very kind and I look forward to working hard and learning all I can."

"Excellent!" Captain Plinius said approvingly. He signalled again and the servants returned bearing platters of roast meats and baked fish, vegetables and crusty bread and butter. Maia's mouth watered; she hadn't realised just how hungry she was. Of course, as they were in port the food was fresh and plentiful, even for the lower ranks. After a long sea voyage, it would be a different matter, unless they re-victualled regularly.

The Captain carved the roast and everyone was served as Cita intoned a prayer to the Gods. Talk soon resumed around the table and Maia found herself the object of friendly scrutiny.

"Are you from Portus, Miss Abella?" Cita enquired.

"I am sir," Maia replied. "I've lived here all my life."

Brought up with the noise of the town, the smell of saltwater and the raucous screeching of gulls.

"Ah, one foot in the sea then. Are you from a naval family?"

"I was a foundling, sir. I never knew my parents or where I came from." A familiar sadness pinched at her for a moment.

"That is a shame, my dear," the old Priest sympathised, "but now you have a family here, is that not so, gentlemen?"

"It certainly is," the Captain agreed, gesturing with his fork around the table. "Lots of new relatives have been sprung on you, whether you wish for them or not!"

There was general laughter and Maia joined in, feeling a little more of the inner ache recede. She noticed that the young Mage, Robin, had said nothing, his blond head bent over his plate as though trying to make himself as inconspicuous as possible. He couldn't have been much older than she, though he might have already been training for ten years. Boys were taken from their families as soon as their Potentia manifested, which was usually very early. As the talk drifted away from her, she decided to ask.

"Mage Robin. Have you been on *Blossom* long?"

The young man lifted his head. The first thing she noticed was the bright blue of his eyes and only then did she see the port wine stain running from his collar up his left cheek, almost to his eye. His sudden flush at being addressed made it all the more vivid.

"A-about a year, m-m-ma'am."

All that and a stutter too. It couldn't be easy for him, Maia thought. And who on earth had named him Robin? It was apt, but maybe a little too obvious.

"Robin is learning fast," Heron said quickly. "He'll be an accomplished Mage in no time."

The youth glanced at her shyly, before shooting his mentor a grateful look and applying himself once more to his food.

"Indeed," Durus said. "We need Mages and Ships too. The Navy's ordered more larger vessels, or so I've heard. The dockyards are busier than ever."

"The Northerners have their eyes on our New Roma colonies, do they not?" Heron asked.

"They do indeed," Durus replied, sourly. There were a few shudders and expressions of distaste.

"Let us pray that the wisdom of the Gods will avert any catastrophe," Cita said.

"Is it true that their god Odin has only one eye?" Durus asked him with interest.

"Yes, and his horse has eight legs. They interbreed with giants and old Earth powers," Cita informed him, waving at a servant for more fish. "They've had a lot of trouble with great dragons lately. They call them firewyrms."

Maia remembered the three foreign Ships she'd seen on her first journey across the harbour. Maybe one of them had been bound to a firewyrm's spirit?

"They can keep the dragons, or firewyrms, whatever they call them," Heron said. "We've enough trouble with krakens. They've been ranging to shallower water lately but we're working on the problem, aren't we Robin?" His apprentice nodded.

Once that course was finished a cream pudding was served, which Maia thoroughly enjoyed, followed by small sweets and savouries. Then the Captain suddenly broke off in the middle of a discussion about the new style of guns.

"A message, gentlemen, Miss Abella. We shall soon be gaining more crew, including some young officers and midshipmen to keep us company." Maia noticed that Robin didn't react and wondered if he dreaded the arrival of boisterous young men. She knew they could be cruel, but then remembered that *Blossom* would keep a close eye on them.

"More young limbs of Pan to keep us busy," Durus growled, but he didn't seem too unhappy. It would be his job to teach the midshipmen, some as young as twelve, the intricacies of navigation and to train them up to be of use.

"As soon as we have our full complement, we are to set sail for Miss Abella's training cruise. A short hop along the coast will test everyone's sea legs, eh?" Captain Plinius smiled. Maia took a deep breath. The next few days would be a challenge, but one she was looking forward to.

Back in her cabin, she perched on her bed, swinging idly to and fro and feeling the movement of the vessel. She was almost too afraid to go to sleep, knowing that the morning could bring all her hard work and hopes crashing down about her ears. A wave of dread overtook her as she stared at the cabin walls.

"Maia?"

Blossom's voice echoed in the cabin, making her jump. She'd been so locked into her misery she'd forgotten that she was never truly alone on board a Ship. She cleared her throat hastily.

"Yes, *Blossom*?"

"May I come in?"

"Yes, certainly."

The panelled wall opposite the window began to bulge outwards to form into the Shipbody, *Blossom*'s features becoming clearer as she appeared. It took about four seconds for her to complete the process as Maia watched, fascinated. The Ship was smiling.

"I just wanted to have a chat about tomorrow, so you'll know what to expect."

"That's most kind of you," Maia said. *Blossom*'s eyes lingered on her face for a moment, as if suspecting that something was wrong.

"I know it's all strange, but it will get easier. I also know that there's a lot of pressure on candidates to succeed these days, more so than when I was training. Some used to drop out before initiation, because when you start on that path there's no turning back."

"You mean I could back out now?"

Blossom's eyebrows raised at the sudden hope in Maia's voice.

"Would you want to?"

What was she supposed to say? Maia thought quickly.

"I mean, I might have to, if I'm not suitable. Perhaps the partnering process won't work."

"Why would you think that you're not suitable?" *Blossom* asked.

This was it. Should she confess now? A warning voice inside her head told her to be silent.

"I…you never know," she said, lamely.

"Hmm. Matrona warned me that you lack confidence sometimes," the Ship said. "Look, nothing will go wrong. Just don't try to use your Potentia when you get the earring. You don't need it as you'll be dependent on mine. I wanted to warn you about that as some girls think they have to make a great show and it can really mess up my channels and linkages."

"There's no danger of that," Maia told her.

"Ah, you can't access your Potentia directly," *Blossom* said, nodding. "That's quite common. Just relax and let me do all the heavy lifting. You'll be working hard soon enough."

"May I ask you some questions?"

"Of course!"

"How long have you been a Ship?"

"A long time," *Blossom* replied. "It will be nearly three hundred years now. This is my eighth vessel and I'm due a new one before too long."

Maia was amazed.

"Do you remember all your Captains?"

"I do indeed," she replied. "I liked some more than others but they were all good men in their way. I've been with Plinius for a while now and it will grieve me to see him go, but that is the way of things. You move on. There's always someone new around the next corner and you just make the most of the time you spend with your crew, while they are with you. I've lost track of the youngsters I've seen grow and take on Ships of their own. I'm a mother to many."

"Don't you wish you could have had your own children?" Maia asked curiously.

Blossom sighed. "It wasn't my path to take. I was chosen by the Gods when I was a child. My parents died and my Potentia manifested through pain and grief. Being a Ship was better than being a slave, alone and friendless."

"Was that in New Roma?"

"Yes. My mother was sold in Africa and met my father in the New Colonias. There must have been a deity somewhere in our line, but I never knew more than that. I don't think it was one of the Twelve, though. My mother worshipped the Orishas, but she was taken far away across the sea. It was another life."

"I was left at the Foundling Home in Portus," Maia told her. "I never knew either of my parents."

"They left you somewhere you would have food in your belly and a roof over your head," *Blossom* said. "Remember that."

Maia nodded.

"Now, is there anything else you want to ask me?"

Maia shook her head, unable to stop a sudden yawn.

"Time for bed, then. Sleep well and don't worry! Everything will be sorted in the morning."

The Ship gave her a reassuring smile before melting back into the wood, which sprang back into its former state as she left.

Maia didn't know whether to feel relieved or not. She undressed and climbed into her bed, wriggling down until she felt comfortable. Tullia and Briseis must have done the same thing, as well as so many girls before her. The thought of her friend lying in the same bed cheered her up and she decided to ask *Blossom* to contact her as soon as possible.

The gentle rocking of the vessel lulled her to sleep before she realised it.

VII

The following morning brought a summons from the Captain. Maia was feeling a little better at the thought that she wouldn't be expected to display signs of Potentia, but the niggling fear that she would fail at this first hurdle remained with her. She made her way up to the quarterdeck, trying to stop her knees from knocking.

The whole Ship's company had formed up and everyone was watching attentively as she was prepared for her first initiation into the Ship Mysteries. Glancing ahead, she saw a small sea of eager faces and squirmed inwardly – she was still not used to being the centre of attention, especially under these circumstances.

The officers all looked very imposing in their best dress uniforms, the gold braid gleaming in the morning sunlight. *Blossom* had decked out her vessel in flags and pennants of celebration, signalling to all that the ceremony was taking place. There were a few gawkers on boats in the harbour as well, though nothing like the amount that would turn up for a Ship Naming. This would only be a temporary installation, but there were always those who were curious to see anything new.

Maia felt her heart thumping as Heron approached her, carrying a small plain wooden box. She knew that inside was the special earring that would bind her to *Blossom*. It was fashioned from a piece of the same branch that *Blossom* used to form her Shipbody and through which she controlled the vessel. Being a training Ship, she had an extra one, twin to her Captain's. The wood, imbued with the Potentia of the Earth Goddess, bound their minds together until either it was removed, or death, whichever came first.

A playful breeze fluttered the flags and danced in the rigging. Maia felt it touch her face like a caress, clean and fresh despite the stink of the docks. Overhead, a gull screamed loudly.

The Captain signalled to Heron, who bowed to Maia. "Maia Abella, do you accept this gift and responsibility of your own free will?"

"I do." She forced the words past her lips.

"Do you swear to abide by the rules and regulations of His Majesty's Navy and to obey all lawful commands given to you by your duly appointed officers?"

"I do."

"Do you swear to honour the sacred trust and to carry out your duties as instructed by His Majesty's Ship *Blossom*?"

"I do so swear, in the name of the Goddess."

"Then let it be so. Long live the King!"

The entire crew answered him with a great shout, "Long live the King!"

Maia steeled herself. Heron opened the box and took out the small earring. Intricately spun gold encased the wood to form a hoop a finger's width in diameter. Heron tucked the box into a pocket in his robe then stood next to Maia. She tilted her head obediently to her left and felt him take hold of her ear in his cool, thin fingers.

There was a sudden heat in her earlobe, followed by a momentary stabbing pain as the ring clamped into her flesh. The Ship's Potentia began to spread through her body like a wave, energy flowing down to her toes and fingertips, making her hair rise and her skin tingle. Maia clamped her lips together fiercely so she wouldn't cry out, then the pain was gone as suddenly as it had come.

<There you are, it's all done now.> *Blossom*'s voice was in her head, warm and approving. <Brave girl! I knew you wouldn't scream the place down, not like some. Didn't she do well, Plinius?>

<Indeed she did.> The Captain's voice, too, bypassed her ears and arrived directly into her mind. She somehow knew he was pleased by her stoicism. Overlaying that, her ears were hearing cheering from the crew and polite applause from the officers.

<I can hear you!> she Sent back, hurriedly adding, <Thank you, Captain, *Blossom*.>

"All is correct, Captain," *Blossom* reported aloud and Maia had the feeling that the Ship was making checks of her own on the new connection.

"Excellent! Maia, how are you feeling?"

"I'm fine," Maia managed to say. The new Potentia of mind-to-mind communication was unfamiliar but exciting. Was this how it felt to have Divine blood? At least she had been granted an idea of what it must be like. She felt a hand on each arm and realised that Heron and the Captain were escorting her to *Blossom*'s side, where a chair had been set for her.

It was as if she were two people. One, a girl sitting in a chair having a cloak wrapped snugly around her and another, huge and heavy. She could feel simultaneously the soft material round her shoulders and the river lapping and pushing at her flanks, the air streaming around her rigging and her furled sails. The doubling of her senses made her feel both dizzy and exhilarated.

"It will take some time to get used to the new sensations," *Blossom* told her. "Rest here a while until the worst of it passes, then you can go and lie down in your cabin. You'll soon settle in." She sounded satisfied, adding, <You're a strong one, my girl. I can feel it!>

Maia watched as the ceremony was concluded by prayers and offerings of incense to the Gods. Cita's voice droned on for a while longer in the background, but Maia was too busy feeling her way around the vessel. She felt *Blossom*'s delicate touch guiding her path, as if she had just learned to walk and a steadying hand was needed to prop up her first few faltering steps.

Gradually, she felt the awareness of her flesh body fade, together with the tiny stinging in her ear. Her borrowed body had so much to explore. She barely knew it when gentle hands lifted her and carried her down to her cabin, where she fell into a deep and restful sleep.

*

The bells for the start of the first watch rang through the vessel. Eight o'clock. The last rays of the sun were just visible above the land to the west and half the crew were preparing to sleep. Hammocks were taken from storage and unrolled, ready for their weary occupants and lit lanterns were echoed by pinpricks of light from the shore. Regis Bay was a pretty enough place, but Maia had no time to sightsee. It had been a busy few days after her partnership ceremony and she still had to get used to the strange sensation of not being alone in her own head. She could feel *Blossom*'s presence like an enveloping warmth, then the Captain's control, sharper but still reassuring. She was beginning to learn to focus when working, using the analogy of adjusting a mental telescope so that things were clearer when necessary, or in the background, blurred and less regarded.

Likewise, she could feel every part of the vessel, from the keel to the topmost yards, with every rope, pulley, chain and winch. Attending to everything at once was proving nigh on impossible and she kept losing herself in tiny details. *Blossom*, tolerance itself, just laughed.

<We've all been there, girl. It will be easier the more you do it, until it becomes a habit and something you don't have to think about. You can't expect to master it all in a week!>

Maia grumbled inwardly to herself, cross when she made a mistake. It was mentally exhausting, even though she had the nights off to eat, rest and sleep. If she was ever fully and permanently installed in a vessel of her own, she would have no need of food and 'at rest' was just another Ship's function, snatched whenever possible and one that didn't really equate to human sleep.

<It's like being half awake and still being aware of your surroundings,> *Blossom* said. <You can't ever stop working, but you can doze. The only time you really have a break is when you're being renewed or refitted and you're uninstalled.>

<How often is that?>

<Depending on what your vessel goes through, about every thirty years,> *Blossom* explained. <Sometimes less if you hit a lot of rough weather, or get shot up in a battle.>

<Have you been in a battle?> Maia asked. The Ship was silent for a moment.

<Yes. There's always a problem with pirates, so we're sent out to deal with them from time to time. Oh, I don't mean the regular patrols, but a full-scale attack to clear the seas. Alas,

they're like rats, always finding a corner to breed in, so needs must we go out and deal with them again.>

Maia sensed that *Blossom* didn't particularly want to talk about it, so she decided to leave the subject to another time and changed the subject.

<Why don't you join us at mealtimes?> The Ship never made an appearance when they dined, choosing instead to stay on the upper decks listening in. *Blossom* sighed.

<I must confess it's the part of being a Ship that I find hardest. Sometimes I think I could give it all up for just a little piece of bread with toasted cheese. Why torture myself?>

Maia thought for a moment. She loved to eat, but what would she miss most? <I would miss potatoes mashed with butter,> she Sent. Since they had been brought from the New Continent, the easily grown and nutritious vegetable had grown rapidly in popularity.

<Pie would be better, with gravy.>

<Spice cake with cream,> Maia countered.

<Apple pie with cheese. Oh no, now we're back talking about cheese!> *Blossom* complained. <It's a good job you're not here with me in body, my girl or I'd give you a clip round the ear!>

Maia's body was in her cabin, magically suspended. Only her mind was needed to operate the vessel with *Blossom*.

<All right, no more talk of food, I promise.> She thought she'd better change the subject. Talking of bodies… <*Blossom*, where's your body?>

<Safely stored away,> the Ship replied promptly. <We have to be kept somewhere very secure, you know and no, I can't tell you where.>

<Is it part of the Mysteries?>

<It is. I hope you'll find out for yourself when the time comes.>

Maia took a few moments to digest this.

<Have you always been the *Blossom*? You weren't ever transferred?>

<No. Transfers are very rare. Ships usually like to keep their name. There was one called *Elephant* once who wasn't that keen.> She chuckled. <Don't blame her either, for all that the creature is a noble beast.>

Maia snickered. <Who chooses the names?>

<It varies. I've heard that it's often the Sovereign who chooses from a list.>

<*Blossom* is a pretty name, but,> she added, <it seems a bit, what shall I say, sweet for a warship.>

This time the Ship laughed uproariously, saying aloud, "Why, girl. Don't you know that some flowers can be deadly?"

A few of the crew, busy working on deck, gave a cheer. They were proud of their Ship and *Blossom* had been happy to broadcast that remark.

"Tough as old boots, she is," Big Ajax muttered. "They'll not put one over on our flower!"

Maia had got to know the crew over the past few days, young, old and in-between. Some were on their first voyage like she was, training on the job and she felt sorry for the two who had discovered the joys of seasickness in the first hours. It had taken about three days before they were anything like back to normal.

"It can affect anyone, even Admirals," the Captain had remarked as he watched the greenish-faced men staggering about. "It's a curse. They can petition Neptune to help them, but they have to offer something of real value."

"Does he listen?" she asked, curiously.

"Sometimes," he replied. "If the offering is truly heartfelt. They're mostly better off asking an Adept for a potion, but some do both to cover themselves on all fronts."

"Have you ever seen him?" she asked.

"Neptune? Yes, once. From a distance." The Captain's face was suddenly grave.

"What was he like?"

"Terrifying." He would say no more on the subject and Maia wondered if she'd get her chance to see him too. The Gods did appear on occasion, but mostly people were happy that they were hidden from mortal view. It could often be dangerous to come to their attention, as they played their games by hidden rules.

Maia's attention was snatched back to the present as *Blossom* showed her how to affect a minor course change. This near to the coast the winds could be tricky. After a while she decided to dig for more information.

<Might I get a new name then?>

<Probably, though some girls end up with an established vessel. It's strange when you've known the previous Ship for a while and then you get a stranger at the other end of the line. I've only known it a few times. When a person leaves, it's more common to retire the name, at least for a while. Maybe you'll get a new, bigger sloop-of-war!> Maia could feel her grinning. <Better defences all round. I'm going to get one of those, just you wait. Three masts and more guns. Maybe even some of those new breech-loaders they've just designed. Or then again, I might just retire when my contract ends. I can live on land and be a fine lady with a carriage and silken gowns, eating toasted cheese all day!>

Her mental laugh was jolly, but Maia wondered if she would really ever consider giving up the sea.

<I hear that Tullia – I mean the *Regina*, has got those new guns.>

She sensed a momentary hesitation from *Blossom*.

<Yes. That one's done well for herself.>

<Why?> Maia asked her, curiously. *Blossom*'s reaction mirrored Branwen's on hearing the news of Tullia's vessel.

<It's not professional to comment on other candidates,> *Blossom* said. <Is it, Captain?>

Plinius joined the conversation.

<What's not professional?>

<Maia was just saying that the *Regina* has some of the new breech loaders.>

<Does she now? Great Gods!> So he didn't like her either. <That's what being an Admiral's daughter does for you.>

<Plinius!> *Blossom* pretended to be outraged.

<Well, it's true,> her Captain said. <All I'll say is that it's refreshing to work with you, Maia.>

The link they shared carried much more than words and tone. Emotions seeped through it as well. Evidently Plinius and his Ship had had an interesting time with Tullia.

<She'll have to behave herself now,> *Blossom* said. <Especially with Silvius as her Captain. He won't stand for any shows of temper.>

<Who's her Captain?> Maia asked. She was beginning to familiarise herself with naval personnel.

<Caius Brigantius Silvius,> Plinius said. <He's a good Captain, but very strict. He was with the *Dauntless* for a few years and this is a promotion. The Navy obviously wants an experienced commander partnered with a brand new Ship. I hear he's well in with the Admiralty, too. One of Albanus' cronies.>

<I hear the King thinks highly of Admiral Albanus,> Maia said carefully.

<Yes, he does,> Plinius said. <Admiral Albanus is a great moderniser and thinks that Britannia should be less dependent on the Empire.>

<Oh, not politics again!> *Blossom* groaned.

<My dear, it might affect us all before too long. The King is young and listens to his friends.>

<Too much, sometimes,> his Ship said, darkly. <But Maia won't be interested in all this.>

Actually, Maia was very interested.

<I met the Admiral,> she said. <He sent me presents. Perhaps it's because he thinks I'm his daughter's friend.> She decided not to mention the conversation she'd had with Tullia.

There was a surprised silence.

<Yes, perhaps,> Plinius said. <He's been generous towards you then?>

<Yes.> She feel her doubt and suspicion seeping through the link and knew that they'd both picked up on it as she wasn't able to mask her true feelings yet.

<You're safe here with us, Maia,> Plinius said. <You don't have to worry about all this. Concentrate on your lessons and you'll be fine.>

<I will,> she agreed.

<Speaking of lessons,> *Blossom* said. <Time to carry on.>

Plinius withdrew from the conversation and *Blossom* began.

<Tell me the difference between a Mage, a Priest and an Adept. You'll be dealing with all three as part of your crew complement, so it's fitting that you know the difference.>

Maia thought about it, recalling her lessons in her head and using her trick of memory.

<Mages deal with the immaterial, using the Potentia of mind and will. Adepts deal with the material, using the Potentia of

intellect and deduction. Priests deal with Deities and use the Potentia of the Divine.>

<Which of them has more Potentia?>

<It depends on the degree of each individual's ability.>

<And where is the overlap?>

Overlap? Maia flicked through everything she'd heard and read.

<I'm not sure about that,> she admitted.

<Thought not,> *Blossom* said. <Each Mystery has its own strengths but there are times when a Mage can prescribe a potion, if that is his bent. He might transmute the ingredients through will, rather than science but the results are the same if he knows what he's doing. Likewise, an Adept can effect change in an object through science. Often the results are the same. Likewise, Priests can control the immaterial if it is Divinely related. It's useful to know these things because if one or other of them is incapacitated or killed, you may have to rely more heavily on the others.>

<It sounds complicated,> Maia said.

<You get used to it and you'll know more with practice and observation,> *Blossom* told her. <Likewise, Ship Potentia can overlap with your Mage's, when raising a defensive shield, for example. He can join his Potentia to yours.>

Talking about Potentia only reminded Maia of her own shortfall but it was all useful information.

<Briseis, I mean the *Patience* when she was Briseis, said that her Potentia had manifested physically and that was why the Navy took her to be a candidate.>

She felt *Blossom*'s nod.

<Yes, the Navy wants physical Potentia, though they'll take mental too, especially if it's enough to be aggressive, such as forced telepathy. There have been a few Ships with that ability.>

She broke off suddenly, as if touching upon a subject that was painful to her.

<Is yours physical?> she asked abruptly.

<I don't know,> Maia replied, as honestly as she could.

<Hmm. Strange, but everybody's different. Perhaps it hasn't fully manifested yet. You're certainly excellent at control and pick things up very quickly. Matrona said you would.>

<I've an eidetic memory,> Maia said, pleased that she could lay claim to this at least.

<Oooh. Lucky you. In some respects, anyway. It can be useful to forget things sometimes,> Blossom added. <Maybe when you're a Ship, Gods willing, that might change or amend.>

Maia thought of the centuries of life that *Blossom* had already experienced and wondered if remembering every little thing in detail would be a good thing after all. She shuddered as an image of Blandina's face flashed before her. Forgetting that would be a blessing for sure.

<I know I'm always telling you not to worry about things, but I mean it,> the Ship said, picking up on her disquiet. <Talking of Mages, Priests and Adepts, there's another method of classification.>

<There is?>

<Yes. Priests drink too much, Adepts are obsessed and Mages are mad, obsessed and often drink too much!>

They both laughed and Maia felt her mood lighten. The next couple of hours took her mind off her worries completely as they raised anchor and set sail along the coast once more, heading back towards Portus and a safe harbour.

*

The last class had finished for the day. Arfon Varus, Overseer of the Portus Foundling Home, was back in his office diligently filling in that day's log entry to include the two new admissions, both girls. He pulled thoughtfully at his lower lip, perusing the list of potential names. They would be an N and an O. He considered the matter carefully, listening to the sounds of the younger children outside in the yard. Play was permitted, so long as it wasn't too noisy. Discipline had to be maintained at all times, especially in this establishment. He prided himself on the strict care he gave the children, to fit them for the world of work they would be entering. Fear of the Gods and respect for authority, those were his watch words and so far, he had not failed in his duty. It also turned the Home a tidy profit when he sold their indentures, with a little sweetener on the side for his own purse. What happened after that was none of his concern.

"Let's see," he said aloud. "N." He wrote Julia Numidia in his careful script. A good name. Being free born she deserved to have two names – Varus was careful to admit no slave born; a simple spell ensured that only the free were taken in. Leaving the rejects outside had soon made his point – they were either taken in by others, reclaimed by their slave mothers or... well, otherwise disposed of eventually. But that was none of his business.

Now, what could he use for O? It was always a tricky one. Olivia? Oenone?

A sudden movement out of the corner of his eye made him turn his head sharply to the left, towards the door. Had someone come in? He could have sworn that a black shape flitted across the room. Varus blinked rapidly, then shook his head, dismissing it. It must have been a bird flying past the window, its shadow flashing across the wall and distracting him.

He shrugged and was turning again to the letter O when thin, bony fingers gripped the back of his neck, forcing his head down towards the desk. An acrid smell of burning, like wood smoke mingled with seared flesh, made him choke and gag. His body jerked once, then was stilled, muscles locked and paralysed, silencing the scream in his throat. The fingers tightened their grip as the stench intensified.

Abruptly, the pages of the logbook began to whip backwards, faster and faster until they became a blur before his watering eyes. Fat tears trickled down his doughy cheeks and dripped on to the paper, until, at last, the pages came to rest at a date many years before.

A voice like the crackling of flames hissed in his ear.

"Tell me about this one."

*

Marcus Novus Placidianus, Prefect of the Portus Polismen, gazed around the Overseer's office with a look of distaste on his patrician features. The lingering smell of burnt meat was enough to make him wish that he hadn't dined quite so well but an hour before. He waved a hand at his two companions.

"Gentlemen. May I suggest that we move next door out of this stench?"

Officer Grumio, stolid and red-faced, hastened to open the door. Placidianus didn't rate his deduction skills too highly, but at least he'd had the sense to send for the departmental forensics team. This looked to be more their line of work than something a beat capere usually came across.

Jackdaw was busy peering at the book on the Overseer's desk, whilst Scabious was poking at the remains of the late Overseer. There wasn't much left of the corpse bar a charred mass of bones and dried lumps of flesh.

"It's strange how nothing else was damaged. The papers should have gone up in flames and taken everything else with them." The young Mage, black haired and as beady eyed as his namesake bird, cocked his head as he squinted to take in as much detail as possible.

Placidianus groaned inwardly. This was going to be one of those cases. He'd prefer a simple murder or robbery any day of the week, but this stank of evil magic. He exited the room of death with relief and escaped to the small living room beyond. This contained various items of furniture, including an old leather armchair, which he felt no inclination to take.

"Well, Grumio, you were right to call for me directly. Who's on guard?"

"Caractacus, sir. He's a good lad, an' 'e'll keep his trap shut. That one was straight on it, sir. Like a dog with a rabbit, 'e is." Grumio jerked his head in the direction of the Adept, who was still absorbed in his work. The capere's moustache twitched in distaste.

"Quite." Placidianus sniffed, then wished he hadn't. "I take it there were no witnesses?"

"Nobody heard or saw anything, sir. The servant found 'im when she brought 'im 'is dinner."

"No screams or noise of any sort. Only the corpse burnt and not its surroundings," the Prefect stated, flatly. Yet something had been very, very angry as a palpable sense of rage still permeated the atmosphere, thickening and clouding it like an unseen fog. No, Placidianus definitely didn't like where this was leading. Surely it couldn't be Divine vengeance – the man had

120

had a good reputation, though of course one never knew what went on behind closed doors. He remembered the case of Marcia Blandina with a shudder.

"Has any God claimed responsibility?" he asked, in the forlorn hope that this could all be settled quickly. If Varus had transgressed enough to warrant this, surely the relevant Priest would want everyone to know that their deity was not to be offended.

Grumio gave him a mildly reproachful look. "Not yet, sir. I've sent discreet messages to all the major temples and I'm still waiting on replies. It wouldn't be like 'em to 'old back if 'e'd pissed one of 'em off."

The men exchanged knowing glances. The might of Divine wrath was better than money in the bank for any cult, but the fact that nothing had come from the Priests was worrying.

Jackdaw finally followed them, the open door wafting a reek of overcooked meat before he hastily shut it behind him.

"Well?" Placidianus demanded, wearily.

To give the young man credit, he didn't flinch when met with the Prefect's undiluted glare.

"There are traces of negative magic," Jackdaw announced. "Some sort of evil creature or other similar agent. I doubt that it's Divine, so, with your permission, sir, I'll pass this on to the Collegium to investigate."

Placidianus heard Grumio grunt in relief. This wouldn't be on them to sort out, thank the Gods. Let the Mages deal with this mess.

"Do you think it will attack again?" he asked.

Jackdaw grimaced. "Hard to say, sir, as we don't know why it attacked in the first place. The burning is alarming as it could mean Stygian involvement, though it's been quiet on that front lately. I had a look in the logbook to see what Varus was working on, but it was open at an old entry."

"Really?" The Prefect was interested. This was more of a clue.

"Yes, sir. The entry was getting on for nineteen years ago, right at the start of the book. It could be related to something historic."

"Hmm." Placidianus stared at the wall, where a cheap print of Neptune and his court, all flowing hair and scaly tails, stared back blankly, their painted faces offering little consolation. "Well then, it might be at that. Smacks of revenge to me. Take what information you have and give it to the Collegium. We'll do what we can, but if it's hostile magic better to let the experts sort it out, eh?"

Creatures that could burn a man to a crisp for no obvious reason were above a capere's pay scale. He sensed Grumio's agreement radiating across the room. It would of course be their job to stop any panic if a garbled version of this night's events leaked out. Rogue magic was nothing new but such targeted and seemingly motiveless destruction was. At least angry deities could be appeased. Maybe one of the names in the book would lead to something, but Placidianus just didn't want to be around when it did.

*

Master Mage Raven was similarly disquieted. Jackdaw's report had been precise – the boy could be irritating but he had a nose for clues, which was why he had been assigned to the polis. That and the fact that he'd point blank refused to consider anything else. He and that Adept, what was his name? - the one who preferred his patients to be no longer breathing - worked well together and had cleared up a number of cases. Raven liked to keep an eye on his students as they made their way in the world but there had been so many over the years. Scabious. That was it. He might be old but he had an excellent memory for names. No doubt the pair of them would be happily examining the remains in the city mortuary at this very moment. Each to his own.

So, Raven thought, the facts. Firstly – a murdered man who had charge of the Foundlings' Home in Portus. Secondly – no God claimed responsibility. Thirdly – a list of names. Whatever killed the Overseer had been looking for something or someone. Most of the children – adults now – had been discounted. Two were dead. Of the remaining three, one had been claimed by his mother and apprenticed to a butcher. Another, a girl, had only been there until the age of five before being taken in by the Temple of Juno, where enquiries were already being made.

The other was Maia Abella.

His intuition screamed at him that she was linked to this. The only problem was proving it. Raven bit his lip in frustration, wondering how to proceed.

Sounds and movement outside his chamber alerted him to the prospect of a visitor. He heard his servant's voice.

"I'll just let him know you're here, Domina."

The door opened. Polydorus rarely bothered to knock as he knew how keen his master's ears were.

"Lady Claudia Modesta, sir."

Raven raised an eyebrow. If the High Priestess of Juno was deigning to visit him at the Collegium building then it must be serious. This had to be related to the attack.

"Greetings, Master Mage. I come on the most serious business!"

The clear, aristocratic voice rang out as the lady swept in. Raven could only hope that Polydorus had managed to get out of the way in time before he was trampled underfoot. Nothing got in Claudia's way when she was in this mood.

He stood politely, angling his face towards the sound of rustling silks. A waft of expensive scent swirled past him and began to explore the room.

"How may I be of assistance, Lady Claudia?" he asked, adding quickly, "Please, be seated. Would you care for some wine?"

"No thank you," the Priestess replied. Raven heard Polydorus hurry off and felt a brief stab of envy. "The whole city is agog with the news of the attack on Overseer Varus," she began.

So, someone had talked then. Raven wasn't surprised.

"A horrible affair," he agreed.

"I was informed about the list of names found near his body." The High Priestess certainly didn't beat about the bush and her intelligence gatherers were second only to his own.

"One of which I understand to be your acolyte."

"Yes, Sibylla Xanthia. What you do not know is that something tried to gain entry to the girls' dormitories last night."

That was unwelcome news and Raven had a moment of doubt. He'd been so sure that Maia Abella was involved, he hadn't considered any other ramifications. He mentally berated himself for the omission.

"The intruder activated our magical defences and woke the sacred geese as well. We managed to keep it at bay, thank the Goddess."

"Did you see what it was?" he asked, sharply.

"Not clearly. It was dark, twisted and stank of corruption and burning. We're having to cleanse the whole area thoroughly." Her voice twisted with disgust. "Sibylla was awake and insists that the Goddess sent her a warning in a dream. She was told it was a Revenant."

Raven was silent for a few moments. "Are you sure?"

"The Goddess was quite clear. Sibylla is one of our more talented acolytes and has already been shown the Goddess's favour. She will go far. The word 'Revenant' was given to her directly." Claudia's tone held just a touch of awe – direct communication with a deity was rarer than people supposed. It was more usual for auguries to be taken to understand the will of the Gods, as too much interaction could often lead to madness or worse. Raven spared Sibylla a moment of pity, but at least she had the shelter of the temple and experienced mentors.

A Revenant. Good Gods.

"I understand that Varus was suspected of involvement with that bad business a few years back," he said. "But why would a vengeful Revenant turn up now?"

"They're born of rage and untimely death," Lady Claudia agreed. "Varus must have been guilty of something."

Perhaps Varus had just been unlucky. Curses that involved the Gods, calling upon the punishment of others might or might not be heard and acted upon. Those cases were written off as Divine vengeance, as the one cursed clearly deserved it and the Priests could confirm that it wasn't just random bad luck. All Gods wanted to show their Potentia, as greater Potentia meant worshippers and influence.

"But why would a Revenant target a child who surely has done no wrong?"

Claudia Modesta hadn't finished. "It wasn't after Sibylla, something else we have since found out through the mercy of Juno. Our defences held, as I said, but it possibly realised that it was after the wrong quarry and departed of its own accord. We have also communicated with the Priests of Neptune, because Varus was a regular worshipper at the Temple and they knew him quite well. They can't shed any light as to why he was attacked, either."

"You have been most thorough, Lady Claudia," Raven acknowledged.

"Thank you. I hope you didn't expect us to sit on our hands," she replied waspishly.

"Not at all."

"Have you found the others on the list?" she probed.

Nobody put one over on the High Priestess, Raven reflected. She ruled the temple with an iron hand and he would definitely not want to get on her bad side. He decided that it was better to share his information, or part of it, anyway.

"We have traced them all and there is one girl that seems to be the most likely target."

"And where is she?"

"At sea, training to be a Ship."

The Priestess digested this information for a moment. "Do you think that it was just going through the names?"

"Probably," he said, carefully. "The others are either dead or were already claimed by their families, who have reported no disturbances. Does Sibylla have a family?"

"She did. Her mother left a token, but died shortly afterwards. She was of good family, but disgraced herself, alas! The father was unknown, but as soon as her Potentia manifested and the Goddess made contact it was thought wisest to send her to us before the Navy could snatch her away. Do you know the other girl's origins?"

"No. We could find nothing at all."

They shared a thoughtful silence.

"Well, we shall have to wait and see what transpires," Claudia said at last. "I pity anyone who stands between her and this creature. You know that Revenants are notoriously difficult to stop until they have achieved their goal. Do let me know if I can help in any way."

"The support of the Goddess is always invaluable," he replied, hearing the rustle of her clothing and the subtle chink of her bracelets as she stood to leave. "Should I hear any more, I'll inform you immediately."

"Likewise, Master Mage. I shall pray to the Goddess that she grants us understanding and guidance."

"As shall I," he assured her. "The Collegium will send a sacrifice to thank her for her intervention. May the Twelve look favourably upon our efforts!"

"Let it be so," she replied, formally.

As he rang for Polydorus to escort the Lady Claudia to her carriage, he was already beginning to formulate his course of action. For the time being, the girl was safely aboard the *Blossom* and presumably out of harm's way but that was no guarantee that there wouldn't be further attacks. This Revenant, like others of its kind, was motivated by one all-consuming purpose. He only wished he knew what it was.

What in Hades could have brought this thing forth, to latch upon such an innocent and unlikely victim? He needed to talk to Jackdaw and his friend down at the mortuary. Extending his awareness, he set off, following the sweet scent of Claudia's perfume, to where the air would definitely be a lot less fragrant.

*

Jackdaw and Scabious muttered to each other as the latter carefully teased apart the burned and twisted mass that was lying in a heap on the polished steel slab. The whole corpse was brittle and flaky down to the bones, only charred pieces of clothing remained, together with some metal buttons that had warped and melted in the heat. It was barely recognisable as human.

"Intense heat, seems to have radiated outwards from the internal organs," Scabious observed, dark eyes peeping over the top of the surgical mask which obscured his wide nose and generous mouth. A white linen cap held his unruly hair in place, decorated with the entwined snake and staff badge of his office.

Jackdaw, younger and similarly garbed but without the badge, jotted down notes on a tablet.

"From within?" he said, puzzled.

"Yep. It's worse on the inside. Come and look."

Jackdaw leaned over. Scabious was right. The Overseer's organs were just like lumps of coal and the bones had virtually turned to ash.

"Are there spells that can do this?" Scabious queried.

"Oh yes," the Mage confirmed. "Takes a lot of skill and Potentia, though. Why bother expending extra energy when you can just set people on fire the usual way, from the outside in, I mean?"

"So…this is real nastiness."

"Looks like it. Definitely magical. I could tell that anyway."

"Well, that's going to be in my report. It'll all be on you lot."

"Funny. That's just what Sergeant Grumio said too."

It was cool under the polis offices, just right for storing bodies. Jackdaw liked the quiet; it helped him think. Scabious, too, was happy working there. No queue of noisy patients constantly complaining about this or that ailment, for which he was eternally grateful, though the odd visitor could be a blasted nuisance. Footsteps and the tap tap of a staff announced the arrival of one such.

The Adept straightened, probe in hand, to meet the Master Mage's milky gaze.

"Good day to you, Master Scabious, Jackdaw." The pair hastily stripped off their masks.

"And to you, sir," they chorused, like obedient schoolboys.

"I take it you've had time to come to some conclusions?"

Scabious quickly outlined his findings, which caused Raven's eyebrow to lift, though the old Mage seemed otherwise unmoved.

"Overseer Varus was killed by intense heat from within, much hotter than normal. I've seen similar cases; a sailor burned by Greek fire which exploded due to careless loading, but it was from the outside in and that doesn't stop once it takes hold."

Raven nodded. "Go on."

"It's supernormal, both Jackdaw and I agree on that. With your permission I'll go and write up the full medical report and have it delivered to you post haste."

"I would be much obliged," Raven said. He knew that he made most people nervous and Scabious was no exception. He waited whilst the Adept gathered his note tablets and made a hasty exit, grinning at his friend who would face the full inquisition. Jackdaw pulled a face back at him and rolled his eyes.

Raven wasted no time in getting down to business.

"I've just had a visit from the Lady Claudia Modesta. She's been informed by Divine revelation that this was caused by a Revenant, which tried to break into the Temple of Juno last night. This cannot be a coincidence, as one of her acolyte's names was written in Varus's book. I need more information. What have you deduced?"

Jackdaw realised that his jaw had dropped and shut it hastily. Gods above – a Revenant! At least that confirmed the supernormal theory.

"I agree with Scabious's findings," he began. "In the light of this new information and the state of the crime scene, I would definitely say that the original victim was burned. The whole place stank of burnt wood and flesh, with a hint of saltwater, as if it happened at sea, but somehow unclean – not like a sacrificial fire, more, well," he plunged on, "like an execution. Are you all right, sir? I know the smell's bad. I'll get you a chair."

Raven felt the world suddenly tilt around him, as though the Earth Shaker, Poseidon himself, had heaved and shifted, twisting everything out of kilter. The blood pounded in his head and he was only dimly aware of being helped to sit down.

"There you are, sir. I'll fetch you some brandy."

"No need," he managed to rasp. "Tell me. Fact or intuition?"

"What's that, sir?"

"Execution. Fact or intuition?"

"Intuitive impression, sir. It's my particular strength."

Memories flooded him. The screams, the madness and finally the fire. He'd thought it was over and long buried, with even the ashes consigned to oblivion in a secret, sealed page in a dusty book of records. He prayed that he was wrong but he couldn't take the risk.

The horrors of the past were rearing up to meet him. It wasn't over after all and now he would be forced to dig up the dead.

VIII

The *Blossom* glided over the calm sea, a gentle breeze filling her sails as the west wind pushed her back along the coast towards Portus and its sheltering harbour. Maia, now linked to the vessel through every plank, rope and pulley felt as though she were no longer flesh and bone, but hemp and wood, metal and canvas, her belly in the salt waves and her head in the sky. Her oaken bones creaked and shifted with the movement of the vessel and her vision expanded to include the entirety of her surroundings, as if she had a whole multitude of eyes instead of just the two that nature had given her.

The sense of exhilaration persisted as she covered the last few miles to her destination, putting into practice the many lessons learned over the past weeks. Truly, she had never imagined it would be like this; the joy of being part of a greater whole that was like the family she had never known. She relished the fact that she was needed and cared for, something she had always longed for. She sensed *Blossom*'s smile and her Captain's presence, as she was enfolded in their warmth.

<Aye. I am mother to many Ships,> *Blossom* agreed.

<This must be what it is like to have parents,> Maia Sent to her. <It was so hard to imagine before.>

<Oh yes, girl. You can always rely on us, even when you have a vessel of your own. It is one of the compensations for the life we lead.>

Blossom's mental touch held love and pride. She had come to trust Maia's control and their partnership had been an easy one. Maia had worked hard to master her new skills and was delighted to receive praise when she accomplished a particularly tricky manoeuvre. Days were spent practising techniques over and over, using the information she had learned at the Academy about wind and weather, charts and reckonings – all the knowledge of the sea passed down by Ships and sailors. It was becoming second nature to take commands and implement the appropriate procedure. *Blossom* had even occasionally let her listen in to the other Ships' chatter, sometimes just gossip from boring night watches as Ships sought to pass the time, but at other times warnings of weather or obstacles. Maia soon realised that *Blossom* was something of a hub, especially if a Ship needed a sympathetic ear. There were many complaints as well, about crew, orders, weather and enforced idleness from Ships who were in port too long. Unlike their crew, they didn't get shore leave and some crews were hard to settle after a riotous time on land.

The *Persistence* was having Mage trouble.

<Tryin' t' tell me me job!> she grumbled loudly to all who would listen. <An' 'im no more 'n' an idler! Does 'ardly anythin' 'cept eat from the stores – big lump 'e is. Thinks 'e's a gift from the Gods. Well, 'e ain't! 'E's annoyin' me Captain too.>

<What's his name?> *Blossom* asked.

<Plover. Should be Turkey the way 'e gobbles.>

Blossom laughed. <You should get him transferred.>

<Already suggested that,> *Persistence* said, sourly. <I reckon that's 'ow 'e was foisted on me in the first place. 'E was with *Scorpion* for a bit an' I reckon she couldn't stand 'im either. If it wasn't fer regulations I'd shove 'im overboard meself!>

When she finally signed off, *Blossom* sighed.

<Ah, Ships love to grumble. It's a lucky one that doesn't have something to complain about. Still, if we were regular women it would be physical ailments. At least we don't have those and the shipworms don't bite as much since we got copper bottoms!>

<So what do you have to complain about?>

<Oh, I'm one of the lucky ones!> They both laughed.

Suddenly she became aware of being watched. It had become a familiar feeling as the voyage had progressed.

<Your friend's back,> *Blossom* remarked. Indeed, a very large black backed gull had alighted on the taff rail and was regarding the Ship with a knowing eye.

<How do you know it's here for me? Or even that it's the same bird?> Maia asked.

<Just a feeling.>

<It could be one of your followers,> Maia teased.

<No, I don't think so. It always lands on the same place at the same time. It must prefer your company.>

<It's a clever bird after scraps,> Maia said.

<Perhaps it fancies Scribo's parrot,> *Blossom* suggested.

Maia snorted with laughter. Scribo's pet, Cap'n Felix was loud and very foul-mouthed. The tale was that he had once told an Admiral to do something anatomically impossible, then added "And you can too!" to sundry other dignitaries. He was now strictly confined below decks under a cover whenever anyone of note came aboard. The whole crew was very proud of him.

<I wouldn't put it past Cap'n Felix to fancy it back, though it would have to get used to the swearing,> Maia said wryly.

Even though *Blossom* and she shared the same body during the day, she couldn't shake the feeling that the gull was watching *her* closely.

<I'm receiving a message from land,> *Blossom* abruptly informed both her and the Captain. Maia felt her thoughts separate away on to a private channel, so she concentrated instead on checking their course, speed and heading, all the while aware of her feathered admirer's intent gaze. It wouldn't do to run aground on her first trip out. Idly, she noted the crew's activities.

Heron was instructing Robin on some aspect of weather-working at the bow. Unlike inanimates, Ships weren't totally at the mercy of wind and weather, having skill of their own to supplement their Mage's. She and Robin had become friends since her lapse, their status as apprentices giving them a common bond though they had little time to do much socialising. Lieutenant Durus was taking the midshipmen through their paces, heads bent over charts and navigational instruments. The rest of the watch was busy as well, though Maia took a special interest in what was being prepared in the galley. She intended to make the most of eating well whilst she could. Tonight, it looked like duck in a sauce and a selection of fish dishes. The officers naturally ate better than the men, but there were no empty stomachs on board one of His Majesty's Ships and for many that alone was a good incentive to sign up. Everyone would be happy that pickled cabbage wasn't on the menu today; though beneficial to health, it wasn't a favourite dish.

Reassured, she resumed her observations. The gull, as if satisfied that all was well, had taken to the skies and was wheeling in lazy circles around her masts. It would surely be joined by more when it was time to throw out the food waste. The screeching and bickering birds would fight over the smallest scraps.

Captain Plinius' mental voice broke into her musings.

<*Blossom*, Maia, could you please attend me in my day room? Maia, in body if you would.>

Maia was jolted. What could have happened to warrant this? He sounded slightly rattled by something – it was harder to hide when Sending and she knew him well enough now to pick up on these things. Carefully, with *Blossom*'s help, she began to detach her anima back into her suspended body. This was the part she disliked; it always felt as if she was being compressed and forced back into something too tight, giving her a brief sensation of suffocation.

She adjusted back into her flesh body gradually, with hearing coming first as usual. There was a voice, Heron's, then she managed to open her eyes. He had removed the suspension spell, though she still felt groggy. He helped her to sit up and she rubbed her eyes, blearily.

The Mage handed her a glass of watered wine laced with some herb she couldn't identify. Maia sipped at it, wriggling her toes to restore her circulation and, after a minute or two, she felt ready to head for the cabin, Heron standing by to offer an arm should she need it.

Blossom was already there in her accustomed place on the wall, as were Durus and Campion. Maia could tell that something had happened as soon as she set foot inside, as all three faces showed concern and not a little apprehension. What could she have done? As far as she knew, everything was going well and there had been no complaints about her work. Perhaps her imposture had finally been discovered? Her panic registered with *Blossom* immediately.

"It's all right, Maia. You haven't done anything wrong."

The Lieutenant pulled out a chair for her and Maia sat gratefully. Her knees had been threatening to give way and her heart was thumping uncomfortably. The four men seated themselves.

"Maia," the Captain began, "I received a message from the Admiralty, as you know already. The contents were…" he paused, clearly searching for the right word, "disturbing."

He glanced briefly at his Ship. "I'm sorry to have to tell you that Overseer Varus has met with great misfortune."

Maia was surprised, but wondered what it had to do with her. Whilst he had not been overly cruel, she suspected that he had known about her last mistress and had sent her there anyway. She certainly hadn't trusted him.

"He's dead," *Blossom* said, bluntly. "Murdered in his office by something very powerful and evil." The Ship knew that Maia hadn't liked the man much.

"Yes." Plinius shot her a look and *Blossom* subsided. "I don't quite know how to tell you this, but it is suspected that whatever killed him was actually looking for you."

Maia could only stare at him in disbelief. Her? What had she to do with this?

"Why me?" she managed to say.

"That's what everyone from the major temples, the Admiralty and the Collegium is trying to discover. So far all we have is a list of names that was found at the scene. The others have been ruled out, which only leaves yours. The High Priestess of Juno has had information that it is a Revenant."

Maia just looked at him blankly. Of all the things she had expected, this wasn't one of them. She'd heard blood-curdling tales of Revenants of course; they were a popular after-lights-out horror story, but she hadn't thought they were real. And why would anyone want to harm her?

"Surely it can't have anything to do with me?"

"It isn't a hundred percent certain, I admit, but apparently the creature was searching quite methodically. It went to find an acolyte at the Temple of Juno, one Sibylla Xanthia, who was admitted to the Home a few weeks before you. It seems to have been working its way through the list of names in the Overseer's logbook."

Maia's forehead creased as she remembered Sibylla Xanthia, a timid fair-haired girl. She must have been very young when she left for the temple.

"There were other names, surely?" she pointed out.

"Discounted or dead," Plinius said, casting her a look of sympathy. "If there's anything that you know or remember that could have a bearing on this, you must tell us now."

Maia could only shake her head and wonder if she was actually in some sort of strange, nightmarish dream. Her palms were clammy and she unconsciously rubbed them on her skirt.

"So there's nobody else it could be?"

"Apparently not, if the clues have been read aright. I hope you understand why we've told you everything we know ourselves – be assured that we are keeping nothing from you."

"Nor I from you," Maia insisted. "If this is something to do with my past, all I know is what I was told at the Home."

"Naturally. However, my orders are clear. We're to drop anchor before we reach the mouth of the estuary and you're to stay aboard until this matter is sorted. Should this Revenant be pursuing you, the hopes are that it cannot cross open water, but we can't take anything for granted. In the meantime, report anything that comes to mind, however trivial it might seem. I will be setting extra watches." He looked meaningfully at his second-in-command, who nodded, his normally open face set in grimmer lines.

"Aye, sir," Maia replied. She wondered if she should mention her friend the seagull, but *Blossom* had noticed it too and hadn't said anything. Still… "There is one thing."

Plinius' head rose and he regarded her intently. "Go on."

"I've noticed a seagull that comes at the same time each day." Even as she spoke, Maia felt increasingly silly. "We've joked that it appears to be watching me."

Campion snorted, but Heron was more interested. "Do you feel watched?"

"Yes," Maia admitted, "but it could be my imagination."

"You're not usually the imaginative type," Heron remarked.

"I've seen it too," *Blossom* interposed. "It is a little strange, but birds are often creatures of habit and we are just off the coast."

Plinius raised an eyebrow. "Heron, would you look into it? Cita is praying for guidance but hasn't received anything yet. He's planning a sacrifice."

"Certainly, Captain." Heron's expression remained sceptical, but Maia felt relieved that Plinius had taken her seriously, even if there would be a few jokes if it all came to nothing.

"Maia, you are excused for the rest of the day. I want everyone on full alert and it isn't wise to leave your body unprotected. Be assured that we will all do everything in our power to keep you safe."

His brown eyes regarded her steadily. "We'll get to the bottom of this eventually. Now, you have some free time, a rare occurrence I know, so off you go and I'll see you at dinner."

Maia left them to finish their meeting and make preparations for whatever was to come. She tried to smile, but felt sick inside. It was bad enough that she was constantly waiting for the other shoe to drop and her guilty secret to come to light. A surge of irritation and disquiet rose within her as she walked along the corridor to her cabin. She didn't feel like going up top today, wanting nothing more than to brood in her quarters away from everyone, but *Blossom*'s voice chimed in her head.

<Keep your chin up, girl. I'll have some food sent from the galley. You need to eat.>

<I don't think I could,> Maia Sent back. <I can't believe all this!>

<Me neither,> *Blossom* admitted. <I only hope that they've all got their breeches twisted over nothing. But don't fret now! If there is something out there, it has to get past me and I eat krakens for breakfast!>

Despite her fear, Maia had to smile as she flopped down on her cot. She really hoped the Ship was right. It would only be a few more hours before they dropped anchor at the entrance to Portus harbour.

*

The remainder of the voyage passed uneventfully, save for the feeling of tension and Maia's rapidly increasing boredom. The Captain had given her some naval history books to study, but whilst the tales of famous Ships had distracted her for a time, the sense of approaching danger refused to leave her. Heron was keeping an eye out for the seagull, or so he said, but it was

135

keeping its distance, for once. She thought she glimpsed it through her window from time to time, but, as he pointed out, they all looked the same and it could be any of the many attracted by the prospect of easy pickings.

She managed to wade through the account of the First Placation of Neptune and the Treaty of the Atlantic before she ran out of patience, her mind losing concentration and focus. At any other time, the story of how the Emperor Augustus managed to speak directly to the God of the Sea and offer tribute in return for his Ships' safe passage would have been a fascinating one, but now the words danced before her eyes and she could feel the start of a headache.

Fresh air was what she needed. She contacted *Blossom*.

<I'm coming up on deck.>

Blossom answered promptly. <We're just rounding the headland now. I can see Portus from here. I'll talk you through the procedure so you'll at least get some benefit.>

Maia needed no further encouragement. It was a good opportunity to get some tuition even though she wouldn't have control of the vessel. She grabbed her cap from its peg and headed for the quarterdeck, not bothering with a cloak as the day was warm enough.

Upon reaching the deck, she felt better immediately. The usual noises and activity served to raise her spirits and she felt her bad mood dissipate, to be replaced by a more cheerful outlook. The wind was light and fresh on her face as she gazed landward to the green and brown of the shoreline and she could already see the smudges of smoke that hung in the air over Portus itself.

A raucous shriek made her glance upwards to where a large gull swooped and wheeled. She squinted at it suspecting that her friend had returned, but couldn't be sure as it was joined by others all calling in excitement at the sight of galley waste. The air was soon full of manic cries and rapidly beating wings.

"Maia! Good to see you out and about." Heron had appeared at her shoulder. He followed her gaze to the squabbling gulls and she thought she saw the shadow of a frown cross his face but it was gone before she fully registered it.

"I needed fresh air," she explained. He nodded, understandingly.

"Of course. It must be frustrating, all this hanging about. Still, the matter will hopefully be resolved before too long. I haven't heard anything more," he added, seeing her hunger for news, "but the Collegium is working on it. Ah, here's Robin."

The young apprentice Mage bobbed his head as he approached. His fair complexion had caught the sun, making his birthmark less noticeable than it had been. She thought that his confidence had grown too as he mastered more of the art of defence and weather-working.

"Miss Abella, M-master."

"How are you doing with the task I set you?" Heron asked, briskly.

"All finished, M-master. If any kraken comes within a m-mile of us the alarm w-will sound."

Heron raised his bushy eyebrows. "You seem very sure of that."

"Yes, M-master. I tested it on the sample to check the response. It was tiny and only just audible, but it w-was there."

Heron beamed, clearly delighted. "Good! I knew I was right to salvage that bit of tentacle. We found a young one dead on a beach on the Isles of Sillina," he explained to Maia. "Even so, it had limbs over fifty feet long. Perhaps a bigger one had attacked it – it's rumoured that they eat each other, or maybe the Mer-people had wounded it; we couldn't tell as it had started to rot. Either way I hacked off a piece and dried it out to use for an experiment with a warning device." He lowered his voice. "*Blossom* wasn't at all pleased. Said it stank the vessel out." He rolled his eyes. "I insisted that it would be of great benefit to science. She forgave me eventually, when the smell abated."

He grinned and she had to laugh.

"I'd love to see how it works," she said. She knew about krakens, because they could be a menace to Ships. Anything that would give an advance alarm sounded intriguing.

"Good idea!" Heron was immediately enthusiastic. "I'm hoping to get the perfected device installed on each Ship as standard. As you know, the beasties can rise up from the depths and attack without warning. I've been studying them for thirty years or more and am convinced that they mistake our vessels for giant orcas, upon which they feed."

She listened with interest as the Mage began to hold forth on one of his favourite subjects. His many ideas and theories as to the nature of these deadly and elusive beasts of the deep ocean were interesting, but when he showed no signs of stopping, Robin flashed her a glance and interrupted smoothly.

"Perhaps I could show M-miss Abella the specimen, M-master?"

Heron paused, caught mid-flow and blinked at his apprentice, as if he'd forgotten he had an audience. "Yes, yes, certainly. I'd accompany you but I must make my report to the Captain about the results of the experiments." He rubbed his hands, clearly relishing the prospect. "We'll be dropping anchor soon, so it's a good idea to do it now before we all get too busy."

Busy watching for anything that might be after her, Maia thought with an inward shudder.

"Off you go then," Heron ordered. Maia and Robin retreated to the Mage's work cabin. It was a larger space even than the Captain's, mostly because of all the paraphernalia required to perform magic and also, as Robin told her, because Heron loved to experiment. She had only seen inside when working with *Blossom* and relished the chance to look around more thoroughly.

It was unusual for a space on a vessel in that every available surface was cluttered with piles of books and notes. Even the ceiling was festooned with strange, exotic objects that swung gently to the roll of the vessel. She was particularly taken by an enormous dried crocodile that grinned toothily from where it was fastened to the full length of the cabin wall. Robin followed her gaze.

"That's Sobek. He's a sacred Nile crocodile all the w-way from Aegyptus."

"He's big," she said, in awe. "How on earth did Heron end up with a sacred crocodile? Did he find it washed up, like the kraken?"

"Oh no. Nor did he k-kill him or anything," Robin replied hastily. "Heron says he w-was a gift. I'm not sure he's actually dead," he added. "I once c-caught him w-winking at me.

Blossom quite likes him. Perhaps it's because he doesn't m-make a m-mess like some of the other pets."

Maia stared at Sobek with interest. He certainly looked dead and somewhat shrivelled. She didn't know what she'd do if he winked at her.

"Heron talks to him too," Robin informed her. She stared at him until his face cracked and he burst out laughing. "All right – he didn't actually w-wink at me, but I did see him talking to him."

She pulled a face at the young Mage before turning to see a long, leathery tentacle fixed to the inner wall. She hadn't recognised what it was at first because it was coiled round on itself like some tanned and vaguely unpleasant seashell. Huge circular suckers, ringed with lethal-looking barbs, studded the surface at regular intervals. It was both simultaneously fascinating and repulsive. Embedded in the flesh was a thick copper wire with different coloured crystals fastened along its length and its end attached to a small array of bells.

"And here it is, the w-world's first kraken alarm!" Robin announced, proudly. "The tentacle retains its…w-well…krakenness for w-want of a better w-word. It's all to do with sympathetic resonance. If one of the beasties comes w-within a three mile radius of us, the bells w-will ring, increasing in strength as it approaches. Heron invented it himself. W-we're trying to increase the w-warning distance, but that takes time and possibly a better sample."

Maia was impressed, despite the look of the thing. She wouldn't have associated such devices with Mages, but knew that they each had their own particular strength. Heron and Robin were clearly mechanically minded.

"Will every Ship get one?"

"Only if a; w-we can get approval of this prototype and b; enough tentacles," Robin said. "W-we're still experimenting to find out how much kraken is actually needed for the optimum result. It might be possible to use a smaller piece. It's got to be field tested yet."

"I don't expect *Blossom*'s volunteering for that," Maia pointed out.

"Er…no," agreed Robin, looking slightly crestfallen, "but it m-might happen anyway when we get into deeper w-water."

He brightened at the thought, then saw Maia's face. She wasn't keen on going anywhere near a kraken. "It w-would be interesting to find out if it w-works," he offered, plaintively. Maia now understood why the two of them got on so well.

"Has anyone pointed out that you're both slightly mad?" she asked, sweetly.

"Of an enquiring nature, if you don't m-mind," he replied, not at all offended.

She moved around the workshop, careful not to touch anything. Her eyes fell on something interesting at every glance; crystals of every colour imaginable, jars containing liquids or strange bits of animal and a model planetarium that moved steadily on its own. Robin watched her with amusement. If he'd been hoping to provide a distraction he'd certainly succeeded. She was admiring a particularly pretty stone when the Ship's bells rang for dinner.

"I didn't realise the time," she said.

"Me neither," Robin admitted. They smiled at each other.

"Come on now you two. Stop gawking at each other and get ready to eat!" *Blossom*'s voice made them both jump and she decided that she was hungry after all. Hopefully it wouldn't be pickled cabbage.

*

The stink of the port crept its way into the carriage as it bumped along over the uneven cobbles of the quayside. The daytime noises had given way to the quieter sounds of evening, broken only by raucous shouts from late night revellers eager to be relieved of their hard-earned cash and the final wagons trundling into the town before the new curfew began. The Master Mage shifted his old bones as the vehicle came to a halt, the creaking of springs and the cessation of hoof beats signalling their arrival. Outside, hushed voices conferred urgently.

A horse snorted, then the door opened and Raven swung himself out, ignoring the hands thrust forward to assist him.

"The boat's ready, sir." Polydorus, who knew more than he would ever tell, was at his elbow.

Raven made his way to the steps, outlined to him by the purplish silver glow that had been a substitute for his human sight for more years than he cared to think about. The Ship's boat would take him out to where the *Blossom* lay at anchor far enough away to deter any unwelcome attention, or so everyone hoped.

This time, Polydorus' proffered arm was accepted as he stepped into the little boat. His pride would definitely not survive a sudden immersion in the filthy water of Portus harbour. As soon as he had made himself as comfortable as it was possible to be on a hard wooden bench and, moreover, one that was moving, they headed out towards the harbour entrance. The moon had not yet risen and, despite his thick cloak, a shiver passed through him.

<I'm on my way to examine the girl,> he Sent to Heron, through his speechstone.

The terse answer was immediate. <Acknowledged.>

Raven had a blurred image of the figures in the boat, but the constantly shifting water made it harder for his sightsense to settle. He cut the Sending off short and huddled deeper into his cloak, hood pulled close. He felt the need to consult with Heron and it was surely good fortune that he and the girl were aboard the same vessel. His thoughts skittered away from the past. Best to forget the horrors and concentrate on the present, for as long as he was able.

If there was anything Maia Abella knew that could help solve this mystery, he would get it out of her, one way or another.

*

It had been a busy day and Casca was glad to be shutting up for the night. The last customers had been gently but firmly encouraged to leave, sent reeling out into the darkness to find their own accommodation wherever they could. Doubtless, some wouldn't make it that far, but that wasn't his problem. He had a few paying guests but they were mostly businessmen and already in bed.

Cara was sweeping up and stacking stools prior to mopping the boards, while he removed the empty barrels and cleaned spigots. A sense of peace descended as they went about their accustomed tasks, lulled by the familiar routine.

Casca's thoughts had turned to food and sleep when, out of the corner of his eye, he saw the front door began to open.

"Cara, didn't you lock up?" It hadn't seemed windy outside.

"Course I did."

He frowned at her carelessness, moving round the bar to remedy the mistake, when the figure entered. At first, what he was seeing made no sense. The woman was alight, sparks drifting and dancing around her body and his first instinct was to rip off his coat to smother the flames. Then the smoke cleared and he saw her face.

Cara's scream shattered the silence. He backed away, hitting a stacked table and spilling the stools across the floor. The thing moved faster than he believed possible, gliding swiftly over to where the woman stood, open-mouthed and forcing her against the wall.

Casca glanced over at the bar. Could he get his cudgel in time? Maybe he could smash the thing to pieces.

"You will tell me what I need to know."

The voice sounded quite normal, belying the horror of the creature before him. Cara had flattened herself as far as was possible, her head turned away from the apparition and tears streaming down her face. The stink of burnt wood intensified.

"What do you want?" he croaked.

The thing's head rotated slowly, to fix him with a staring eye and Casca felt his bowels turn to water.

"There was a girl here. Maia Abella." The creature lingered lovingly over the syllables of the name, drawing them out. "Where is she?"

"The polismen took her."

"Where? Tell me or this one dies," she said, gently.

Casca shook his head in frustration. "I don't know where she is!"

"She's a Ship-in-training!" Cara screamed suddenly.

The thing's head snapped back to her, eagerly.

"Are you sure?"

"Yes!" Cara moaned. "I saw her in the parades!" Her clothes were beginning to smoulder.

A gaping split opened in the creature's face and Casca realised that it was smiling.

"Yes, it is fitting."

The thing broke off its attack and stepped backwards towards the open entrance. As it did so, its wooden feet scraped along the floor, leaving a trail of orange flames that raced to devour the alcohol-soaked boards.

Soon, a curtain of fire concealed it from view and Casca ran for the mop bucket, yelling at Cara to get out. He only hoped he could save his guests in time.

*

Raven is on his way," Heron reported to the Captain.

Plinius nodded. "*Blossom* is expecting him. I haven't seen him for a while. How is he?"

"The same as ever," Heron replied. "Wizened and scary."

They exchanged a smile.

"Isn't he needed on land?" Plinius asked. He was puzzled that the Master Mage was coming at all.

"We need information," Heron explained, "and he specifically wants to examine Maia. There must be something about her that we don't understand. Why has she been singled out like this?"

"It can't be her," Plinius said. "It must be something to do with her origins. Hopefully he can find something out. The crew doesn't suspect anything, but it's only a matter of time."

The lamps were lit and darkness had fallen by the time the boat was sighted by human eyes. The sound of oars in the water heralded its arrival, though the *Blossom* had already informed her Captain of its approach.

Raven dispensed with the ladder, as Heron suspected he might. It was harder to levitate on water, but the wood of the boat gave him the surface he needed to push against, ensuring he rose smoothly up past the side of the vessel and over the rail to land gently on the deck. He was gratified to hear a few gasps and muttered oaths. He rarely showed his Potentia so openly and a little demonstration now and then not only kept his hand in but also ensured proper respect.

The shrilling of the Ship's whistle brought them all to attention.

"Welcome aboard, Master Mage Raven." *Blossom* and her Captain spoke as one, signalling the unity of their intent.

"Thank you, I only wish it was under happier circumstances," Raven replied. He nodded to Heron and the other officers, who saluted.

It was definitely warmer below and Raven gratefully accepted a glass of wine from Victor, who waited on his master's guests. It had been a chilly crossing. Heron, at Raven's request warded the cabin against outside eyes and ears as an added precaution. Immediately everyone felt as if they had been plunged deep under the sea and the men had to resist the urge to yawn widely to equalise the pressure.

The Captain presented his officers to the Master Mage. Durus and Campion were suitably overawed; both had heard of him by reputation.

"So, how may we assist you?" Plinius said, once Victor had left them.

"I need to gather information," Raven replied. "If the lessons of the past have taught us anything, it is that these things move swiftly."

Plinius cleared his throat.

"You seem certain now that Maia is the target."

"As much as anyone can be." Raven looked grave. "There have been no further attacks, but the Lady Claudia Modesta, Flamenica Prima of Juno's Temple in Portus was granted a Divine Sending through one of her acolytes, who incidentally was also on the list of names found in Varus' office."

"The Goddess has taken an interest?" Heron asked.

"Certain sacrifices were made and Juno spoke," Raven stated. "Her sanctuary was attacked and her acolyte threatened and we all know that no God takes kindly to that, least of all a deity of her power."

"Message from shore," *Blossom* said. "I think everyone needs to hear this. Portus is locked down. The Revenant has attacked a waterfront tavern, setting it alight though everyone got out safely and the Vigiles have managed to extinguish it. The landlord reports that the thing looked like the remains of a Ship."

Raven's heart sank. He realised that he'd been clinging on to the hope that it had all been a mistake and nothing would come of it. Now that hope was well and truly scuppered.

"It wanted to know Maia's whereabouts."

An appalled silence filled the cabin as *Blossom* finished speaking.

"A Ship?" Campion asked, casting a puzzled glance around the room. Plinius' face was stony and Durus looked grim. Heron was staring at the ceiling. There was good reason that Campion was confused as the execution had been classified as top secret, though most sailors got to hear about it sooner or later.

"She was called the *Livia*," Raven said quietly, "and she murdered her Captain in a fit of jealous rage."

Campion's mouth fell open.

"When was this?"

"Eighteen years ago. She found out that he had married and was going to leave her. She snapped and killed him. The King ordered her execution out at sea."

"Dear Gods!" Campion muttered. "So, this Ship's back as a Revenant? Why?"

"So," the Captain cut in. "Let us draw inference from the facts laid before us. Firstly, this angry Revenant has been generated by the *Livia*." He ignored the jolt of horror that hit him from *Blossom*. "Secondly, it is looking for Maia. Lastly, we can presume that anyone standing between this creature and its desires is in extreme danger."

"That's us then," remarked Campion.

"Quite."

"Why now?"

Blossom's voice echoed through the wall, then suddenly she flowed out of the wood, coalescing into her figurehead form, armoured and ready for battle. Her bright bouquet had been replaced by an impressive war axe.

"Indeed," her Captain agreed. "The *Livia* went down many years ago. Why has it been so long?"

"Maybe conditions weren't right," Raven said. "I suspect that Maia has been protected by a friendly deity of some sort, which has already intervened to save her life."

"It could have been a time sensitive working as well," Heron offered, "with a temporal limit perhaps, to allow Maia to grow."

"She's an unlikely target," Plinius said. "She fades easily into the background, maybe too easily eh?"

"Then there was the death of her former mistress," Raven mused. "A Priest of Mercury confirmed that that was Divine vengeance and, from what we found out about the woman's crimes, justly deserved, but nothing was done until she attacked Maia. It must be a subtle protection indeed."

"She thinks a bird has been watching her," *Blossom* said.

Raven's eyes opened wide. "You didn't think to mention it?"

"We weren't sure," she said quickly.

"Hmmm. I can see a pattern, of sorts," the ancient Mage concluded. "I sensed some anomaly but couldn't place it. It was like trying to grasp an eel that was always slipping away out of sight." Then, more to himself than to the others, he muttered, "what did I miss? She appears fully human."

"But with Divine blood, of course," Plinius said.

Raven sighed. "None could be detected."

Everyone in the cabin was stunned.

"But she must have some!" *Blossom* was shocked. "How can she be expected to go through initiation without it?"

"Why was she enrolled as a candidate in the first place?" Plinius demanded.

"It was the will of the Gods," Raven told him.

"Does she know?" *Blossom* asked angrily, "or does she think she has - ah! That's why she's constantly afraid. She thinks she's going to fail! How could the Navy do that to her?"

The Ship was furious and, from the look on Plinius' face, he was in agreement with her.

"These are unusual circumstances, I know," Raven said quickly, "but we weren't going to argue with a God. We just assumed that things would work out somehow."

"This casts a different light on things," Heron muttered. "Divine sponsorship and now an angry Revenant. We have the pieces but still can't see the picture."

"No wonder she was so evasive about her Potentia," *Blossom* continued. "It's so unfair! She's very capable too."

"Is she?" Raven asked.

"Oh yes, unlike the last girl we had. Maia has performed excellently. We've been lucky with the weather; she hasn't had to contend with any bad storms yet, but she's taken to Ship work like a duck to water."

"Interesting," Raven mused. "Where is she now?"

"She's resting in her cabin. The poor girl has had a lot to bear and now this. I'd swear that she doesn't know anything."

"I agree. We need to find out how and why the Revenant formed," Heron said, practically. Plinius knew that his Mage was always interested in why things happened. "Something must have been left to anchor the spirit."

"How can it be the *Livia*? She was totally destroyed," *Blossom* said. "Isn't that right, Master Mage?"

"Yes. We made sure of it," Raven agreed. "We dealt with everything of hers we could find, lest any trace remain. Even what few possessions she had left in storage."

"Yet you must have missed something."

Raven lifted his arms, then let them fall in frustration. "I don't know what it could be. She had no flesh and blood kin that would be close enough either; she was three hundred years old and more at that point. Everything went up in flames, vessel and bodies, Ship and flesh. There were no keepsakes."

Involuntarily, Heron found that the scene rose before his inner eye, its horror engraved into his memory despite all he had done to forget.

*

It was a cold morning on the water. The sea was calm, with an oily sheen that heaved gently under the leaden sky. A slight breeze moved lazily around the two Ships, prowling through the rigging like a stalking beast, as if anticipating the events to come. Heron stood on the deck with the other five Mages, their minds firmly locked on their task.

The *Livia*, a first-rate Ship of His Majesty's Britannic Navy, was being held forcibly at anchor above the Atlantic. It had taken all six men three days to restrain her and drag her out to sea, using every ounce of brute Potentia they could muster. The journey had taken its toll as they struggled in shifts to overcome the resistance of the furious Ship. Even now, Heron and the others could sense her straining to snap the compulsion laid upon her as she desperately fought to break the magical restraints and regain control.

The only sounds were the low chanting of the Mages and the soft slap of the waves on her hull.

The Lord High Admiral, grim-faced and pitiless, stepped forward to read the Royal Decree of Execution. His Majesty, Artorius the Ninth, Rex Britannica and Defender of the Roman Empire, had signed the death warrant and now it was time to carry out the sentence. The penalty for mutiny and murder was death.

Heron hardly heard the words, concentrating on the binding that blocked the doomed Ship from linking to the mechanisms of her vessel. He could feel her insane rage as she probed and pushed, seeking a weakness, any weakness, in her captors' wills. To his right, the ancient, blind Master Mage stood like carved granite, his mouth moving as he chanted, whilst before them, fixed in her position on the quarterdeck, the *Livia*'s Shipbody stood like a beautifully carved statue. Her face was immobile, though her eyes darted and rolled like those of a trapped animal waiting for the killing blow.

A shrouded bundle lay at the Ship's feet – her body, held in suspended animation and removed from storage. Human flesh and living wood, linked by ancient magic, would burn together.

The Admiral finished the pronouncement and snapped the scroll shut, the tiny sound loud in the sudden silence. Heron struggled under the weight of the spell, feeling the demand increase as the Ship silently raged. She was bound, but they hadn't been able to sever her mental link to her sister Ships and he thanked the Gods that he couldn't hear what she was Sending to them. Their orders were to bear witness to their sister's fate, as both a lesson and a warning.

It wouldn't be long now. The small party of officers and crew turned and made their way across the deck for the last time, footsteps hollow on the boards, to where they could go over the side and climb down into the waiting boats.

None of them spoke or looked back. Any tears would be shed later, in private.

It was only when they were clear that the Mages began to slacken their spells; not enough to relinquish control, but just enough to allow them to make their escape. One by one, they stumbled to the rail, faces lined with exhaustion and slid more than climbed down the ladder. As the chanting voices decreased in volume, the *Livia*'s Shipbody began to twitch, jerking spasmodically as she regained some movement, but not enough to free herself. Her eyes ceased to roll, fixing instead on the retreating men and, beyond them to her sister Ship, the *Augusta*. Finally, Heron and Raven, the Master Mage, were the last ones remaining and only Heron could see the *Livia* as she strained to speak, her wooden lips opening and twisting soundlessly.

It was enough. He forced himself to move across the deck, knowing that Raven would be close behind him, and climbed down to the waiting boat. Hands reached to catch him as he continued to concentrate on the form of the binding, keeping the net-like shape of it in his mind.

The boat lurched and Heron knew that Raven was aboard. He was conscious of the quiet order from the bow and the boat sped swiftly away, pulled by the *Augusta*'s will. The wooden wall of the *Livia*'s flank receded and more of the vessel came into view. She had been stripped of her guns, which had been melted down and destroyed and her only cargo was heavy stone ballast and many barrels of oil and gunpowder.

They were over halfway to the *Augusta* when Heron felt the binding began to slip. Hoarse shrieks of pain and fury echoed across the water, causing the men in the boat to flinch, some shutting their eyes as if that would ease the horror. Pleas and threats in equal measure filled the air, followed by pitiful sobbing and a name, repeated over and over.

"Gods above!" an officer muttered. "She calls for her Captain. Can't she remember she killed him?"

Suddenly, Raven straightened and Sent the mental command to his fellow Mages. Heron felt only relief as he joined with the others to push the ignition spell towards the insane Ship.

At first, nothing seemed to change, then a tongue of fire shot up through the hatches. The sound of the explosion followed, booming out like the voice of Jupiter himself and debris hurtled outwards in all directions. The *Livia* began to burn, great gouts of oily black smoke ascending from her funeral pyre. The fire spread quickly over what was left, running along her decks and racing up her masts to punch great holes in the slack sails which began to shift and billow in the up draughts as if life had returned one last time, even as the canvas was replaced by sheets of flame.

The Ship's final, desperate screams were lost in the roar and crackle of the blazing inferno. Heron watched the sparks fly upwards, pale, flitting things that quickly transformed to black ash which settled quickly on the water. A sudden gusty breeze sprang up, spurring the fire to even greater frenzy, creating a whirlwind of leaping shapes that pranced and cavorted around the Ship as if delighting in its destruction.

They reached the safety of the *Augusta* at last, to join the lines of men watching in silence, their faces lit by the weak morning sun and the reflection of the fire on the water. The *Augusta* herself, over five hundred years old and the proud Flagship of His Majesty's Royal Navy, remained impassive, her regal face showing no signs of the emotion she must be sharing with her far-flung sisters. She would be ensuring that they all knew that justice was being served.

It took longer for the Ship to die than Heron had supposed. It seemed an age before she finally sank, her masts cracking and groaning as she heeled over to show her hull, stripped of the protective copper plates and fatally weakened by her carpenter. Soon, all that was left was a slick of charred destruction drifting on the current. Any larger pieces would be magically disintegrated and sent to the depths. Nothing could be permitted to remain.

The *Livia* was dead.

A fair breeze guided them back to port, as if the Gods themselves were showing approval.

*

"Everything was done properly. Only ash remained. Something else must be tying her to the earth," he pointed out.

"We both helped bind her," Raven said quietly. "If she, or whatever she has become, wants vengeance, she will no doubt remember our part in her destruction."

Heron winced.

"So, we just sit and wait?" Plinius asked.

"That's all we can do here," Raven replied, "though of course the Collegium has Agents watching on land. I'll let Maia rest for tonight and question her in the morning."

Blossom was silent. She, too, remembered that day. Every Ship in the service had borne witness to the penalty for killing her Captain and, unlike the other observers, they had heard everything. The *Livia* had raged, pleaded and threatened in her agony and madness, right to the end. She had died screaming vengeance on her destroyers.

"Her Captain," she said aloud.

The men stared at her, puzzled.

"What of him?" Plinius asked, his forehead creasing as he tried to follow her thought.

"Just suppose he had something of hers. A souvenir no-one knew about. I know some Captains take a tiny splinter of their Ships with them when they retire, even though it's forbidden. It's hard for old sailors to let go."

"Surely it would have been discovered," Durus said.

"It would have hardly been fitting for him to be buried with anything of hers," Raven agreed. "His mother would never have permitted it and, as I said, we burnt all that we could find."

"Is she still alive?" Plinius asked.

"No, she died two years ago," Raven answered.

"What is known of his wife?" the Captain said, thoughtfully. "Did she really just simply vanish into thin air after his death, as was the rumour?"

Raven sighed. "We could discover nothing about her, save her name, Julia Aurelia and that she was twenty-five. Where they met and what happened thereafter is unknown, save that they married in secret. An old Priest of the Temple of Mercury in Portus remembered them and their nuptials were recorded, but he couldn't – or wouldn't - answer any questions. I thought that perhaps his wits were addled with age, but now I wonder. There are secrets within secrets here. It was presumed that Valerius kept everything quiet because of his Ship's jealousy, especially in the light of what happened subsequently."

"I have an idea. What if it is an actual piece of her Shipbody after all?" Heron said, slowly. Raven began to object but the other Mage continued. "What if it's lodged in him? Deliberately?"

"What do you mean?"

"In him. His body. I saw what she did to him, remember?"

"You were there?" Campion asked.

"I was her Mage," Heron replied, his voice full of anguish. "She clutched Valerius to her and it was all we could do to rip him from her embrace. What if she drove a piece of her Shipbody into him, to somehow keep him?"

He swallowed convulsively. It had been horrific. The *Livia* had seized the Captain before anyone could stop her, enfolding him in her unyielding arms and crushing him. He hadn't even been able to scream. The man's face had been undamaged, though she'd reduced his ribcage to splinters by driving her fingers into his back.

"It would have been easy for her to release a portion of herself, a finger perhaps, smoothing over the wound and reshaping any missing part." The memory made him feel nauseous; he'd been fond of the man, they all had.

"Dear Gods," muttered Campion. "There'd be no way of telling afterwards, without cutting the body open and I doubt they did that. Anything driven in deep would have stayed there."

"It's a distinct possibility," Raven said at last.

"All this time," *Blossom* said. "She could have him still, working through his corpse and somehow feeding off his remaining anima vita."

"What do you mean?" Campion asked, curiously.

"We are trees. We have roots," *Blossom* said. "It is part of our Mystery. It could have been her plan all along, or just a mad impulse."

Plinius, having an inkling of her meaning, wasted no further time. Aloud, he began.

"*Blossom*, Send to the Admiralty, mark top priority. To stop Revenant, exhume and burn Captain Valerius's body. Possible Link to the *Livia* in his remains. Signed, Gaius Plinius Tertius, Captain, HMS *Blossom*. End Sending."

"Aye, sir."

Even as the Captain was speaking, Raven accessed his speechstone and made a Sending of his own.

"I've informed the Admiralty that I'm activating a suitable Agent to carry out this task," he reported, "and I've also updated the Collegium. Unfortunately, even if we are right, the whole thing will take a few hours to execute. I understand that Captain Valerius is interred in the family tomb outside Durnovaria."

"Your Agent must travel west with all speed then, unless there is anyone nearer," Plinius said.

"Alas, there is no-one else I can trust with this," Raven said regretfully. "In the meantime, we must remain on our guard. We have to hope that we're right."

"And if we're on the wrong track?" Plinius asked.

"Then we'll think of something else."

It was going to be a sleepless night for most of them. Raven sent a prayer to Mercury, the swift one, asking that Milo would be able to get to Durnovaria in time. He would speak to the *Blossom*'s Priest as well, who was even now making sacrifice on their behalf.

They would surely need any help that the Gods were willing to grant.

IX

Milo was sitting unobtrusively in the corner of the highly disreputable tavern, hat pulled down low and staring into a small cup of what passed for wine. He was cursing his luck that such a filthy hole was the preferred meeting place of his newest informant, vowing to have words with the imbecile if he actually appeared, when the heat of the speechstone against his chest signalled that his link to the Master Mage had been activated.

Milo sighed inwardly. What could be the problem now? Despite his constant surveillance of the harbour and its surrounding streets, nothing else had turned up as yet. No more fiery deaths either. A word from the Master Mage had got him access to the polis mortuary to see the Overseer's remains, but there had been nothing gained from that to add what they already knew. Neither Jackdaw nor Scabious had been able to shed any further light on the matter, despite every test in the books of both Mage and Adept. Since then he'd kept watch, making regular reports that amounted to the same thing. Absolutely nothing. This latest informant was actually to do with another, less vexing case because Milo didn't see why his other work had to suffer whilst he twiddled his thumbs over this conundrum. He glanced round the tavern, his patience evaporating. The cook shop over the road would have been a better and far more salubrious place to wait and he already missed the familiar bar at The Anchor. Oh well, needs must.

<Master Mage,> he Sent.

<Milo. Good. I have a new task for you, of the most extreme urgency. Go to Durnovaria as quickly as possible. I've ordered you a flyer. Find the tomb of the Valerius family, get a Priest, exhume the corpse of Captain Lucius Valerius Vero, salt it and burn it with the appropriate rites. Beseech whichever Gods favour you to grant you their blessing. Leave immediately, as lives depend on it. You have the full backing of His Majesty's Government and the Collegium, but be discreet. Do you understand?>

Milo realised that his jaw had dropped. He quickly replayed the orders in his head. Go to Durnovaria. Find a Priest. Burn a corpse. Right, then.

<Do you know where near Durnovaria?> he asked hopefully.

<They were an ancient and wealthy family and his mother was only buried two years ago so the local Priests should remember. The tomb will be of some substance somewhere along the main road in from the east. I can't get more information without arousing suspicion and there just isn't time.> Raven sounded tetchier than usual, so Milo decided not to push his luck.

<Understood.>

<May the Gods be with you.> The contact ceased abruptly.

Milo thought quickly. Captain Valerius? He knew the name, of course. A cold shiver ran up his back. It had to be to do with the ill-fated HMS *Livia*, though that was an old tale, from before he had entered the service of the Collegium. Ferreting out gossip and rumour was his trade after all and old sailors would talk in their cups or for a shiny coin or two. He knew that the repercussions had rumbled on for years, as much as they tried to bury the story. Ships going rogue – it was the stuff of nightmares, a horror story whispered in dark corners and, though he'd heard at least five different versions, the ending was always the same.

Even as he was running through his options, he rose to his feet and slipped out the door, sidestepping two happy drunks and fending off a hopeful doxy, before reaching the street and cleaner air.

Durnovaria, fast.

Horses would get him there, but it would take too long and he would need regular changes of mount. It would be complicated, even with his Agent's badge, if he cared to show it. Transport spells over that distance were impossible without a prepared receiving circle and even a short one knocked him sick. Several would leave him totally incapacitated. That left him with only one viable option, as Raven had pointed out. Damn the man to Hades! Why wasn't there anyone nearer?

Milo hurried through the darkening streets towards the Polis Offices at the other end of the Forum. He knew that they kept at least one flier there for emergencies and it didn't seem as if he had much choice.

He arrived at the front desk slightly out of breath and slammed his badge down on the counter in front of the startled desk capere.

"I need a flier. Now."

The uniformed officer eyed him, glancing at the badge briefly before fixing him with an 'I'm not to be hurried' look that polismen everywhere seemed to specialise in.

"Please wait 'ere, sir," he said at last, before shouting over to a spotty youth at a desk who was laboriously filling in a form. "Oi, Caractacus! Get off your arse and get the Chief. Quick now!"

The youth frowned, thought better of it and trotted off into the back offices.

"And Jackdaw!" Milo bellowed after him. The Mage knew him from previous adventures and, with any luck, he would be able to speed things up. He didn't want to waste time explaining everything to a load of plods.

"Thought I'd seen you around 'ere before," the officer said. His face was familiar and Milo groped for a name.

"Sergeant Grumio, isn't it?"

The polisman nodded. "That's right sir. Quite a memory for names I see. Going somewhere in a hurry, then?"

Milo was saved from answering by the sound of a door closing and rapid steps announcing the Prefect's arrival. He looked as though he hadn't slept for a couple of days and could do with a trip to the baths. He probably had private ones, Milo thought enviously. At least he was on Revenant watch like the rest of them. Grumio snapped smartly to attention.

"This man says 'e needs a flier, sir."

His tone implied that this was the last thing Milo deserved; a good kicking being the most likely reward and one that he, Grumio, would be more than happy to provide gratis.

"He's authorised, Sergeant," the Prefect said, wearily. "See to it immediately." Grumio's large moustache twitched with disappointment. "Is there anything else we can do for you, Agent?"

The Prefect clearly knew which side his bread was buttered. He'd probably had half a dozen priority messages in the last five minutes and he wasn't going to stand in the way.

"I'd just like a word with Jackdaw if I may, sir," he replied politely. Placidianus nodded.

"Of course. He's waiting for you at the stables." Placidianus nodded graciously, dismissing him and returned to his office, no doubt to assure his superiors that his duty was discharged.

"Don't forget your badge, sir," Grumio remarked, as Milo turned to leave. "Enjoy your flight."

"Thank you," Milo replied glumly, fancying that he saw the trace of a smirk on the polisman's face as he reclaimed the copper plaque. Caractacus' eyes were openly popping as he watched the Agent leave.

The stables were at the back of the building, which was a lot less impressive than the frontage as was usual for all civic offices. Several polismen stood muttering in a group and the smell of straw, leather and manure hung in the smoky air. A lone figure hurried to meet him and it was only then that Milo realised how dark it was getting as he could barely see Jackdaw's face in the evening light.

"Milo!" The two men clasped arms. "I heard you're on an urgent mission."

"Very. I had a Sending from Raven."

"Me too." He lowered his voice. "What's going on?"

"I have to get to Durnovaria tonight."

"Now? Can't it wait until morning?"

Milo wasn't thrilled himself at the thought of flying in darkness. It was bad enough in daylight and he'd only done it once before, under extreme duress. He made a moue of regret.

"Unfortunately not."

Jackdaw shrugged. "Rather you than me. Come on then and I'll introduce you to Nix. She's a good girl and she'll do as she's told. Strong too."

They tramped along the cobbles, Jackdaw holding up his robe to avoid the scattered puddles, to where a lamp burned outside a large barn door.

"She's in here," he said. "Aeron!" A small, wiry man bustled over.

"Yessir. She's all saddled up and ready to go. Just needs telling."

"Thanks. Could you bring her out then?"

Aeron scuttled inside the cavernous space, emerging a few seconds later leading the pegasus. Black as the night which had given her her name, the mare tossed her head and snorted, iron-shod hooves ringing on the cobbles. Her huge, feathered wings were laid neatly across her flanks and she regarded Milo with an interested eye.

Aeron gave the agent a toothless grin.

"'Ere you are, sir. Ain't she a beauty? 'Ave you ridden before?"

"Once." Milo felt his stomach sink at the prospect.

"Ah, yer'll be fine. She's a clever one is our Nix. She won't let yer fall, will yer, me darlin'?" He patted the glossy neck and the pegasus whickered softly in return.

"Just one more thing, sir. Yer'll be needin' this." Aeron handed him a fur-lined cap with earflaps that tied under the chin. "Stow yer 'at in yer coat. Yer don't want ter be losing it over the 'arbour!"

Milo accepted the cap, knowing that he'd be glad of it shortly. Aeron nodded approvingly as he removed his battered felt hat and tucked it away in an inner pocket. Gritting his teeth, he swung himself up into the saddle, which had a high horn at the front and a solid rear cantle to keep him firmly fixed on Nix's back.

Jackdaw stepped forward and whispered something in the mare's ear. She tossed her head, as if acknowledging her instructions and Milo gripped the coarse mane firmly. Unlike horses, pegasi didn't need reins. They were far more intelligent than horses and most understood some human speech.

"There you go. She has her instructions. East road, Durnovaria. It should take less than an hour in these conditions." He paused, looking hopefully at Milo. "I don't suppose you can tell me what all this is about?"

"No, sorry." Milo had to admire the Mage for trying.

"Alas, my curiosity must remain unassuaged," he sighed in mock sadness. "Never mind. Good luck and may the Gods go with you!"

Milo sent up a quick prayer to Mercury the God of messengers, travellers and underpaid Crown Agents as Nix, knowing that her time had come, flexed her wing muscles in preparation for flight. He remembered to nudge her gently with his knees to urge her forwards and the pegasus responded, wheeling towards the arch that led to the runway beyond. Torches were placed along its length to give some illumination, but beyond that, in the direction of the harbour, the city lamps pointed the way. The moon was just rising, her swollen face peeping above the rooftops and he offered a prayer to Luna as well, that his way be illuminated this night.

Nix clattered through the archway, clearly eager to be about her business. Her speed built up rapidly to a brisk trot then a canter and, as her hooves hit the sanded earth of the runway, to a full gallop. Milo crouched low over her neck, feeling her massive wings unfurl as she suddenly leapt skywards, the initial thrust of her hind legs being taken up by the heavy downbeat. The air resistance forced him backwards as he leant into it, eyes closed with fingers entwined in the thick mane, feeling his body tilt and the rushing wind hit his face.

It seemed an age before Nix attained the proper height and levelled off. He risked a glance, slackening his cramped fingers from their death grip and saw that they were already heading south over the sea before their westward turn. Portus had fallen away behind them and the full moon to the south-east cast a silver glow over the calm waters of the harbour. At any other time, he would have enjoyed the sight. Few people had the privilege of a Gods'-eye view, he told himself, although presumably the Gods had more of a head for heights than he did.

Below and ahead of him he could see the lights of vessels as they rode at anchor, or made their way into harbour on the incoming tide. The dark bulk of the island of Vectis lay beyond.

Briefly, he wondered what had happened to the girl he had investigated, the one he could find nothing about. It was an odd thought to have out of nowhere and an icy premonition ran down his spine. A foundling child, a burnt corpse, an angry Revenant and now a mission to burn a body.

He turned his focus westward as Nix adjusted her bearings and hoped that the locals in Durnovaria could provide a sensible Priest at short notice.

And a spade.

Blossom was well into the first watch of the night, when the Ship sensed the huge flying shape overhead. A pegasus on some urgent mission westbound. She wondered whether there was a connection – the Agent that Raven had mentioned, perhaps.

Poor Maia, she thought, having to live with her burden for so long, knowing that the end could only lead to failure and heartbreak. She prayed to the Goddess Yemoja on her behalf, the way her mother had taught her long ago when her name had been Ifede, before her Potentia had manifested to set her on a new path away from all she had known.

"Lady, grant us your protection. I beg you, keep her safe, keep Maia safe," she whispered.

Out in the dark night a gull called and a sudden blast of wind made her timbers creak like old bones, the vessel rising and falling as the waves were whipped into life around her.

*

The moon rose higher as the night drew on and Nix's wings beat steadily as they crossed the vast harbour where Vespasianus had commanded his troops ashore during the Great Conquest of Britannia. If it had been daylight, he knew he could have seen ahead and to his left the huge limestone quarries from which the finest building materials were taken, but his way led inland to the old city of the Durotriges, dominated by the ancient ramparts of Mai Dun. He regretted that it was too dark to see this wonder, or view the new amphitheatre that had just been recently rebuilt.

On they flew, the pegasus' instructions spurring her on to their destination. Milo hoped that they were accurate; he'd get there in pitch darkness and be expected to find one particular tomb among many on an unfamiliar road. Unlike an experienced messenger, he was feeling the cold and although the flight was smoother than that of a horse, the knowledge that a fall meant certain death tended to outweigh the advantages.

The rhythmic wingbeats suddenly stopped as Nix glided, losing altitude and jerking Milo from a brief doze. His ears popped and he yawned to equalise the pressure. He realised that he hadn't given much thought as to their landing, assuming that by the time of their arrival he wouldn't care so long as he was safely back down. A chill breeze from the west carried the smell of civilisation, smoke and dung. Though not the largest of cities, Durnovaria still had a sizeable population.

Their descent was more pronounced now as Nix began to glide lower, guided by her orders and angling her wings to reduce her speed. The full moon, high in the south, cast her light on fields, heathland and patches of woods that covered the gently rolling land. The road became visible, paved with pale stone chippings, running straight as an arrow from the east and continuing on to Isca in the far west. Nix was aiming straight for it. He hung on for grim life and trusted in his mount's ability to find her way.

Abruptly, the great wings rose to brake against the air and Milo felt an enormous surge of relief as Nix's hooves connected with the smooth road, her gait changing to a regular gallop. At least the way was relatively quiet at this time of night and, for once, he couldn't see any other traffic. He was grateful that would be spared the inevitable crowd of daytime gawkers and the pleas of small excited children to pet Nix.

The mare cantered gently, then slowed into a smooth trot, wings tucked away over his legs and providing some welcome warmth.

"Good girl! Thank you, Nix."

Her ears pricked up and she snorted cheerfully, a satisfied sound as if to reproach her rider for ever doubting her abilities.

Durnovaria lay ahead and they made good time, passing no-one, until the first tombs loomed out of the shadows. This was the abode of the dead who were buried outside the city bounds by Roman tradition; thirteen hundred years' worth of burials, rich, poor and in between, remembered or lying forgotten in the earth they had walked above when living. The oldest were long gone, or smoothed into weathered fragments by time's rough hand. The grandest memorials still bore their carvings; a soldier, a mother, a family sharing a meal, painted features long gone and inscriptions barely legible. They watched silently as he rode past.

The flare of a match caught his attention and Nix slowed to allow him to get a better look. She whinnied gladly, as if seeing an old friend and Milo spotted a tall fellow wearing Priestly robes and carrying a lantern.

"Hello there! Greetings!" The cheerful voice was that of a young man with dark, curly hair and a smiling, open face. "Are you Agent Milo?"

"I am indeed." He patted Nix, then dismounted carefully, groaning quietly as his cramped muscles complained.

"Just a short hop from Portus, eh?" The Priest gave Milo a broad grin.

"Thank the Gods it wasn't longer or you'd have needed a crane to get me down," Milo winced.

"Call me Nuntius," the Priest said. "I've come to give you a hand. I know why you're here."

"Then I hope you have some salt and a spade."

Nuntius fussed over Nix, who snorted and butted him happily.

"Whoa, girl! No, no spade needed. There's a family mausoleum, all above ground and so…"

He produced a crowbar from somewhere beneath his robes.

"That's a good trick," Milo said, impressed. He was relieved that he wouldn't have to dig.

"Thank you. Come on, we don't have much time, alas!"

The pair of them set off up the road a short way before his companion indicated they should turn off.

"It's here."

Raven had been right about the wealth part. Milo gazed at the recently repainted portico, which was carved from the finest marble and elegantly surmounted by a crouching sphinx. The whole thing spoke of privilege and a long line of distinguished ancestors.

"Big local family," Nuntius informed him. "The Captain was the only male left of the direct line, though I believe there was a younger second cousin left to inherit. Tragic."

"Like something out of Euripides," Milo agreed. "I don't think the Navy's ever got over it."

"No." The Priest's face clouded. "But it's time to finish it. You grab the crowbar and I'll start the prayers to appease Pluto. The doors are unlocked."

"Really?" Milo was surprised. Tombs like these were usually fortified with the strongest magical locks and wards.

"Oh yes. That's all been sorted. Someone owed me a favour."

He was really far too chirpy for this time of night, Milo decided wearily. In the meantime, Nix was doing her best to tidy up the long grass and seemed content enough. Belatedly he remembered to send a brief message to the Master Mage to confirm his safe arrival.

"Right then," he began.

Nuntius suddenly cocked his head, listening. Milo followed suit, but heard nothing.

"*Merda!*" the Priest exclaimed. "We've got to get a move on."

The urgency in the Priest's voice was undeniable. They mounted the steps towards the heavy metal-studded doors, past two more guardian sphinxes and entered into the realm of the dead.

*

The moon shone silver-white on the streets and houses of Portus, with no clouds to bar her rays save the ones currently occupying the face of one very tired, hungry and generally fed up apprentice Mage. Wren's feet ached from patrolling since dusk and now it had to be past eleven o'clock. The only consolation was that it wasn't too cold and wet. He could see well enough in the moonlight but, just to be sure, he'd supplemented it with a small sun orb because he really didn't want to mess up his new boots by stepping in something nasty.

The orb glided just above his head, keeping pace as he walked. For once, the town was quiet and the streets empty as a result of the authorities' curfew, backed up by the order of the Collegium. It was hoped that innocent bystanders would be spared the consequences of any battle magic that might have to be thrown about, not to mention the wrath of a mad Revenant. Wren and the other juniors had been bound to secrecy and sent out as scouts.

"Remember – just report anything suspicious to Buzzard or myself immediately. You are not, I repeat, *not* to take the creature on. It will be dealt with by those of us who know what we're doing."

Mage Goldfinch's words had been stern, reinforced by glares at several of the more headstrong members of the Collegium School. There had been a few muttered grumbles from the keener lads eager to try out their newly acquired battle skills, but Wren hadn't been among them. All he wanted was a quiet life with his healing potions and his small collection of adopted stray cats. He definitely didn't want to meet the thing that had everyone in such a panic, wishing instead for a tasty meal and a warm bed, neither of which looked likely in the near future. His stomach rumbled forlornly and he wondered if it was too late to move to one of the Adept Colleges. The Aesculepians were always wanting trainees and his magical grounding would come in useful. He could even go into the veterinary section and specialise in the healing and care of small animals.

He was mulling over this happy thought, when movement in an adjoining alley caught his eye. Probably another rat. They were taking full advantage of the lack of human activity and it was said that there were more of them in the city than there were people, despite all the measures taken to try to keep their numbers down.

Or then again it could be a cat. He stared into the shadows before remembering his orb, giving it a mental nudge into a better position.

The dark shape emerged silently, its outline wavering as if it were made of shifting smoke. An acrid smell of burning made Wren's nostrils flare in disgust and stung his eyes with its pungency.

He acted without thought. Operating in sheer blind instinct and instant terror he leapt away down the street, his robe flapping and his mouth wide in a silent scream. Behind him the sun orb winked out and the shape slowly withdrew, pouring itself back into the concealing blackness and away from the pale rays of the moon's light.

Wren didn't stop running until he literally crashed into a figure coming the other way. It only managed to haul him to a standstill by dint of grabbing his robe and hanging on.

"What in Hades?" a sharp voice spat.

Wren could only whimper, eyes bulging, until he recognised the voice and realised that it was Kestrel, another more willing conscript to the night's activities.

"Saw it," he managed to gasp, between huge panting breaths.

"What?" Kestrel snapped.

"The...the...thing. Back there in the alley. It stank of fire."

Kestrel's eyes lit up. "Did you now? Look, you report it. I'll go and check."

Knowing Wren, it was probably nothing more than a smelly old drunk who had set himself alight, Kestrel thought, but he had been bored stupid for hours and furthermore knew of a particularly destructive spell he wanted to test. What better time and place than here and now?

"No, Gods, you can't!"

Kestrel scowled and shook Wren harder.

"Look, we're not all scared little kitty-cats. You call it in and I'll check, that's all." His eyes narrowed in contempt as he stared down at the smaller youth. "Now do it!"

Wren's breathing had eased. "All right, but I wouldn't go near that thing if I were you. You heard what Goldfinch said."

"Yes, yes, I know!" Kestrel emphasised impatiently, shoving Wren away. "Just bloody well get on with it. I'll only be a minute."

He left Wren fumbling for his speechstone and headed off eagerly in the direction from which the little Mage had run. It hadn't been too far away, surely? The idiot couldn't have got more than a couple of intersections without collapsing from fatigue. Kestrel was confident that he could deal with whatever it was, unlike poor pathetic Wren who jumped at his own shadow. Probably smelled himself, he snorted. If this turned out to be a false alarm, he'd make sure the little worm paid for it later.

Kestrel murmured a word to conjure a sun orb of his own, being careful to raise it up so that he wasn't blinded. Another syllable sent it zipping away from side to side, zigzagging from doorway to doorway to flush out anything that might be lurking. He could feel his pulse increase. This was more like it! It was a welcome break from dull routine and endless supervision and when he nailed this, he would surely be given a top assignment

– perhaps even as a battle Mage with a legion! He imagined the speeches of praise he would receive and the envious faces of his fellow apprentices. Goldfinch would have to pass him at the top of the class.

There! Ahead, down a side street, something black, moving but indistinct like a dark cloud drifting over the cobbles. Tiny orange flecks rose from it like a swarm of fireflies and Kestrel saw that they were sparks swirling skywards and vanishing, to be instantly replaced by others. It was definitely on its way to the harbour he decided, watching its progress as it glided downhill towards him.

One good blast would disperse it, then it would be gone and he would be the hero of the hour. He ran through the attack spell in his mind, holding the spiky shape, before drawing back his arm to let it loose.

The Revenant halted before him. The fiery orange glow intensified as the smoke cleared and it revealed itself, its outline shimmering to create a hazy nimbus surrounding the charred and blackened husk that had once been the living wood of a Ship. One eye socket was a gouged and empty pit, though the other still held a trace of blue. Remnants of colour clung to what had been carved folds of drapery and a sash crossed the worm-eaten bosom, but he couldn't make out the name. His gaze was dragged back against his will, to where the lone eye blazed. Beneath it the nose and lips were gone; the rest of the face was a crumbling mass of sodden, rotted wood.

Kestrel's muscles locked. His arm remained aloft, the spell disintegrating even as he struggled to retain control of it, everything burned away by the staring blue eye as it drew closer and closer. He couldn't even scream as the heat and bitter stench engulfed him.

*

The portal spiralled open on to a sloping lane lined with tall, shuttered warehouses. It dispelled some of the choking smoke, but not enough to prevent Goldfinch and Buzzard from coughing and wiping at suddenly streaming eyes. Buzzard recovered first. Spells at the ready, he scanned the street ahead.

"We're too late," he spluttered.

A few lonely sparks rose in the still night air over the smouldering heap that lay, collapsed, on the burnt cobblestones.

*

"The stupid young fool!"

Captain Plinius banged his fist on the table, while Heron groaned and held his head in his hands. Raven had shown no emotion as he relayed the news, his face a mask, though inwardly he seethed. It had all been handled badly; old men forgetting the recklessness of youth and the hunger to prove oneself with newly-acquired Potentia, something he knew all too well. It just proved yet again the old adage 'there are young foolhardy Mages, but few old ones'.

The reckless apprentice had paid dearly for his misplaced confidence.

An image surfaced unbidden before the old Master Mage but he forced the ancient memory back into the chamber of the past and slammed the door shut.

"It was probably heading for the harbour," he said quietly.

"It won't be able to get to us here, surely?" Plinius asked. Raven shrugged.

"Unknown. I would have thought not, but Revenants are totally single-minded. They only stop when their purpose is fulfilled."

"And what might that purpose be?"

"We know it's looking for Maia. Beyond that, I can't say."

"It's clear that she's in danger. I'm tempted to up anchor and sail away, put some miles between us and this thing."

"Not a bad idea," his Ship cut in. "I'd feel happier too. There's an uneasiness in the water."

"We'll do it," Plinius decided. "*Blossom*, inform the Admiralty that we're heading east as soon as the tide allows, which will be in...?"

"Just under an hour, Captain."

"Good. We can anchor off Noviomagus until this is sorted and it's safe to return."

"It may only be a stopgap," Raven warned him.

Plinius shrugged. "It's better than doing nothing. I won't compromise Maia's safety."

"I'll inform the crew," *Blossom* agreed, relief in her voice.

As far as she was concerned, the sooner they were out to sea again, the safer they would all be.

*

The tomb was opulent, the floor decorated with colourful marble mosaics and artfully painted plastered walls that emphasised the wealth and influence enjoyed by the Valerius family. Traditional niches contained carved urns, each inscribed with the name of the deceased whose cremated ashes rested within. A long line of illustrious ancestors indeed, descended from King Artorius Magnus himself and related to both the Britannic and the Imperial Royal families.

Milo knew that these days half the country claimed descent from Artur, but in this case, it happened to be true. The only strangeness was at the far end of the tomb, which had been remodelled to include a whole wall of painted reliefs bearing not Latin or Britannic writing but Egyptian hieroglyphs. Animal-headed Gods guarded inscriptions in neat pictures, speaking of ancient rites that came from far away in the land of the Nile. Milo recognised the Goddess Isis standing protectively next to the figure of a female who was presumably the Captain's mother. Behind her was another God with the head of a huge crocodile, hovering protectively.

Milo peered at the hieroglyphics, feeling the hair on the back of his neck stand on end. Before the frieze and raised above the floor was a large shrine also covered with pictures. The colours were fresh and vibrant, newly painted in reds, blues and yellows. Over their heads, in the light of the lantern, golden stars twinkled in a dark blue sky.

"Very impressive," Milo remarked, his voice muffled in the confined space. "I take it that the good Captain wasn't cremated then."

"No, she had him buried in the traditional Roman way, then became a devotee of Isis. She was mummified, but ordered that both their bodies be put into a shrine. There's an ante room with all their belongings piled up too."

"She wanted to be prepared, then. I hear it's nice in the Egyptian afterlife. Beats crossing the Styx."

Nuntius shrugged. "It's become fashionable, but the Twelve are fighting back. Rumours are that Pluto has been ordered to improve conditions but I think that personally I'd rather go to the Elysian Fields. Anyway, the Nile Priests are really cashing in at the moment." He sniffed in disdain.

"Pity he wasn't mummified too, or just cremated. They might have found something," Milo observed. There weren't many reasons for burning a body so long after a funeral, but destroying an evil attachment was definitely one of them.

"Should have stuck to the usual," Nuntius agreed.

While they spoke, Milo was checking out the shrine. It had a heavy wooden lid, but wasn't made of stone, thank the Gods. The sarcophagus inside would be and that could prove tricky to get into.

"Well, we'd better get the lid off this first," Milo said, matter-of-factly, hefting the crowbar. Nuntius grunted in reply and produced a bag of ritual supplies before kneeling to begin the rites of appeasement. If something nasty had been left to guard the tomb, these would keep it at bay.

It didn't take too much effort to prise the wooden lid loose and force out the nails that were keeping it in place. Once Milo had got enough leverage, he pushed it to one side to get a better look at what awaited him. Inside, there was a standard stone sarcophagus with the usual peaked top. Resting beside it was an elaborate mummy case with the moulded face of a high-ranking lady, her eyes inlaid with precious stones and her expression calm. Milo repressed a shudder. Death masks were all very well, but he preferred them to be on stands away from the bodies they depicted.

There wasn't enough room in the shrine to move the sarcophagus lid, so Milo used the crowbar to lever away the side nearest to the Captain's resting place. He sent a silent apology up to any God that might be watching and kept a wary ear open for any noises or movement that might signal the presence of something undesirable. He'd seen a play once about a mummy

169

coming back to life to avenge the desecration of its tomb and, though he knew this was only a fantasy, the thought made him nervous. There were enough undead things around this night. Nuntius cleared his throat and began the standard prayers of appeasement, which reassured him a little even though Milo wondered if they worked on the Gods of Egypt. The shrine finally gave way with a mighty crack, splitting halfway down, but Milo didn't have time to feel any regret. It would give him the space he needed to work. As Nuntius' voice rose in volume, Milo fancied he heard noises just outside the tomb, as of soft feet pacing up and down. Or paws. He glanced across at the Priest who was concentrating fiercely on his prayers, while feeding pungent herbs into a flame contained within a small brazier.

Outside, a dog howled mournfully. Milo swallowed, hoping it had only one head, then worked the edge of the crowbar underneath the lid of the sarcophagus and pressed down with all his might until a tiny crack appeared. The sense of being watched by unfriendly eyes increased, heralded by an ominous prickling on the back of his neck. Nuntius' chanting continued, but underneath it, Milo became aware of the rumble of voices outside, muttering in an unknown, throaty tongue.

"Nuntius," he hissed, in warning. The Priest glanced over at him then nodded, switching to a prayer in what sounded like the same language and raising his voice in command. Low growling answered him and the mutterings stopped. A sense of stillness returned and the feeling of immediate danger subsided. Milo only realised that he'd been holding his breath when it escaped him all at once in a quiet rush.

"That should hold them," Nuntius remarked, seemingly unconcerned.

"The sphinxes?"

"Yes. I think I've appeased all the Gods with any interest in this, including Pluto and Hecate and negated the protections. I'll replace them later, or you can bet that this tomb would be stripped pretty rapidly. The Egyptian pantheon should be all right with it, as we're not going to be bothering Lady Valerius. We'll have to get the remains outside though, so as not to cause any more damage. They hate for any inscriptions to be spoilt."

Milo considered the Priest's choice of words. Bothering was putting it mildly.

"Can you lend me a hand?" He gestured at the wedged crowbar.

"Yes." Nuntius' face was ghostly in the lamplight. "Let's do this."

X

Maia was lying in bed reading, when *Blossom*'s voice echoed through the Ship.

"All hands! Prepare to weigh anchor. We're sailing eastwards with the tide. Departure in precisely fifty minutes from now."

Her announcement was followed immediately by the thuds of running feet overhead and the raised voices of officers and men as they took up their positions.

<*Blossom*? Why aren't we staying in Portus?> Maia Sent through their link.

<I'll come down to you,> the Ship replied. Maia put down her book and sat upright, watching the cabin wall for the tell-tale ripples that presaged her arrival.

She could tell that *Blossom* was on edge, though on the surface the Ship retained an air of calm as dictated by protocol.

"What's going on?" Maia asked, as soon as *Blossom* had fully materialised.

"The Captain and I both think that it's safer to put some distance between us and Portus at the moment," *Blossom* said. "The Revenant has attacked again."

Maia's stomach lurched. Was it someone she knew?

"Where?"

"It went to The Anchor. No, no-one was killed there, though it was close. She set fire to the place."

"Are Casca and Cara all right?" The thought that the affable landlord had been repaid so badly for his kindness to her was a barb in her heart.

"Yes, they escaped, along with the other staff and guests, though it did kill a young Mage who was foolish enough to challenge it. We can't underestimate how dangerous it is."

Maia was horror struck. She couldn't help feeling guilty, even though she couldn't see how any of this was directly her fault.

"I still don't know what it wants from me," she said, after a time. "Poor Casca!"

"It knows you're a candidate," *Blossom* said gently.

"Matrona…?"

"The Academy's under guard and the staff have been moved out for their own safety. Now do you see why we have to leave? We're hoping it can't cross water but it's better to be safe than sorry."

Maia nodded dumbly.

"One more thing," the Ship said. "Master Mage Raven has arrived and he wants to ask you some questions."

Worse and worse, Maia thought wearily.

"I don't know anything," she insisted. The ancient Mage would be only wasting his time questioning her.

"That's as may be," *Blossom* told her, "but I want you to stay here. Don't come up top until I tell you to, got it?"

"Yes, *Blossom*. I just don't understand why…" A horrible thought hit her. Every tale she'd heard rushed back, leading her to a dreadful conclusion. "Oh, Gods! This Revenant. It's not Marcia Blandina, is it?"

Blossom looked puzzled. "Who?"

"My former mistress."

"No. It's something else."

"What, then?" Maia felt relieved that the evil woman hadn't returned to haunt her.

Blossom hesitated. "I'll explain later. For now, my priority is leaving the area as quickly as possible."

Maia wasn't satisfied with her answer and *Blossom* knew it, but it was the best she could do for now. The Ship withdrew, leaving her alone. For a few seconds she considered appealing directly to the Captain but she didn't think she'd get any more answers out of him, either. What weren't they telling her? And why did fate and ill-fortune dog her footsteps almost every day of her life? There had been hardly a day during her stay at the Academy that she hadn't expected to be thrown back out on the streets.

She groaned and threw herself back on the bed, staring at the white-painted ceiling. Absently, her fingers went to her little necklace, running over the pearls and smooth stones and she wished that she could talk to her friend.

She couldn't wait to put Portus behind her and move on to somewhere new.

"You grab that end and push."

Nuntius braced himself and together they used brute force to loosen the lid of the sarcophagus. The harsh grating of stone made Milo wince, but the two men managed to shift it far enough over to get a look at what lay within.

"Thank the Gods that she didn't wrap him in lead." Milo said. "That would have been messy."

"Not to mention much harder to burn the remains," the other agreed.

The lantern revealed a shrouded shape, the cloth stained with decay. Withered flowers rested on its breast, a final gift from a heartbroken family. Nuntius reached in and gently moved them to the side, before they leaned over and lifted out the Captain's body. There was some resistance at first, as the linen was stuck to the bottom of the sarcophagus, but a few tugs ripped it free. The corpse was light and Milo was glad that its face was covered; he would rather pretend that they were dealing with a bundle of old rags instead of something that had once been a living person.

They placed the corpse on the floor whilst Nuntius checked outside to make sure the coast was clear.

"We'll take it further into the cemetery. There's a clearing in a wooded area among the yews, where rituals are held."

They carried their grisly burden down the steps. Milo noticed that the sphinxes were now standing, their unblinking eyes tracking every movement. He hurried as fast as he could away from the guardians, feeling their stares boring into his back and very grateful that they didn't have to disturb Lady Valerius' mummy.

The moonlight guided them into the dense shadow of the trees and along a well-worn path, until Milo could make out the bare patch of earth ahead, ringed with stones in the ancient manner. It felt as if this place was older, the circle marking a site of worship from long before the Romans had come bringing their Gods with them. Here, the land was watchful and other deities held sway from when the forests stretched for miles, wild and untamed, home to creatures that had now disappeared into myth.

A long flat stone lay in the centre of the circle. The remains of multiple fires scarred its surface, ashes mixed with the bones of small creatures that had been sacrificed to the Genius Loci. Its presence hung in the air and thrummed through the ground like a note too low to hear, powerful and aware. There were no carvings, so clearly no-one was sure what form it took, if any. Perhaps it was too old and had the shape of the land itself, the stones as its bones and the earth as its flesh.

Nuntius directed him to lay the corpse on the weathered slab and step back. Milo's hand automatically went to his lucky phallus amulet, gripping it tightly, for if ever they needed protection surely now was the time. He was just glad that the young Priest knew what he was doing.

*

Maia was woken by a noise she couldn't identify. She sat up, yawning; she must have dozed off, lulled by the movement of the vessel and sheer boredom.

Tap, tap, tap. She looked towards the door in puzzlement, before realising that it was coming from outside the vessel. Something was rapping on the window. She could see a large shape moving rapidly and the point of what looked like a finger hammering at the glass. No, it wasn't a finger, it was a beak. She jumped to her feet to shoo it away, but instead the noise intensified as the screeching gull tried to smash its way in.

She backed away from the window, yelling for help.

There was movement on the wall behind her and she turned with relief to welcome *Blossom*.

The Revenant was forcing its way in through the panelling. Two blackened arms clawed at the wood as it heaved and strained to reach her. The stink of it filled her lungs and made her eyes stream, but she could just make out the charred and disintegrating form of a Ship. One intense blue eye fixed on her as it writhed, but the rest of the features were a mass of pulpy, crumbling rot.

A final crack behind her made her start as the gull finally broke through the glass. Heedless of the damage to its wings, it launched itself at the intruder with a scream. Maia tried to reach

175

the door but was beaten back by a flailing mass of feathers and splintering wood as the huge bird attacked. She fell to the floor, protecting her head as best she could, while above her the screeching and shrieking seemed to last forever. Underlying it, there was a frantic pounding on her cabin door.

<Maia! What's happening?> The Captain's voice echoed in her head and she tried to reply through her terror.

<It's here! The gull is fighting it but I can't get out!>

<Stay down!> he commanded. <We're coming in!>

The noise stopped abruptly. Maia peered up to see the Revenant standing triumphant, the ripped and bloodied gull's body dangling from her hand. The bird's head lolled, lifeless, but Maia fancied that she saw a silvery wisp fly from the broken corpse and disappear into the air. Feathers spiralled down, landing silently on the boards.

The creature threw the carcass aside with contempt and it burned as it fell, adding to the stench in the room. Maia gasped and choked, her vision blocked by the acrid smoke.

Hands reached down to lift her, pulling her to her feet. When her sight cleared, the dead Ship's face was inches from her own.

"Don't be afraid," the Ship crooned, her ruined features shifting as she spoke. Maia sagged in shock, but the wooden arms held her tight. "I won't hurt you, my darling daughter."

"Release her!"

Plinius' voice thundered from the doorway. They'd taken an axe to the door and he was standing in the shattered remains. The Revenant swung around, still clutching Maia to her flaking bosom.

"I am the *Livia* and I have found my daughter. You will stand aside!"

"Madam, I am Gaius Plinius Tertius, Captain of the *Blossom*. You will explain your presence here!"

"I have come for my daughter," the *Livia* said calmly. "They tried to hide her, you know, to keep her from me."

Blossom's voice came through the link. <Keep her talking but don't threaten her, Gaius! She'll kill you, I can feel it!>

"I see," the Captain said. He took a step backwards, trying to defuse the situation. "And what are you going to do with her?"

Maia stared with terrified eyes first at the Captain, then at the creature that claimed to be her mother. Was it her imagination, or was the Revenant undergoing some sort of change? She could swear that her features were becoming more defined, as if the Shipbody was restoring itself. She sensed the Potentia draining from the *Blossom* as the wood smoothed out, regaining colour and definition. From the look on Plinius' face, he'd noticed it too.

"We're going to find her father, of course," the Ship said happily. "Then we can sail away together. My daughter will be our Ship and I will be with Valerius for ever and ever!"

"Ma'am, your vessel isn't here."

"Oh. It isn't, is it? That's all right. The *Blossom* can take us to it. Hello, *Blossom*," she said brightly. "Do you remember me? We haven't spoken in a long time."

"Hello, *Livia*. No, it has been a long time."

Maia could feel *Blossom* straining to pull away from the undead Ship but the Revenant was too strong, feeding on their link like a leech and greedily siphoning the Potentia in the living wood.

The *Livia* was almost fully complete now. Her Shipbody had the shape of a beautiful woman, with brown hair and sparkling blue eyes. She smiled, showing white teeth and dimples. Her Imperial crown glittered in the lamplight and she looked every inch the image of an Empress. Even her name had reformed, picked out on her sash in purple and gold. She shifted, cradling Maia to her breast and stroking her hair.

"It's time to go, my baby. Your father is waiting and then our family will be together at last."

The floor rippled and *Blossom* rose to stand before her former sister. The *Livia* watched, smiling triumphantly.

"Maia hasn't finished her training," *Blossom* said. Livia laughed.

"Don't worry, I'll bring her back. She has to pass her initiation after all, otherwise how will she be a Ship?"

"But she can't be initiated," *Blossom* told her. "She has no Potentia. No Divine blood."

The other Ship looked at her blankly.

"What are you talking about? Of course she has. Lots of it."

177

"She's been tested. There is none."

The *Livia* rolled her eyes. "You're talking nonsense. Now, let me pass."

She moved forward, still gripping Maia tightly. *Blossom* backed off and nodded to Plinius to do the same. The thing that the *Livia* had become could burn her vessel and she had to put her crew first. Plinius followed her lead as the Revenant advanced, dragging a reluctant Maia with her.

They moved into the corridor, the men giving way before them step by step and up to the quarterdeck. The *Livia* was smiling beatifically at everyone, seemingly unaffected by the looks of horror on the faces of the crew. There was no trace of fire about her now, though no-one could hazard a guess at how long that would last.

Raven was waiting for them in the darkness, the fresh breeze blowing his robes around his slight form. Heron stood to the side, his face set into a tragic mask, whilst behind him, Cita was at the Ship's altar casting terrified glances over his shoulder as he gabbled prayers, his voice a continuous murmur in the silence.

Maia was glad of the air on her face after the oppressive confines of her cabin but when she tried to wiggle free, the *Livia*'s grip tightened.

"Don't struggle, dearest one." The blue eyes regarded her pitilessly, despite her affectionate words.

"Why are you here, ma'am?"

Raven's whispery voice broke the silence. The dead Ship fixed her gaze on him.

"I have come for what is mine. What was promised. My child!"

"You are a Ship. How can you have a child? It's beyond the bounds of possibility."

"She's mine! I was promised!"

Raven cocked his head. "Promised?" he asked sharply. "By whom?"

The Ship seemed surprised. "Why, Diana of course! She told me I would hold Lucius' child in my arms! She promised!"

Cita's voice stopped as they stared at her, appalled.

"My child will be a great Ship. Better than that old worm-eaten *Augusta*, or any of them. She will be unstoppable!"

"Ma'am." The Master Mage's voice was calm and polite. "What do you remember?"

Clearly the Revenant's memory was incomplete. She had blotted out her crime but not its fatal consequences for herself. Her expression changed as she regarded the Master Mage.

"I remember enough!" she growled fiercely, her face filling with anger. "You burned me. I burned, my vessel burned-,"

"Yes, you burned," Raven interrupted. "Do you know why?"

The *Livia*'s pretty face twisted.

"Perhaps we should ask Captain Valerius?" the Master Mage continued.

My Captain!" Livia's eyes raked the vessel, checking amongst the crowd for the man she desired above all others. "Where is he? Bring him to me!"

"Don't you remember?" Raven said, his voice still eerily calm. "We burned you because of what you did to him."

Confusion, rage and fear swept across the Revenant's face.

"You're keeping him from me," she snarled. Her beauty began to decay as her true nature reasserted itself and the stench of charred wood intensified. Maia struggled harder to free herself.

"No, ma'am, we are not. Captain Valerius is long dead. You murdered him."

Raven took a step forward, his face like stone.

"You crushed the life from him in a jealous rage. Maia is not your child. Lucius Valerius Vero was not your husband. You are a dead thing and I order you to begone!"

There was a moment of total stillness. Even the wind had dropped and nothing moved save a few rising sparks that drifted in the blackness of the sky.

Without warning the Revenant shuddered, eyes wide, gasping as though she still needed to breathe. Her Shipbody rippled as if to ward off the truth, before she gradually relaxed. Her triumphant smile reappeared, even as her form rotted away before them.

"You lie, Mage. I have reclaimed my child and my Captain awaits. You are powerless against me and you're going to suffer for everything you did."

Her gaze hardened and her smile grew sinister. "I have a little unfinished business to attend to, don't I?"

She was beginning to burn again. At this rate she would destroy the whole vessel and everyone in it. Maia struggled frantically, feeling the sudden heat against her face and body as the Revenant gathered itself to attack.

"Stop her!" Plinius yelled. Both Mages hesitated, weighing up the cost of casting a spell that could kill Maia as well as the insane Revenant.

Maia finally tore free of the crumbling Shipbody. "No! Don't hurt them!"

The Revenant stared at her in confusion.

"Child?"

She stood in front of the *Livia,* shielding Raven from her view. Plinius' orders to step aside and *Blossom*'s desperate appeals faded into the background as she stared defiantly at the undead Ship.

"You're not my mother. You can't be."

Maia threw a last, loving look at the *Blossom* then rushed forward, grabbing the Revenant round the waist and plunging them both over the rail into the ocean's dark embrace.

They burned as they fell.

*

The moon cast her glow on the sacred grove, outlining the dark branches of the ancient yews and Milo was once again thankful for her pale light. There was no sound amongst the stones; even the night creatures were absent and not a breath of air stirred the trees. Milo felt the Genius stir to attention as it became aware of them and decided to take an interest. It didn't seem unfriendly, just old and watchful.

Suddenly, Nuntius cocked his head, alerted by something Milo couldn't hear.

"We have to hurry. There isn't much time."

Milo wasn't going to argue. He pulled a box of vestas from his pocket and selected one. They were so much handier than the old flint and steel.

"Hang on," the Priest said, producing a bottle from his bag. "This will get it going quicker." He uncorked the top and sprinkled the contents over the shrouded body. "Try it now."

The decayed linen caught light immediately, the oil feeding the flames, which ate greedily into the shroud. The familiar smell of a funeral pyre rose into the air.

"We'll need more oil or wood," Milo said. Nuntius spoke a phrase that transformed the fire instantly into a leaping, white-hot conflagration that devoured the body rapidly, lighting up the whole area so that for a few moments it was as if the sun had risen early.

Milo blinked, temporarily blinded but relieved that the job was done. All he wanted was to collect Nix and go in search of a bed and a hot meal. He would arrange for the pegasus to be returned in the morning by someone else more accustomed to high flying. There had to be a decent inn this near to Durnovaria and he was more than ready to find it.

"That's it then," he said, his night vision returning. He could see that the Captain's body had been reduced to a pile of fine, smouldering ash, which was spiralling upwards in a sudden breeze.

The least he could do was stand the young Priest a good breakfast and slip him a few coins for being so incredibly helpful.

"How will we know if it's worked?"

He turned to Nuntius, hoping the man would have more of an idea than he had about what was actually going on, only to discover that he was quite alone.

Despite the heat, Milo shivered.

*

The pain was agonising, doused only by the enveloping cold of the sea. She couldn't breathe, couldn't move; but the Revenant held her up and prevented her from falling into the inky blackness.

The Ship's voice rang in her head, the blue eye staring into her own even as her Shipbody crumbled and melted away into ash.

<My last gifts for you. Fire and mind! Remember!>

The *Livia*'s wooden fingers clamped on to her head, digging in with the last of their strength as Maia convulsed.

*

For a second, everyone stood frozen in shock.

"She can't swim!" *Blossom* screamed. Durus stripped off his coat and made a rush to dive in after her, but Raven gripped his arm.

"No, wait!"

There was a commotion amidships, yells, oaths and Heron's booming voice.

"Stand back! Let him through! He won't hurt you, move!"

The vessel's lights gleamed on a huge, leathery body as the ancient crocodile heaved himself across the deck through the line of startled mariners. His shrivelled body swelled as they watched, leathery skin expanding and filling until he was almost twice his original size. Newly moist eyelids opened to reveal glowing, slit eyes filled with the wisdom of ages. Heron darted in front to open the rail for him and Sobek opened his jaws in acknowledgment, showing crooked rows of pointed teeth as he squeezed his vast bulk clumsily through the gap, clawed feet scraping on the wooden planking.

The crew backed hastily out of the way as the tip of his serrated tail finally disappeared over the side, followed by a mighty splash as he slid into the water. The crew rushed forwards to fill the gap, staring open-mouthed as the avatar swam off.

"He'll find her and bring her back!" Heron shouted. "Let him work!"

Blossom prayed that he would reach Maia in time.

*

Maia surfaced, freezing, her mouth filled with cold, salty water and her lungs on fire. She tried to kick her cloth-tangled legs but the waves closed over her head once more and she sank into the lightless depths, feeling her senses slipping away into the darkness.

A last fragment of thought intruded. *Perhaps it's better this way...*

*

The sun was rising over Portus harbour and a fresh breeze had dispelled most of the lingering stench aboard the *Blossom*. Her carpenter was shaking his head over burnt decking and the damage caused by Sobek's claws as he'd scrambled aboard with the limp body cradled in his jaws.

Most of the crew had managed to snatch a couple of hours' sleep before dawn. The exceptions were the senior officers, subdued and hollow-eyed, who were gathered in the Captain's quarters. They were all present save the Adept, who was tending to Maia.

"Campion thinks that she'll live, but she was badly burned."

Plinius looked older than his years, his face drawn and heavily lined. *Blossom* stood behind him, her hand on his shoulder in support.

"I've made my report to the Admiralty," he continued. "Divine involvement complicates the situation considerably. It seems that we have been caught between feuding Gods. Cita, do you have anything to add?"

The usually jovial Priest shook his head, miserably. "They're staying tight-lipped about the whole thing. I've Sent to the temples in Londin to see if any of the High Priests have more information, but nothing's come back yet."

"We know that the Swift One and the Huntress appear to be on opposing sides," Raven said. "Mercury was Maia's sponsor, or she wouldn't be here. Now it seems that the *Livia* was influenced by Diana, but as to why is anyone's guess."

"She had help in getting aboard unnoticed," *Blossom* said, angrily. "I didn't detect anything was amiss until the window was smashed and that shouldn't have been possible."

"There's also the way she drained your Potentia, like a leech," Raven said. "This whole matter screams of Divine interference."

"She said that the Goddess made her a promise," Heron said thoughtfully. "That she would hold her Captain's child in her arms."

"And the Gods don't lie," Cita said. "They obfuscate and twist the truth but they don't tell outright lies. And they never break their promises."

There was silence around the table while the implications of the *Livia*'s statement sunk in.

"Maia? Is it possible?" *Blossom* asked.

"The timing fits," Raven said. "We don't know exactly when she was born, but we know when Valerius died and that was shortly before she was taken in at the Foundling Home. Her mother must have abandoned her."

"But why would the *Livia* have been targeted by Diana?" Plinius asked. He rubbed a hand over his eyes. "The more we know, the more confusing it becomes. Simple jealousy and madness we can understand, but why are the Gods involved?"

"Insult," Cita said. "Breaking a law or decree. A terrible crime, perhaps?"

"But in this case, everything seems to follow *from* the terrible crime," Durus pointed out.

"We're going in circles," Plinius said wearily. "We just don't have enough information. Heron, did you glean anything from the dead bird?"

"I was coming to that," Heron said. "As you know, I have some experience with avatars, especially animal ones, after my service in Kemet – Aegyptus to you. I can say with some certainty that this bird was one such. The remains were still charged with traces of magical energy."

"Maia said that it attacked the Revenant. It certainly smashed through the thick glass, which no ordinary creature would do," Raven agreed.

"Another deity?" Plinius asked.

"Of a sort, but not a major one as it was quickly overcome," Heron said. "Perhaps it thought that Maia could escape, or perhaps it had a hatred of the *Livia*. It could even have been an agent of another." He spread his hands helplessly. "Who knows? Then there's Sobek's intervention."

"About that," Raven said. "I've just had several interesting conversations with my Agent, the one who dealt with the Captain's body. He notified me as soon as he burned it, causing the *Livia* to disintegrate almost immediately afterwards so we got something right. He also believes that he was assisted by a God."

"Directly?" Cita asked, his eyebrows shooting up.

"He was met by a Priest called Nuntius, who suddenly disappeared as soon as their business was concluded. It was a young Priest of the same name who spoke up for Maia at her initial interview."

"The Messenger," Cita said. "Sounds like him and, of all the Gods, he's the best at human disguise."

"He fooled me," Raven said in irritation.

"What an absolute mare's nest," Plinius muttered to his Ship. "How can we act with certainty when the Gods are playing their games?"

"Also, and this might have some bearing on the matter, Valerius' mother was buried in the Egyptian style. I questioned my Agent and he said there was a prominent relief of Sobek in the tomb."

"And if she happens to be Maia's grandmother it would give Sobek an excuse to intervene!" Heron announced, excitedly. "Another missing piece, gentlemen."

"Possibly," Plinius said, quelling Heron's enthusiasm. "We mustn't jump to conclusions."

"Incoming message, Captain."

The cabin fell silent as he conferred with his Ship.

"New orders," he said at last. "We're to put into Portus. The Navy wants to get to the bottom of all this. They want to transfer her back to the Academy as soon as she can be safely moved."

"Which won't be for a long while," *Blossom* said. "I'll tell them so as well. It's not like we have any other candidates and if she's that injured, she can leave her body to heal without having too much pain."

"Good idea," Plinius said. "Ask Campion for his opinion, as Maia's under his care."

"Aye, Captain." The Ship's eyes became distant as she focused elsewhere.

"In the meantime, we're to impress on the crew that the Navy is forbidding any talk of this. They don't want any sensationalism or scandal. The Gods know it was bad enough the first time around."

"I think that it would be better if I put a binding on them, so they can't spill their guts to outsiders," Heron said.

Plinius nodded. "Do it. I'll be able to grant shore leave without worrying it'll be all over Portus by tonight. There'll be enough gossip as it is with the other attacks."

"Yes, shame about The Anchor. Good beer," Cita said dolefully, adding quickly, "and the young Mage, of course."

"Well, unless someone has something else to discuss, I suggest we follow orders," Plinius said. "We go in with the tide. Gentlemen, you are dismissed."

*

The Adept's quarters were split into four sections. One part was Campion's private space, another was the pharmacy, where all the medicines were stored and the last two were a surgery and a hospital respectively.

Blossom materialised in the hospital and gazed sadly at the bandaged shape under the tented sheet. Maia was still mercifully unconscious. Campion had done what he could for her, applying light bandages to her burns and making her as comfortable as possible. The Ship looked to see if her earring was still intact, but couldn't tell.

The curtain separating the hospital from the pharmacy parted and Campion appeared.

"Ma'am."

"What is your prognosis?"

"Extensive burns to both inner arms and up her left side, from chest to scalp."

"Where she touched the…" *Blossom* couldn't say her name.

"Yes. It was a very brave thing to do."

Blossom's eyes never left Maia's face. "She's a brave girl. Do you really think she'll live?"

Campion shrugged, helplessly. "It's hard to tell in these cases, but she's a fighter. If she survives the next few hours, she's got a good chance, though her recovery will be long and extremely difficult."

"The Admiralty want her transferred to the Academy."

The Adept's normally placid features changed to a look of outrage.

"That's completely out of the question for at least a few weeks, until she's started to heal. Any movement will be excruciating for her and it could endanger her life."

"That's what I thought," the Ship answered. "I'm concerned about the link through her earring."

"You should be," Campion replied. "It's undamaged, but I recommend that it's removed. If not, you'll probably get feedback from her pain. I'm going to give her poppy juice to take the edge off it and to try and help her sleep."

"If enough Potentia remains to power the link, she can come with me and be free of it," *Blossom* said.

Campion shot her a look of sympathy.

"I'm sorry, but it doesn't work that way. If she remains in stasis, her body won't heal and she'd be having to return to it in the long run. It's just something she'll have to go through."

"Damn it to Hades!" *Blossom* swore. "You'll just have to tell the Captain that she can't be moved."

She gave Campion a meaningful look and he nodded slightly.

"I will. I'll make my report now. Please could you ask Heron to come down?" He bent over his patient, checking the dressings with skilful hands.

"Yes. He's in his quarters, probably checking his crocodile."

"That's not something you hear every day," he remarked.

The Ship left her Adept to his work, flowing upwards to her place on the quarterdeck where she would be visible to the crew and settled down to wait for the tide to carry her into Portus harbour.

*

"How is she?"

Robin looked up as Heron entered the Mage quarters, followed by Raven. The young Mage had just returned from assisting the Adept as he worked to stabilise his patient.

"C-campion has induced c-coma," Robin said. "It's bad."

Raven seated himself as Heron, shaking his head, went to inspect Sobek who was now fully dried out and in his

187

accustomed place. He scattered some incense on a little dish and set light to it, murmuring a prayer of thanks in the ancient language. The reptile shifted a little, then settled down into torpidity once more. Robin watched him warily. He'd been ordered to stay below during the attack and had nearly swallowed his tongue when the beast had wrenched himself from his straps and lurched across the floor.

"Will there be much scarring?" Raven asked.

"Yes. Her head, chest and arms w-were b-badly b-burned."

"Does she retain her earring?"

"For now, b-but it w-will have to b-be removed."

"That's a pity, but we can't have Ship functions affected and keeping it wouldn't help her anyway." Raven turned his head to the young Mage. "We'll have to do something about that stammer, young man. Pebbles in the mouth worked for Emperor Claudius, so it should work for you too. Heron, you have been remiss."

"He manages, don't you, Robin?" Heron said.

Raven muttered something under his breath. Heron, unabashed, went to get a bottle.

"We need some of this, I think."

He poured them all a glass of wine.

"It's a shame that Maia can't stay here indefinitely," Raven said, "but it'll be a while before she recovers enough to be moved. I'm afraid that she has a hard road ahead of her."

"We might have more information by then," Heron said, practically.

"We might. I just have the feeling that we're caught up in the middle of something; a story that started a long time ago. It's like entering the theatre half-way through a play, when you don't know the characters and the plot is a mystery." He frowned.

"I take it that you're leaving us when we get to Portus, Master?" Heron asked.

"I am. I have business in Londinium."

They all heard the rattle of chains as the *Blossom* raised her anchors and began the short journey to land. The tide must be flowing. Heron poured them all another glass.

"Perhaps, while you're here, you'd like to examine my new kraken detector?" he asked Raven, hopefully.

XI

It was a perfect day.

Maia was standing on a beach, the silver sand soft under her bare feet. Bright sunlight reflected off a sea bluer than she'd ever known and the lapis sky above was cloudless and full of heat. The little bay was ringed with lush, green hills that shimmered in jasmine-scented air. Maia drank in the idyllic scene and felt at peace, watching little waves curl over and over on to the sand.

Nearby, a couple were walking arm in arm, the woman laughing at something the man was saying. Tall trees swayed, their long fronds rustling in the breeze that ruffled the woman's pale hair. A sudden gust caused the man to chase after his hat, while the woman gestured, seeming to move it farther away until it lodged in a bush full of flowers.

She couldn't hear what they were saying but she envied them their happiness. The man, a young Captain, broke off a bright bloom and tucked it into his lady's hair. She laughed again and danced away from him across the shore, her tasselled shawl fluttering in the air like wings.

"Maia? Can you hear me?"

The voice was familiar but Maia ignored it.

"Maia, it's *Blossom*."

She tried to resist, but the bright scene before her was starting to collapse in on itself and slip away in shards of light and colour, leaving only darkness. A new, more uncomfortable awareness began to intrude, along with a growing sense of pain.

"She's waking." Another voice. Campion?

Maia opened her right eye. The other one didn't seem to be working. Two blurred faces resolved into the Ship and her Adept.

"Don't try to speak," *Blossom* said quickly. "You're in the hospital."

Maia reached for the Ship link but got nothing but a void where the connection had been. She tried to raise her arm to touch her earring but it wouldn't move. A croak was all she could manage.

"We had to take the earring," *Blossom* said. "I'm so sorry, Maia. You saved us all, you know and we'll look after you. Now you must rest and get better." Cool liquid dripped between her cracked lips and she swallowed, thirstily.

"There. This will help you to sleep," Campion's soothing voice comforted her as the terrible pain subsided and she fell into the dark.

This time there were no dreams.

*

"It's a good job we put into Portus," Plinius remarked, staring at the boiling thunderclouds approaching from the west. "I wouldn't want to be out in this."

Blossom followed his gaze. "Indeed. The meteorologists have issued a severe unnatural weather warning."

"Angry God?"

"Seems so. It just came out of nowhere. Someone's extremely pissed off."

"Do we know who?"

"It's localised to just off shore, with about a five mile range, but with severe winds further afield. The link's alive with speculation and several Ships are running for shelter. There'll be some vessels caught out, too."

A flash of lightning caught their attention, the rumble of thunder a few seconds behind.

Plinius rubbed at his face.

"This is all we need. I knew I shouldn't have granted Cita shore leave. I suppose we could go and drag him out of the nearest tavern."

"I think he's due for retirement," his Ship said, lips pursed. "He was never very effective at the best of times. There must be some youngster who'd like a crack at his job."

"I'll make a discreet suggestion that he'd be better finding a place in Neptune's Temple," Plinius said.

The harbour was getting crowded now, as more and more vessels and Ships jostled for space and shelter from the rapidly developing storm. *Blossom* tuned into the link to see what everyone else was saying.

<*Blossom* here. Any news?>

<*Blossom*!> The *Patience*'s voice came over the link. <I'm five miles out and towing a merchantman with a snapped mast.>

<You might be better heading south.>

<Impossible!> She sounded worried. <We're in the storm now...oh!>

<What is it?> *Blossom* asked in alarm.

<I don't know,> *Patience* replied. <It's parted around us, like a corridor of storm clouds! There's - good Gods, it's Cymopoleia! She's forming above the altar! My Priest is making sacrifice.>

<Show me!> *Blossom* commanded.

Instantly, the scene began to play out through the link as the *Patience* relayed. She could see through her eyes and sensed other Ships in the harbour joining in to watch.

The Goddess looked as if dark clouds had been blown into a gigantic glass vessel in the shape of a woman. She was fully twenty feet tall, her swirling form looming over the *Patience*, whose crew cowered before her. The remains of a goat lay on the altar, expertly butchered by the Priest who was laying the fat and bones on the sacred fire. Cymopoleia leaned over and inhaled the smoke, darkening and swelling with the Potentia the worship granted her.

<She's after offerings,> *Blossom* told her sister Ship. <We'd all be as well to follow your example.>

The *Persistence*, anchored in the harbour, chipped in.

<Aye and right quick! She ain't to be trifled with an' summat's got her dander up. I'm lucky I've a sheep left aboard.>

Blossom relayed the information to Plinius, who cursed quietly.

"I'd better sort our sacrifice myself. What have we got?"

"Nothing much," his Ship answered. "I'll send some of the lads to commandeer something quick, before the rest of Portus catches on. If she's after Potentia, she'll make as much fuss as she can."

<If she needs strength, perhaps that's why she spared the *Patience*?> timid little *Cameo* offered.

<Aye, probably,> *Persistence* said. <Dead crews can't light fires. Funny how she had a go at that merchantman.>

<Couldn't help herself, I expect,> *Dauntless* grumbled, quietly. <We all know what she's like.>

The other Ships murmured agreement.

<She's building up to something if she needs all this Potentia,> *Blossom* observed.

Thick black smoke was boiling up from most of the decks now and even a few spots along the waterfront and further into the town. The Priests were busy.

<You ain't wrong, sister. She's going ter 'ave a pop at someone all right, mark me words!> *Persistence* said.

<As long as it's not one of us,> the *Scorpion* chimed in. <There are some Northmen further up from me. She can have them with pleasure!>

There was some nervous laughter from the other Ships and a loud snort from the *Persistence*.

They watched as the Goddess finished her meal. *Patience*'s Priest, younger and more daring than most, raised his arms in salutation.

"Hail, O Cymopoleia, Powerful Storm Bringer! This Ship and crew salutes you and offers you worship! Spare us your wrath, O mighty Goddess, we beseech you."

Cymopoleia turned her huge head towards him, regarding them all with inhuman eyes. Her voice rose and fell in gusts, like the storm winds she commanded.

"Insult has been done to me and mine!"

Blossom listened, fascinated. The *Persistence* was right, she was accumulating Potentia ready for a fight.

"Who would be foolish enough to cross you, O mighty Lady?"

Cymopoleia tilted her head and her eyes turned black with rage.

"They know who they are. I will tolerate it no longer!"

She raised an arm to the heavens and shook a fist. Lightning speared into the clouds and the boom of thunder shook the firmament as she gathered the Potentia to her. The wind from the sea increased, almost blowing Ajax and Hyacinthus off their feet as they struggled back to the *Blossom*, dragging a frightened goat behind them.

An answering flash and boom, louder and longer lasting, split the sky above them and everyone flinched. Cymopoleia was powerful but not as much as the one who spoke now. *Blossom* cast a glance at the Captain, who had covered his uniform with a Priestly robe and was preparing to do his secondary duty in the absence of her Priest. The sailors and goat clattered across the deck towards her altar and she left him to it, knowing that he would do a good job.

"You all might want to throw in a prayer to Jupiter too," she added, keeping one eye on the horizon. It seemed that Cymopoleia, hot-headed as she was, might be biting off more than she could chew this time.

Meanwhile, the *Patience* was in the thick of it. The Goddess stared down at her as if considering her options.

"You, Ship, have been of service and have my favour. I will not forget," she said abruptly. Without warning, her form exploded outward into a roiling storm mass which shot up and dispersed into the sky. One last flash of lightning and she was gone.

Everyone, Ships, crew and the townsfolk of Portus breathed a huge sigh of relief. There was some damage, especially to the crippled trader, but on the whole, they'd got off lightly. Cymopoleia needed Potentia more than destruction.

With the Goddess' departure, the sky began to clear and the wind dropped back to normal levels. All traces of heaviness and oppression dissipated and the Ships settled back into their routines.

<Hey, *Patience*! Thought you were a goner!> *Persistence* cackled. <Why does she like you, then?>

<I've no idea,> the young Ship replied, puzzlement leaking through the link.

<It must 'ave been a right good goat.>

<She fancied your Priest,> *Scorpion* sniggered.

<Who can fathom the ways of Gods?> *Blossom* said. <The main thing is that you're all right. As to what's got her knickers in a twist, the Priests can sort that one out. I don't think the Thunderer was all that pleased she was kicking off.>

<Too right!> *Persistence* cut in. <More sacrifices all round, ladies. Our lads'll eat well at least!>

It was true that her crew were looking more cheerful. It would be goat stew on the menu tonight.

Other Ships linked in, curious about the recent events and *Blossom* updated as many as she could while keeping an eye on the *Patience* as she came into harbour, towing the stricken vessel behind her. She was doing well for one so young and *Blossom* was proud of her. She had shaken down to become a dependable Ship.

Her thoughts turned briefly to the newest addition to the Fleet. The *Regina* had a brand-new, state-of-the-art vessel but how she'd turn out remained to be seen. *Blossom* had had her doubts from the start.

If ever anyone had an agenda, that person was Tullia Albana.

*

Lying in the Adepts quarters, Maia was making slow progress, drifting in and out of consciousness over the next few days. People were with her constantly but she mostly couldn't make out who was there and barely managed to stay awake long enough to take in food, water and medicine. Any movement hurt and several times she was aware of someone crying out and wondered who could be in such pain.

"Hush, Maia, I'm here," a familiar voice said.

"Matrona?"

"Yes and Branwen too. Sleep now."

She'd thought it was another dream, but when she awoke properly at last, it was to see her former guardian sitting by her bed, sewing. She wasn't sure how long she'd been asleep but her head felt clearer and the pain was more manageable. Her movement alerted Matrona immediately.

"Ah, you're awake. Good. Feeling hungry?"

"What are you doing here?" Maia whispered. Her face felt stiff down the left side and she still couldn't open her eye properly.

"I've been here a while now. Someone needed to look after you. I've been taking turns with Branwen and Campion's been supervising the pair of us. He's an excellent healer."

"Are we in Portus?"

194

"Yes. You were too ill to move, so we came to you."

A sudden vision of the *Livia* flashed into her mind, followed by the searing pain as she barrelled into her, feeling the furnace heat, before the shock of the icy water. She shuddered and cried out at the memory. Matrona leaned over her, gripping her good shoulder to calm her as she screamed. Behind her, Campion rushed in, a bottle in his hand.

"You can't keep dosing her up," Matrona told him, firmly. "She has to get it out of her system. She can't forget either, more's the pity!"

Eventually, Maia's cries turned to sobs. "*Blossom…*"

"I'm here!"

The Ship rose through the floor and glided over to the bed. "I've been here all along. Brave girl! Look what I have for you."

Maia stared through her tears at the string of pearls and gems in *Blossom*'s hand.

"My necklace!"

"I thought you might want it with you. It was damaged but Heron and Robin restored and restrung it for you."

"Do thank him for me. It was a present from Briseis," she explained to Matrona.

"She's in the harbour right now and has asked after you every day," *Blossom* told her.

"Give her my love," Maia said. She could already feel her eyes beginning to close but Matrona insisted that she drank a little soup.

"Enough excitement for now, I think," Campion said. "Finish that and get some rest."

Maia did, then sank back into the pillows gratefully. She knew that she was probably crippled for life, but what did that matter? She could never have become a Ship anyway and now the Navy would surely grant her a pension. Perhaps she could stay at the Academy with Matrona and Branwen, visiting her friends when they were in Portus and building some sort of life for herself here?

Strangely enough, despite the pain, the thought cheered her.

*

195

"I checked with the Central Records Office, as you asked. There's been no daughter registered to the Valerius family for the last two generations."

Milo helped himself to a drink then took a seat opposite the wizened Master Mage. Raven was sitting in his high-backed chair, its arms worn from many years of use. He rubbed the pale oak thoughtfully.

"The *Livia* was quite clear. She would 'hold the child of Lucius in her arms', according to a promise made by the Goddess. Unless she was fantasising about the whole thing, the only person that could apply to is Maia Abella."

"And you said the dates fitted?"

"As far as we know. It's strange that we know nothing about Valerius' wife."

"I couldn't find out anything," Milo said. He hated cases that petered out into dead ends. "Too much time has passed to get concrete information and I had to be discreet."

The afternoon light slanted into the small office that Raven used in the Londin Collegium, backlighting the heavy oak chair and its occupant. Milo subtly angled himself so that the sun didn't blind him.

"The one clue is the mention of the Huntress. Sounds like one of her games," Raven said, his lip curling.

"She's not the most stable of deities," Milo said.

"Quite. And forgiveness isn't part of her repertoire." He paused, considering the problem. "The question is, who insulted her? Valerius? His wife? It must have been bad to cause subsequent events."

"It could have been something as little as a word in the wrong place, or a boastful remark," Milo stated, contradicting him. "What I don't understand is, what happened to the wife?"

"Maybe she was so grief-stricken at her husband's murder that she abandoned their child for fear of reprisals and killed herself?" Raven suggested.

"Then why isn't she buried with him? You might be right about the child, though. She could have been pregnant when he died and feared that the child was under threat. It would be like the Goddess to take the grudge to the next generation."

"But she wouldn't kill a pregnant woman. If the wife had insulted her, she would have been dealt with in no uncertain fashion later on. The Lady isn't subtle. There's something else we're missing."

Milo sucked his teeth. "Can't help you there, unless another piece of information comes to light. Have you asked her Priests?"

"I have contacts there," Raven admitted, "but they clammed up. Claimed to have no knowledge."

"And you believed them?"

"No."

"Strange. The Gods love for us to know when they punish someone, especially when the death is dramatic and messy. Why would she be silent?"

"Perhaps she acted rashly and offended another God? She wouldn't be inclined to boast about it then."

Milo nodded. "We know that the Messenger is seeking to mitigate some of the effects. He sounded saddened by the whole thing."

"It seems likely that Nuntius is either his agent, or the God himself."

"I think it was the God," Milo said. A shiver ran up his back at the thought. "He became involved for a reason. Sympathy? Orders? We know who gives him his orders."

"The one person that keeps the Huntress in check."

"The Thunderer." Milo groaned. "Please don't ask me to question Aquila." The last thing Milo wanted to do was to have to face Jupiter's High Priest.

"Not yet. Have you heard? The Lady of Storms appeared off Portus, throwing a fit about some insult and gathering Potentia. Apparently the Thunderer warned her off but it doesn't bode well."

"Off Portus? All the places in the world she could go to and she manifests there?"

"Do you see why I'm worried?" Raven asked him. "This is God versus God, with us caught in the middle." He sighed. "If I were you, I'd make an offering to the Temple of Mercury."

"I already have."

"Then make another and, this time, ask to be granted information."

197

Milo glared at him. "I'm adding it to my expenses."

The Mage grinned at him. "Make it a good one, then. I'm billing the Navy."

*

Maia's burns healed slowly. After a few weeks, she was able to leave her bed and sit in a chair from where she could see something of the outside world. She'd resisted looking at the damage to her face but, at last, she felt that she couldn't put it off any longer. Others were seeing it every day, so she should have to as well.

"Branwen, could you fetch me a mirror, please?"

Her maid stiffened, then went and brought her a small mirror from a drawer. Maia took it gingerly, concentrating on getting her fingers to close around the handle as they were still very stiff.

She stared at her reflection. The right side of her face and neck was mostly clear but the left side was a mess. Most of her hair on that side had been burned away and the rest had been cut close so that bandages could be applied. Her face looked half melted, like candle wax that had run. She thought of Robin and his strawberry birthmark, but that was nothing compared to her scars.

"It's not as if I was beautiful to start with," she said, then burst into tears.

"It won't matter when you're a Ship," Branwen said, fetching her a handkerchief. "You can choose whatever form you like. And anyway, handsome is as handsome does. There are plenty of pretty faces that hide ugliness beneath."

"I suppose so," Maia sobbed, though Branwen's well-meaning attempt to cheer her up was having the opposite effect. She fought to pull herself together. "At least I can see out of my left eye a bit now."

"Yes, that's an improvement. You'll be able to go up on deck soon and get some fresh air. That'll be nice, won't it?"

"Yes." Maia glanced over at what she jokingly referred to as her offering table. She'd had some visitors lately, mainly the *Blossom*'s crew who had brought her little gifts as a thank you and to cheer her up. They regarded her with even more awe and respect now.

The memory of Big Ajax standing there, twisting his cap in his enormous hands like a small boy, brought a smile to her face. Well, one side of it anyway. The left side still didn't move very well. He'd brought her a little ivory dog that he'd carved himself, from an orca's tooth and she promised him that she'd treasure it. She hoped that her injuries would provide the excuse as to why she couldn't become a Ship.

A few minutes later, a knock on the door heralded the arrival of the Captain. He visited her every day and his presence was a constant reassurance. He smiled at her as he entered.

"And how's the patient today?"

"Getting better," Maia told him. "Bored."

"Good. I'm just glad you're alive to be bored." He fell silent for a moment and she saw in his eyes that he had news.

"What is it?" she asked, suddenly wary.

"The Navy want you to go to Londin, Maia."

She looked at him in astonishment. "Why?"

"They want to find out about your origins. There's a mystery there and it's possible that we might know who your father was."

You'd better tell me what you know," Maia said, emphatically. "I need to know. I'm sick of surprises. I remember what the *Livia* said."

"Me too," Plinius said. He took a deep breath. "You remember when she said that she would hold Lucius' child in her arms?"

"Yes. Do you know what it means?"

"Possibly. Lucius was the praenomen of her Captain, Valerius Vero. The man she murdered."

Maia digested this information. "So, you think that he might be my father? You do know she was totally insane?"

"There was method in her madness," the Captain said. "As to the rest, we can't be sure, but wouldn't it be better if you knew which family you came from?"

Maia could scarcely believe that she might be a part of anything. "How could anybody tell?"

"Oh, the science is beyond me," he said, "but Heron has assured me that there is a way, using a living relative of the

Captain. Something to do with sympathetic magic and resonance, whatever that is. Don't expect me to explain, I only sail Ships for a living."

She joined in with his chuckle. "It would be nice to know," she admitted. "But do I really have to go to Londin? Couldn't Heron do something here?"

"It needs an Adept who specialises in such things," he said. "Now, if you were related to a kraken or a crocodile, I've no doubt he'd be your man."

"Perish the thought!"

So, she could be related to a naval family? Maybe she would inherit something more than a cursed lineage? A villa in the country would be nice.

"When am I to go?"

"When you're fit enough to travel," he said. "Until then, you're my responsibility."

"You and *Blossom* have taken good care of me," she said. "I'm sorry that I can't become a Ship after all."

He shrugged. "Don't worry about it. You won't be abandoned, that I can promise you, even if I have to adopt you myself!"

He saw the look of hope on her face and smiled broadly. "My wife would love to have a daughter after three sons. Keep it in mind, won't you?"

"It's more than I could have wished for!" She smiled lopsidedly, not wanting to hurt him by saying that she'd rather not be a burden.

"Don't worry," he said, as if sensing her unease, "and that's an order!"

"Aye, Captain."

She wished it were that simple.

*

It was more than four months before she was deemed well enough to travel and that was only as far as the Academy. It felt strange to saying farewell to the *Blossom* and Plinius, though the latter assured her that he would visit as often as he could.

"There aren't any other candidates as yet but that doesn't mean that there aren't young officers and the like to train up," he said on their last morning together.

Early autumn sunlight was glinting through the windows of his cabin, which made a change as the season had been unusually wet and stormy. Even *Blossom* had decided to break her unspoken rule and join them for breakfast.

"The *Patience* sends her love," *Blossom* said. "She's taking a trip around the Mediterranean, ferrying diplomats. She says that she'd rather deal with pirates. They're more honest!"

They both laughed. "I'll see her when she gets home," Maia said. "I don't think I'll be in Londin for long."

"I don't think so either," the Captain said. "A few quick tests and then you should be back."

His Ship nodded in agreement.

"I'm hoping that I might get a pension," Maia said. "I've got to have some way of supporting myself in the future and I don't fancy returning to my former line of work."

"Gods forbid! That won't happen," Plinius said. "A pension is the least they can offer you." He looked meaningfully at *Blossom* who raised her eyebrows at him. "A word in the right ear might be of use."

"Already on it," his Ship said promptly. "I know people."

"You certainly do. You've trained most of them."

Blossom grinned at him.

"So, you'll have a few days on land to adjust, then you should be strong enough to undertake the journey. Have you been to Londin before?"

"Me? No!" Maia snorted. "I never left Portus before I came here but I always wanted to see more of the world."

As long as it doesn't see me, she thought privately. She might be healing but nothing could hide the savage scars that covered her face and scalp where her hair had burned away. She'd been protected aboard the *Blossom* but knew that she would be stared at when she left the safety of the Ship.

"It will be exciting!" *Blossom* encouraged her, "and you won't be on your own."

"No. I'm afraid you'll have a couple of travelling companions," the Captain said. "Matrona and I will be accompanying you."

Maia was relieved. Travelling by herself would have been daunting.

"Here's to a successful trip!"

She joined in with the toast but couldn't help a feeling of apprehension at the thought of entering the world again.

*

"*How* much?"

The farmer crossed his arms across his broad chest and raised his eyebrows at Milo.

"Best ram I've got, 'e is. Yer wouldn't want to offer the Gods anything less than the best, would yer?"

"Who said anything about the Gods?" Milo adopted an injured expression. "I've a family of six hungry mouths to feed and we fancy fresh mutton tonight, that's all."

The man smirked at him. "Yes, and I'm Queen Kleopatra. You're 'eading for a temple. Which one is it?"

Milo opened his mouth to protest his innocence, then sighed and gave it up as a bad job.

"Mercury's."

The farmer's face brightened. "Ah, 'e's all right, he is, not like some of 'em. Keeps an eye on 'is people, 'e does. We worship 'im as Lugus down our way. 'Elped you out, did 'e?"

"Yes. In person as far as I can tell."

The farmer's eyebrows nearly hit his scalp and he whistled through his teeth.

"You do need the best! Look, I'll sell you this one, but I'll do you a discount if you add my name in. Just mention Madoc, son of Brennus. 'E'll know who I am," he added, with pride.

Milo envied the man his faith in his God, though he had to admit that he was praying more to Mercury now it seemed that his prayers might be heard.

"I'll do that," he promised and they agreed on a price that was more than fair. Madoc went to put a halter on the ram, which regarded them both with a steady eye.

"'E shouldn't give you any - oh! Would yer look at that? That's a good omen if ever there was one."

The sheep trotted meekly out of the pen and stood next to Milo like a faithful dog.

"I reckon you can keep your rope," Milo said. Madoc beamed.

"Good fortune to you, sir!"

"And to you, Farmer Madoc. I think this is your lucky sheep."

He left the man pointing in excitement, telling the next customer how his animals were favoured by the Gods and walked across the Forum to the Temple of Mercury. It was a smaller building, somewhat squashed between Apollo's grander façade on one side and Juno's on the other. It was probably due for an upgrade, since trade and commerce were the lifeblood of Britannia and her capital city, as more and more new routes were opened up. He could see plenty of market stalls full of exotic goods, all shipped across the Empire in exchange for wool, tin, copper, lead and gold from the mountains. Business was good.

He glanced down. The ram was walking placidly enough but he decided not to push his luck by browsing and nipped round the side to where the Priests were accepting offerings.

For a heart-stopping moment he thought he saw Nuntius in the crowd, but when he looked again it was another Priest. He blinked and told himself to concentrate. The ram let out a low, rumbling bleat.

"Come on, sheep," Milo told him. "At least you seem happy enough with your lot."

He waited in the queue behind a woman with a basket of eggs. When he reached the front, the Priest looked him over, then down at the sheep.

"I wish to offer this sheep to the God Mercury, on behalf of His Majesty's Navy," he said. The Priest nodded, jotting notes on a tablet. "With gratitude for his timely aid. Also, on behalf of Madoc, son of Brennus, worshipper of Lugus, who sold me this sheep at a discount when I told him who it was for."

The Priest looked up and laughed.

"Yes, we know him. Anything else?"

"I would be grateful for any information the God can impart."

The Priest smiled. "Haven't you had enough help? He's done all he can for now, but you can have hope of a fortunate outcome."

Milo was startled, before realising that this was a stock answer. The Priests would select one of many that fitted each petition. He let out his breath and nodded, turning away to let the next person be seen.

"Be careful, Milo."

He swung around. The Priest was staring straight at him, a half-smile on his lips. Then a puzzled expression crossed his face and he shook his head slightly, before returning to his task once more.

*

"Hey, Ferret! Over here!"

Milo spotted his fellow Agent waving from a corner of the crowded tavern. He shouldered his way through the market day crowd and joined him at a table.

"Hello, Dog. What's happening with you then?" He took a good swallow of ale, glad to be off his feet for a while.

His friend Caniculus, or Little Dog, ran a freckled hand through his thinning, sandy hair and adopted his usual lugubrious expression.

"This and that. We broke up another gang last week. I tell you, I'm sick of smugglers."

"They cost the Empire money," Milo pointed out.

"Yes, but I'm sick of freezing my backside off wading through Thamesis mud in the dark. What have you been up to?"

"Burning a corpse and other bits and pieces for Raven."

"Ooh, lovely," Caniculus said. "At least you were warm. Weren't you down Portus way recently?"

"Yes."

"Did you hear? The Lady of Storms turned up just off the harbour and grabbed a load of smoke."

"Really? That's not like her. She's more likely to wreck you than flaunt herself."

"I know! She wasn't happy, one little bit. You won't get me anywhere near a boat for the foreseeable future, not when she's in that sort of mood."

"You hate sailing anyway."

"Too right. Oh, and your favourite watering-hole burned down."

Milo sighed. "I know. They're rebuilding. So, where're you going next?" The ale wasn't bad. Not as good as The Anchor's but decent all the same.

Caniculus shifted in his seat and lowered his voice.

"Palace duty. This new King's not really got his head round ruling yet, if you see what I mean. There's a lot of jostling for favour and his cousin's gathering a crowd of hangers-on."

"Marcus is the heir now," Milo pointed out. "Artorius should be concentrating on marrying some Gallic princess and producing lots of little Pendragons, instead of hunting every hour the Gods send."

Caniculus snorted.

"No sign of that yet. I'm expecting blood on the corridors before too long. What about you?"

"I'm in between jobs," Milo admitted, "but I think they need agents to keep watch on our Northern friends. I'm expecting a call anytime."

"Good luck with that," Caniculus said with a sniff. "You can grow a beard and paint on tattoos to hide that ferrety face of yours."

Milo made a rude gesture at him. "Could be worse, I could look like you."

They both grinned, then Caniculus grew serious again.

"That could all change. Rumour is, the Gods are squaring up for a scrap and that was why *she* was sucking up Potentia."

Wise folk rarely mentioned a deity by name, unless you wanted them to hear you.

"That's bad news, if true. We'll just have to keep our ears open and wait for the collateral damage," he said, tapping his arm where his speechstone was hidden. Like Mages and Priests, the Agents had their own communication network. Caniculus nodded glumly.

"Well, I must be going. I'm due to start my stint hobnobbing with royalty. Enjoy your free time."

"Won't be for long," Milo groused.

Caniculus finished his drink and slipped out, leaving Milo to ponder on the state of the nation. The little statue of Mercury he'd purchased was digging into his hip through his coat pocket. He pulled it out and looked at the figurine thoughtfully.

"What do you know that I don't?"

For once, he was glad there was no reply.

*

The chilly breeze blowing across the harbour was busy reminding everyone that winter was on the way. Maia was glad of its icy touch because that gave her an excuse to wrap up in a hooded cloak that would hide her scars.

She bade a tearful farewell to *Blossom* and the crew that weren't already ashore, including Robin, Heron and Campion, who had saved her life. The Adept had given her strict instructions to keep using his salve and to contact the nearest hospital if she felt unwell.

"Don't forget," he said, sternly.

"As if I could," Maia replied. There had been many times over the past few months when she'd wished that some of her memories would fade. The nightmares were fewer now but still terrifying when they invaded her sleep.

When she arrived at the Academy, Matrona was waiting for her in the vestibule, as she had done nearly three years before. It seemed like a lifetime now, though the statues of the Royal Ships were just as forbidding. She'd had little contact with them through *Blossom* and she averted her eyes as she made her way across the familiar tiled floor.

"Welcome back!" Matrona said warmly. "I've put you in your old room. Do you feel sick at all?"

"A little," Maia admitted. The ground didn't feel quite steady under her feet and even the short journey had left her feeling tired.

"That's to be expected. Landsickness is common after so long on a moving vessel."

Maia followed Matrona down the corridor. The familiar furnishings brought a lump to her throat and she almost expected Tullia to make an entrance, complaining about something or other. She would have returned here before now, after her partnering was completed but she'd never dreamt that she would come back under these circumstances.

"I'll let you settle back in. Branwen's already unpacked your things."

Maia glanced over at her sea chest, standing empty against the wall.

"Do you need anything?"

She shook her head, wearily. "No, thank you. I could do with a rest."

After Matrona had left, Maia sat on the bed and wondered what on earth was to become of her? Before she lay down, she got up and turned the mirror to the wall.

XII

The summons came just over two weeks later. The Navy was tired of waiting and demanded that she travel up to Londin so that they could decide what she was, once and for all.

"I'm not sure that you're well enough," Matrona told her, looking her over.

"I'll manage," Maia said. "I just wish that I had more energy. Every little thing wears me out."

"Hopefully that will pass as you get stronger."

Maia stared at the floor. "It might, I suppose."

Part of her was looking forward to the Navy's final decision so that she could just get on with her life without this constant uncertainty. The other part was dreading that she would be separated from everything and everyone she'd come to depend on. It had been nice to have status and possessions.

Her hand moved automatically to her necklace. It was important to remember that she still had friends.

The next couple of days were taken up with preparations for the trip.

"We'll be stopping at an inn halfway," Matrona said, "and you'll have another night to recover before the actual tests."

Maia nodded.

"I bought you some more clothes for the colder weather," she continued, "including a veil for when you want to go out. Everyone will think that you're an aristocratic lady."

Maia snorted. "As if."

"You might be. Captain Valerius was from a well-respected and noble line."

"*If* we're related. I still don't see why I ended up dumped in the Home."

"It's a mystery for sure," Matrona admitted.

Maia was still wondering about that as their carriage set off in the early morning, leaving Portus behind. She'd ended up with three travelling companions because Branwen had insisted on coming too, to look after them both. Plinius mostly dozed, his hat pulled down over his eyes and arms folded across his chest. Once they were clear of Portus, she amused herself by rolling up the blinds and watching the countryside as they travelled. It looked well- tended, the farmers' fields bare now that the harvest had been gathered in, though the trees blazed with autumn colour. Maia watched everything with great curiosity as she'd never been inland before and it felt strange to be so far from the coast. She was glad when the sun finally appeared and the air became warmer. Plinius woke long enough to unbutton his coat before settling back down again. The three women chatted a little and Maia soon found herself nodding off, lulled into sleep by the swaying carriage.

The journey was uneventful, broken by a night at an inn. Maia had put on her veil and stayed in her room, though the hubbub of voices drifting up from below reminded her of her time at The Anchor. They set off early the next day and the noise and traffic increased steadily as they approached Londin itself. Matrona pulled down the blinds as they entered through the great south-western gate, so Maia only caught a glimpse of the arches as they rumbled through. She hadn't slept much at the inn, despite the place being comfortable enough and had hardly managed to force down food during the day.

"We'll be there shortly," Matrona said, at last. "We have to cross the river first."

"The Thamesis?"

"That's right. There are several bridges now, thank the Gods. There used to be only one and it took forever to get from one side to the other. Captain!"

Plinius opened his eyes.

"Ah, I take it we've almost arrived. I can tell by the stink. They can't build those new underground sewers fast enough for me." He checked his pocket watch. "We've made good time I see. I've arranged to be dropped off at the Club and I'll meet up with you tomorrow morning."

"The Club?" Maia asked.

"Yes. The Royal Naval Officers' Club. It's a place for Captains and senior officers to stay while we're in Londin," he explained. "We get to see our friends and catch up on the news."

"Gossip and drinking, you mean," Matrona said, smiling. "Don't be up all night."

Plinius grinned back. "You have to allow us some pleasures after months at sea."

"Hmm."

The afternoon light was fading when the carriage stopped and the Captain alighted. The coachman helped him down with his bag and they wished him a good evening.

"Indeed! I'm off to the baths," he said, waving them farewell.

"I wish I could go," Maia said as they set off again. It wasn't possible in her condition. A careful wash was the best she could manage.

Branwen and Matrona gave her the sort of looks that she was becoming used to. She hated being an object of sympathy but knew that they meant well. Her first real test would be when she had to meet strangers.

The Navy kept other accommodation for its people when they came to the capital, a large building with everything anyone might need, situated to the rear of the main offices for ease of access. Maia didn't take in most of the details, not only because darkness had fallen but also because she was exhausted. Matrona took one look at her face and hurried her inside. A servant guided them to their quarters for the next few days.

The rooms were sparsely furnished and clearly for only temporary stays. Branwen bustled about, whilst Maia sank down on to the bed, so tired that she could barely keep her eyes open. Gentle hands helped her to undress and she crawled under the covers, heedless of the strange surroundings and the challenges of the morrow.

A few minutes later, the door opened and Matrona came in. Branwen put her finger to her lips and indicated the bed. Matrona beckoned and both women left the sleeping girl, moving to the adjoining room. The older woman's things were already arranged; Branwen would be staying in Maia's room to keep an eye on her should she need anything in the night.

Matrona told Branwen to sit and took another chair for herself. The servant looked at her expectantly.

"Branwen, I need to ask you some questions before tomorrow," Matrona began. "I know you are close to Maia."

She paused for a moment, gathering her thoughts. "Is there anything you've noticed that's out of the ordinary in any way? I need to know now."

Branwen answered without hesitation. "No, Matrona. Only her memory. She never forgets anything. It's like a game. She can read a page of a book, close it and quote it right back at me, word for word. Then I'll make up some nonsense and she remembers that, too. Whole strings of numbers, even."

"Yes, her trick of the mind," Matrona said thoughtfully. "Prodigious, but not uncommon. I once knew a storyteller who could recite the whole of Homer and Virgil, plus some others, though he had some training. No, I mean anything else. Does she talk to people you can't see? Do things move without human agency?"

Branwen shook her head. "No. I'd tell you, honest, ma'am. I haven't seen anything."

"I have to warn you, you might be questioned. Don't be afraid and just say what you've told me."

Branwen's eyes were like saucers. "What do they think she can do?"

"I don't know," Matrona admitted. "We must help her as much as we can. We'll know more in the morning."

"They'd better be kind to her," Branwen said fiercely. "She's been through enough."

"What will be, will be," Matrona told her.

After Branwen had left, she sat for a while, watching the flames dance in the grate, then took out a little portable shrine. She set it up on a table and gently opened the little doors. Inside, instead of a statue, was a tiny twig, polished smooth by years of handling. Matrona took it out reverently and raised it to her forehead.

"Mother," she whispered. "I pray for your guidance."

A sense of calm flooded her body as the ancient Goddess responded. The fresh smell of the deep forest filled the room and her spirit sank into the sacred place, to commune with the deity.

It was late when she returned, her mind full of fear.

*

The next morning, Matrona was up early. She hadn't been able to sleep much after the Mother had given clear warning and she was haunted by the terrible feeling that they were all in over their heads.

In the end, she threw on her clothes and went out into the communal rooms to call for a servant.

"I need you to take a message to Captain Plinius Tertius at the Club," she told him. The man bowed and took the note, promising to be back soon.

There were covered plates of food on an adjoining table, prepared for any who needed it, but her appetite had deserted her. She had been in charge of candidates for over twenty years and thought that she'd seen it all, but this was new. She realised that she was prowling around the room like a stalking tiger and forced herself to be seated to wait for the Captain. If anyone could put this into perspective, Plinius could.

It wasn't long before he appeared, shaved and ready and she wondered that he could have arrived so quickly.

"I was already up," he explained. "I couldn't sleep for some reason."

"Me neither," she said. "I've had a warning."

Plinius' face was grave. "From…?"

"The Mother."

He looked at her with worried eyes.

"There's a lot at stake," she told him. "There are other powers at work and a lot of interference."

"What sort of interference?"

"I have a feeling it concerns the Twelve. We already know that some of them are at loggerheads. She told me to be prepared."

"For what?"

Matrona sighed. "Some sort of trial. I don't know what Maia is caught up in but I do know that it's not of her own making. She's simply a tabula piece to be moved as others will it. I did gather one thing, though."

"What's that?"

"The Goddess is angry that her sphere is being compromised in some way. Trouble's brewing, all right."

"Who would dare obstruct her?"

Matrona lowered her voice. "Some of the Twelve have been meddling in places they shouldn't. We can all see that their power and influence have grown over the past centuries and not everyone's happy about it. They're not the oldest Gods in Britannia, after all."

Plinius raised his eyebrows. "They don't want to annoy *her.*"

"Too late," Matrona said. "In the meantime, prepare yourself. I think-," She broke off suddenly as someone entered the room. The robed figure was unmistakeable.

"Master Mage," the Captain greeted him.

"Good morning to you both," Raven answered. "Up early, I see."

"We both had a bad night."

"I'm not surprised," the Mage replied. "I sense something in the wind. Times of change are always trying. I felt I had to be here today, of all days. I take it Miss Maia is ready to be tested?"

"I think that she should be allowed to recover her strength first," Matrona said. "The journey took a lot out of her."

"It can't wait," Raven said. "I'm involving myself because I want to see this done properly. I also think she deserves recompense for her courage and I mean to see that she gets it."

"Hear, hear," Plinius agreed.

"I'm afraid for her," Matrona told him flatly. "I've lost candidates before, but not like this, hunted and scarred when she shouldn't even have been admitted in the first place. I don't know what to say to her."

"She must see her journey through to the end," Raven said. "Speaking of which, someone's coming."

Sure enough, footsteps heralded the arrival of a messenger, but not a naval one. The slave was dressed in Temple colours. He stopped before them and bowed.

"I bear a message for the Lady Helena Quintilla."

Matrona shot Plinius a look then accepted the message. What did a Temple servant want with her? Her face went white as she read the note.

"Our presence is required at the Temple of Jupiter at ten o'clock. It's signed by Aquila."

Her eyes filled with tears and Plinius leaned over to place a hand on her arm.

"It might not be as bad as it seems, Helena," he said quickly. Matrona gave a short laugh. The hand holding the note shook slightly.

"The Thunderer himself? He doesn't intervene without cause."

"I'm coming with you," Raven announced. "I don't like any of this and I know Aquila of old. He'd better have some answers for us. Personally, I'm sick of all this cloak and dagger stuff."

"The Admirals want to question me at the same time," Plinius said, "or I'd be there to support you. I can at least plead Maia's case."

"Talking of Maia, you'd better get her ready," Raven said. "I know you won't worry her unduly."

"I know my job, Master Mage," Matrona said, stiffly. She'd recovered her usual composure.

He stood and bowed respectfully. "Indeed, ma'am. I meant no offence."

"I'll go and see how she is. Hopefully she slept."

"I'll eat here and wait for you," Plinius offered. She nodded.

"And I'll do likewise," Raven said.

Matrona hurried off to check on Maia.

*

Branwen was bringing Maia a tray, when the young Adept stopped her in the corridor.

"Good morning, ma'am. I believe you are a servant at the Portus Academy?"

"I am," she said, cautiously.

"Excellent!" The young man flashed her a smile and she felt herself colouring. He was rather handsome, with his olive complexion and dark, curly hair. "I've a gift for your patient."

"Oh yes? And you are?"

"Forgive me, I'm Speedwell," the Adept said. "And you must be the beauteous Branwen."

She pursed her lips at him, secretly flattered, but not to be swayed so easily.

"You're a one!"

214

He grinned at her. "A friend of mine said you'd be here. I was given orders to mix up something to help Miss Abella get through the day. I hear that Campion's done a good job healing her."

Branwen relaxed a little at the mention of the *Blossom*'s Adept.

"You know Campion?"

"By reputation. Here's my badge if you don't believe me."

He showed her a gilded medallion with the symbol of the God Aesculapius in relief. She peered at the staff and its snake before nodding.

"You can't be too careful," she told him. "I need to get the Matrona's approval, though."

"Of course," he agreed. "Please, lead the way."

Branwen balanced the tray and rapped quietly on Matrona's door.

"Come in."

"We've a visitor, ma'am."

Matrona had finished washing and dressed with care, wanting to look her best to visit the most important temple in the country. She turned away from the mirror to greet her visitor.

"This is Adept Speedwell. He's brought something for Maia."

"I am Helena Quintilla."

"Ma'am." The Adept bowed. "I've brought Miss Abella a tonic, to give her strength."

"That's most kind of you," Matrona said, once she, too had established his credentials. "Do you need to examine her?"

"No, I won't disturb her," Speedwell said. "As you can see, the bottle is stamped."

The glass bottle did indeed bear the seal of the Adepts.

"Just mix it with water and take it with food," Speedwell told her. "I hope it helps."

"Thank you," Matrona said. She felt as if she should ask more questions, but the thought slipped away from her before she could grasp it. Naturally the Navy would want Maia to be able to undergo her test with confidence.

"Everything's fine," the Adept assured her. Matrona smiled at him, noting his penetrating dark eyes. Such a nice young man and so considerate.

"Of course. I'll give it to her with her breakfast."

"Excellent! Well, I must be off. It was lovely to meet you both."

A blushing Branwen saw him out and was rewarded by another dazzling smile, while Matrona went to see if Maia was awake and to prepare her medicine.

*

Maia had just finished breakfast when she had two visitors.

"Captain!" Her face lit up when she saw Plinius. "I'm so glad you're here!"

"Good morning, Maia. Did you sleep well?"

"Yes, thank you." Behind him, the wizened Master Mage raised a hand in greeting.

"Master Mage Raven," she said, politely.

"Hah. I can see who the favoured one is in this room," Raven said, grinning like a death's head.

"Very funny," Plinius told him and Maia realised that the Master Mage just had a very dry sense of humour. She rolled her eyes at the Captain, who winked.

"I am indeed the favoured one," he said. "Now, Maia, I have some news for you. You aren't going to be tested here, but at the new Temple of Jupiter. They probably have more skilled Adepts there," he forestalled her, as she opened her mouth to question him. "It's an amazing building, so you'll get to see something of the capital after all. Raven and Matrona will be going with you."

"Not you?" Maia asked, disappointment on her face.

"Alas, not. I'm to report to the Navy Board this morning," he said. "On the plus side, everything should be cleared up by lunch time, for you at least. My meeting might take a little longer."

"Can't be helped, I suppose," Maia said. "Is it far to the Temple?"

"No, but you'll need a carriage. The old Temple's just across the Forum but it got too small so they're building this one. Ten years and it's still not finished, believe it or not. It's set to rival the one in Roma."

Raven harrumphed. "I prefer oak groves. More sincere."

"Will I see you later?" Maia asked.

"Oh yes. We can meet up and compare notes before planning your future," Plinius told her. "No more uncertainty, eh?"

She nodded.

"Well, I must be off. Wish me luck."

"Luck!"

He smiled at her and set off.

Maia expected that Raven would leave too, but the ancient Mage remained where he was.

"I wanted to say something to you in private," he began in his whispery voice. "I understand the pain that you feel. I wasn't always as you see me now."

She frowned, puzzled. "I'm not sure what you mean, sir."

In answer, his hands went to the collar of his robes and he parted them just enough for her to glimpse what lay beneath.

His neck and chest were reamed with deep channels that looked as if molten metal had been poured over the skin, eating it away as it ran. She tried to suppress her gasp but knew he'd heard it nonetheless.

"As you can see, I have had my fair share of torment."

"You were burned too," she said, quietly.

He nodded, refastening his robe.

"Yes, but not by fire, as you were. The effect, however is similar and I assure you, just as agonising. I wanted you to know that you are not alone and that you have as much protection as I can offer."

Maia was touched. Despite her initial reservations about the Mage, he really did seem to be concerned for her welfare.

"I'm sorry you had to suffer that," she said. "Thank you."

She looked into his clouded blue eyes and knew that he would not break his word. If he could help her, he would.

*

It wasn't a long journey to the Temple of Jupiter. The huge complex dominated the waterfront, with entrances from the town at the front and the river at the rear. The great triangular pediment towered over all the other buildings in the city, larger even than the palace and making it abundantly clear that the Ruler of Olympus was the most important and feared God in the Empire.

217

Maia alighted from the carriage, tilting her head back to stare up at the painted and gilded columns that towered above her. It was truly massive and already famous. Britannia was up and coming and wanted everyone to know it.

She shut her eyes hastily, suddenly feeling that the tons of marble were about to topple and crash down on her head. Crowds of people were already thronging around the entrance and she was glad of the gauzy veil Matrona had provided for her.

"Big, isn't it?" Raven sniffed. He didn't sound impressed. "Come on. It'll take us long enough to climb all these dratted steps."

Matrona gathered her skirts with one hand and took Maia's arm with the other.

"Do you think you can manage?" she asked anxiously.

"Oh yes, thank you. I feel much better today," Maia said. It was true. She did feel better for a good night's sleep. Even her burns weren't hurting anything like they normally did, in fact, she could almost forget they were there.

"Good," Matrona said. She thought of mentioning the Adept's visit to Raven, but again the notion melted away like ice in summer.

They proceeded up the wide steps and went in through the enormous panelled doors. The temple was dark and smelt of smoke and incense, under laid with burnt offerings from that day's sacrifices. It was already full of worshippers of both sexes and all stations, who were presumably here to petition the God for Divine favour.

Beside her, Maia heard Matrona gasp as the statue of Jupiter came into view. Its head almost touched the ceiling, lit by artfully placed clerestory windows that allowed the daylight to pour through. The shafts illuminated the golden hair and jewelled eyes, inlaid into the finest ivory from Africa. It must have cost a fortune. Temple staff, in their white woollen robes, were stationed here and there to marshal and direct the worshippers. Their small party was soon spotted by a short, harried looking man who threaded his way through the queues towards them.

"Mage Raven, Lady Helena, greetings! The Pontifex is expecting you. Please come with me." His brown eyes flicked towards Maia, but other than that he made no acknowledgement of her presence.

They were escorted to the front of the queue, through fragrant, cloying clouds of scent-laden smoke. The only sounds were the muted chanting of prayers and petitions, wafted upwards by the perfume to the Divine ears.

Their guide took them to a burning brazier, where each of them offered up a pinch of incense in worship, as was customary, then they left by a small side door. Another set of steps ran alongside the side of the massive building and led to a wide-open space.

"We're heading to the administrative buildings," their guide explained. "That is where business is conducted and the Priests are housed."

"It's like a town in itself," Matrona commented.

"Probably bigger than some," the man agreed.

More steps took them into an atrium that reminded Maia of the one in the Admiralty office in Portus, though instead of naval themes the walls were covered with elaborate mosaics showing scenes from the lives of the Gods. Jupiter was there again with his thunderbolt poised to threaten enemies, or receiving the tribute of the Empire. In one, he was the bull carrying away Europa on his back with the maiden clutching at his horns for balance. He'd certainly fallen for a lot of mortal women, Maia reflected. Half the Empire could probably claim descent from him, though the demi-gods and heroes of old were long gone now.

Maia concentrated on her breathing and looked straight ahead, ignoring Matrona's concerned glances in her direction.

Their escort took them along a corridor, before knocking at a door and stepping aside to allow them in. To her surprise, the room they entered was less of an office and more like a lounge with small tables and couches, whose opulent upholstery and delicately carved armrests displayed the wealth of the temple. There were dishes of sweets and savouries as well as glass decanters of wine and goblets set upon silver trays. The man and woman who glided forward to greet them were a Priest and Priestess of the highest rank. Both were clad in fine woollen robes and bore themselves with the assurance that came from an aristocratic upbringing.

"Master Mage, good to see you again." The man spoke first, extending his arm to clasp the other man's in greeting, adding, "Lady Helena. And this must be Maia Abella."

His voice was deep, rich and resonant, a real public speaker, Maia thought. He was of middle height but broad with it to the point of corpulence, his fine robes hanging round him like a tent. She was just about to dismiss him as yet another over-indulgent Priest, until he turned to her and she met the force of his regard.

Green eyes, rimmed with golden flecks bored into her like gimlets through wood, sharp and quite at odds with his outer appearance. She felt a sudden shock, as if needles were being inserted under her skin and recoiled instinctively.

The woman was older than he, her curly grey hair gathered back and crowned with a tiara from which a fine woven veil fell down her back. Her brown eyes crinkled at the edges as she turned to Maia, stepping forward to take her hand.

"I am Vibia Laelia, High Priestess of Juno. Do come and sit down. Would you like something to drink?"

They demurred and, at her gesture, took seats around one of the tables. Maia was aware of the High Priest's continuing stare as he scrutinised her every movement.

I've fought off worse than you, she thought, sourly. *You're not even undead.*

"So, Miss Abella. I am Gnaeus Proculus Aquila, High Priest of Jupiter here in Britannia. I understand that this is your first visit to Londin," Aquila began.

"It is, sir," Maia replied.

"Hmm. You've caused quite a stir lately. I understand that the past returned in a most unpleasant fashion."

Maia didn't know what to say to that, but Vibia spoke instead.

"We know about the recent…events. What remains to be seen is where you fit into all this. It is for that reason that you have been brought here, so that we may ascertain your origins and how they bear on the situation. It is vital to know the wishes of the Gods. Do they desire you to continue in the Navy, or move elsewhere?"

Maia found her voice. "I have no Potentia."

"We shall see," Vibia said, not unkindly. "The Gods have yet to speak. Until they do, or do not, we have called for an Adept to do some basic scientific tests. He should be here shortly. Master Mage, I understand that you detected no Potentia?"

"That is correct," Raven said. "I hope that this meeting will give us clarity once and for all."

"That is our hope, too," Vibia agreed.

"What sort of tests have you arranged?" Matrona asked, curiously.

"A paternity test and another for Divine heritage, just to confirm your findings, Raven," Aquila answered. "I can't pretend to understand the process, but they have it down to a fine art. Ah, the wonders of modern science!"

So that was how imposters were weeded out. Ever since Jupiter's ban on demi-gods, there had been those who claimed a Divine parent in order to advance their cause. Unless they could be proved insane, their journeys ended not in Olympus but on the bloody sands of the arena. Maia didn't believe Aquila's claim that he knew nothing about it; here was a man who would take great pains to learn everything he could that could affect the relationship between humans and the Gods.

"I'm sure that this will all be sorted out quickly," he said to her, smiling patronizingly.

She regarded him from under her veil, then made a decision, lifting it away from her face and over her head. To Aquila's credit, his face registered nothing but politeness, though he blinked a little more rapidly.

"Don't be alarmed, my dear," Vibia assured her. "The test is routine in these cases. I myself am descended from Juno through her son, Mars, though of course that was many generations back. Aquila here has the blood of Jupiter in his veins, which is why he is able to communicate with the God."

Matrona looked suitably impressed, though Maia thought privately that Aquila looked like any other man, only fatter. Their Divine heritage must just give them enough Potentia to mediate and possibly some other abilities as well, but if Aquila had been very skilled in magic the Collegium would have taken him.

Maia was spared any further conversation by a quiet rap on the door.

"Ah, this must be the Adept," Aquila said. "Come!"

The door opened to admit a tall man wearing the blue robes of a scientist-healer. His hat was tucked under his arm, allowing the light to glint off his bald head which shone a rich brown like a glossy conker. A ginger-haired youth followed him in, carrying a medium sized chest with a domed lid.

"My Lords, Ladies," he bowed. "I am Juniper, at your service. I understand that you have called for tests?"

"Indeed we have, Adept Juniper."

Juniper signalled to his companion, who placed the chest on the floor, unlocked the lid and began to unpack the contents carefully.

"My apprentice will prepare the equipment," Juniper explained. The youth kept his head down and Maia watched with interest as he removed piece after piece, placing them on a nearby empty table. There was a shallow glass bowl, several vials and jars and two strange devices the like of which she had never seen. One was all tiny wheels and polished metal that rested on a stand, the other some sort of box with an eyepiece on top.

"This young woman is the subject," Aquila said. "Please proceed."

The Adept turned to Maia, his expression unchanging and Maia once again felt like an object laid out before him to be studied.

"I will need blood and hair," Juniper told her, signalling to his apprentice. "Parsley, the scalpel, a vial and a slide, if you please."

Parsley hurried to do his master's bidding. Juniper took the metal blade in one hand and a small vial in the other and approached Maia.

"I just need a little blood from your finger," he told her, his brown eyes regarding her dispassionately. "I hope you aren't squeamish."

"Not at all," Maia said, briskly. She offered her left forefinger and he examined it carefully.

"Hmm. Extensive trauma," he remarked clinically, making her feel more like a specimen than ever. He took a scalpel and carefully made a little cut.

Bright red drops welled from the nick, which the Adept caught deftly in a little vial. One further drop was then transferred to the centre of a small rectangle of clear glass. He hurried over to the first contraption, discarding the scalpel into a jar and placed more glass on top of the one holding her blood.

Parsley appeared at her side and deftly bandaged her cut finger. She smiled her thanks, then turned her attention back to where Juniper was adjusting the machine.

"First, for the paternity test," he said in his dry voice. "We have obtained a sample from the last of the Valerius line to compare with the one from the subject."

He opened a flap in the machine and uncorked a small vial, pouring in a few drops of what was presumably blood. He checked through the eyepiece and nodded.

"Now for the young lady's."

He poured hers into another slot and peered intently into the device. Maia could feel her heart beating in time with the throbbing in her finger. She hoped it wouldn't take too long.

After what felt like an age, the Adept straightened.

"It is a match," he announced. "The young lady is of the Valerius line through her father."

Beside her, Matrona gasped with relief and Maia let out the breath she'd been holding. She had a family name after all.

"Congratulations!" Vibia said. "I am very pleased for you, my dear." Even Aquila seemed satisfied and Raven nodded his head as if unsurprised. She could call herself Maia Valeria now, she supposed. Was a house in the country and a large bag of money too much to hope for? She hoped that this heir, whoever he was, hadn't spent it all. She could feel herself relaxing as her confidence grew.

Meanwhile, Juniper was bent over the other device. He slid the glass into a space underneath and peered through what she saw was an eyepiece, while fiddling with the little wheels at the side.

"That's a microscope," Raven whispered to her. "They magnify things. A chap I know demonstrated one at a dinner party. You wouldn't believe what lives in a drop of water, so take my advice and stick to wine."

So that's what he's doing, Maia thought. He's checking the composition of my blood. The Divine markers must show up somehow. She wondered what they might look like and how he could tell, but that would be a Mystery known only to Adepts.

Everyone waited for the inevitable negative result. Juniper looked, adjusted the microscope once more, raised his head and then bent to the eyepiece again as if checking his observations. Was it her imagination, or had he turned slightly paler?

After what felt like an hour, but was in reality only a few minutes, the Adept seemed to have come to a conclusion, though he appeared uncertain.

"Lord Aquila, Lady Vibia, I would beg a word in private if I may."

"Has something gone wrong with the test?" Raven queried. Juniper looked apologetic.

"I must beg your indulgence, sir," he said, not looking directly at the Master Mage. The Adept's smooth pate was definitely shinier than it had been. Something had him severely rattled.

"Please excuse us for a moment." Aquila glanced briefly at Maia and she felt his equilibrium falter. He swept from the room followed by Vibia, who looked as puzzled as her fellow Priest. She gave Maia a slight shrug of her shoulders as she passed. Juniper hastened to follow them and the door shut with a click, leaving Raven, Matrona, Maia and the dumbfounded Parsley staring after them.

"What in Hades is all this about?" Matrona said, to the air. She rounded on the unfortunate apprentice. "You there, Parsley. Do you know what's going on?"

Parsley, who looked to be about fourteen and still had some of his boyhood chubbiness, looked puzzled.

"Don't know, ma'am. Never seen 'im like that." His broad accent told of northern birth, somewhere up in Brigantia. "Whatever it is, it's got 'im worried." He studied Maia with great speculation.

"It's something he's seen, isn't it?" Raven said. He eyed the microscope warily. "Do you know what it might be?"

The young Adept was clearly weighing up the perils of keeping silent against the obvious authority of the Master Mage.

"I could 'ave a quick check sir. Just to see if the instrument is workin'."

224

He listened for a moment, but no sounds disturbed the peace. Emboldened, the youngster scuttled over to the microscope and peered in, turning the little wheel as his master had done. He whistled softly.

"Bloody 'ell. That ain't normal."

"What isn't?" Matrona demanded.

Parsley opened his mouth to reply, just as rapid footsteps echoed from the corridor outside. He leapt aside like a startled colt and assumed an air of innocence as Aquila, Vibia and Juniper returned. Aquila immediately poured himself a large glass of wine. Vibia declined, seating herself back next to Maia and looking shaken. Juniper was openly sweating now, his gaze fixed on the Priest before remembering Parsley's presence.

"Boy. Out now." His apprentice wasted no time in showing a clean pair of heels.

"We have the results," Aquila announced, having downed most of the wine. "I would recommend that you leave too, Lady Helena."

"I'd rather stay, if it is permitted," Matrona replied. Maia shot her a look of gratitude.

"It is best that you leave, for your own safety," Aquila repeated, fixing her with his unsettling eyes. Matrona swallowed, before carefully embracing Maia and exiting. Maia watched her go, feeling sick with fear.

"I have verified it with a divining glass that answers yes or no," the High Priest continued. He took a deep breath and this time, when he looked at Maia there was no smugness or condescension. She saw instead respect and not a little fear.

"Miss Abella…you are of Divine parentage. Directly."

"Directly?" Raven asked, startled. "You mean…her mother?"

Aquila swallowed visibly. "Yes."

The word hung in the room and Maia felt her insides drop away in horror. Her mother? That meant that she had defied Jupiter's decree and had gone beyond a mere dalliance. She had had a half-Divine child. She glanced upwards, expecting at any second a bolt of lightning to come smashing through the temple roof and down on her forbidden head.

"This can't be right," Raven insisted. "I felt for her Potentia and she has none."

"It can't be accessed," Juniper clarified. "It has been occluded, blocked somehow. However, the markers remain. I stand by my findings."

Raven looked as though he was about to argue, but Aquila held up a hand.

"The Gods don't lie, Master Mage. What was hidden from you is not hidden from them and they have spoken."

Raven reluctantly subsided, his mouth a hard line.

Maia remained, paralyzed with fear. She had just been handed a death sentence.

"There is another test," Aquila said into the shocked silence. "We don't know which Goddess is responsible. It may help if we knew."

Maia looked dumbly at Vibia and was shocked to see tears pouring silently down her face.

"I'm so sorry, Maia," she whispered, "but we've nothing to lose now and it's better that we know. At least," she added, "we know that there are powers friendly to you. It isn't perhaps as clear cut as it might seem."

"Possibly," Aquila agreed. "Juniper, do the test."

This time, the Adept had to get his own equipment. He left the microscope alone, going to the bowl and uncorking a vial of some silvery substance over it that poured like thick treacle until the shallow base was coated.

"Lady, I shall need some of your hair," he said. She saw the fear in his eyes as he waited, unwilling now to approach her so readily. She took pity on him and pulled out a few strands. He took them gently, almost reverently and dropped them into the substance. They floated on the surface for a few seconds, before sinking down and disappearing. The mixture began to bubble and froth, then abruptly a miniature whirlwind rose from the bowl, spiralling rapidly upwards. Gusts of air burst forth from it, rippling invisibly through the room before dissipating and falling back into the bowl, causing the liquid to become inert once more.

Maia looked on numbly. It must mean something, but she didn't know what. Aquila and Vibia must be able to interpret what they had seen.

"Aura," Vibia said, her lined face bleak. "So that was her crime."

"What do you mean?" Raven asked. The old Priestess sighed. "Jupiter banished her from Olympus. We all thought that it was because of her feud with Diana. They used to be boon companions until Aura made some disparaging remarks – or so it was said. It seems instead that she took a lover and the virgin Goddess would never stand for that."

"We must consult with the Gods." Aquila shot Maia a look of pity. "It is in their hands now. Thank you, Juniper."

Dismissed, the Adept bowed and left, not bothering to gather his paraphernalia.

"I take it we can rely on his discretion?" Raven asked.

"Absolutely," Aquila answered firmly.

After a moment both Aquila and the Priestess began the summoning, eyes closed in prayer. Slowly, the silence in the room grew thick and heavy with unseen presences. Maia felt the hair on the back of her neck prickle in warning as the Divine approached closer. Time itself seemed to slow as the attention of the Gods moved over her like a heavy weight, pinning her like an insect beneath their scrutiny and their examination of her very being. Raven sat rigid beside her, his blind eyes focused on something she couldn't see. Abruptly, Aquila jerked once and Vibia slumped forwards, breathing heavily.

"So Maia Valeria, you are training to become a Ship." The voice was coming from Aquila's mouth but it was subtly different, even deeper with a low rumble that reminded her of faraway thunder. She looked at the Priest, only to see that his irises were completely golden. They were not the eyes of a human and she shuddered.

"Yes," she whispered, her mouth dry.

"That was my son's doing. He has been active on your behalf, both because of your mother's pleading and to spite my daughter."

Maia remembered the Priest, Nuntius. He had spoken for her when no-one else had. The God must be referring to Mercury.

"My wife, Juno, has also spoken up for you," Jupiter continued, every word dropping like lead into the charged atmosphere. "And your Aunt Cymopoleia is threatening violence. It seems to me that the easiest way to resolve this matter is to remove you from the board entirely."

Raven's hoarse voice broke into the heavy thrum of the Olympian's Potentia.

"Why not remove her by permitting her to offer a life in service?"

Aquila's head turned towards Raven, the slow movement reminding her of a Ship. The God stared at him through his Priest's eyes and Raven bore the gaze calmly, his blindness an asset for once.

"She has shown herself willing to die to protect others," the Mage persisted.

"Ah, Raven. Still going, I see." Aquila's fleshy lips peeled back from his teeth in a terrible smile.

"Yes, Lord. I'm still here."

"It's an option," Jupiter said, considering his suggestion. "She would be confined and controlled. What do you say, Maia Valeria?"

Maia stared at the possessed Priest. Her skin crawled, her scars contracting painfully.

"I have no Potentia," she managed to croak.

"You have what I say you have," the God replied, "and I say you have enough for this. Plus more than you bargained for, courtesy of the *Livia*. If you wish, I can end your earthly journey now. Your choice."

"I'll be a Ship," Maia managed to stammer. *Some choice.*

"Very well, though my daughter may not be finished with you. She still seeks to torment your mother. Be warned. I look forward to seeing how you fare."

"My mother?"

"Aura is forbidden to contact or aid you. Your sister has already been punished for helping you. She, too, is brave, so I will permit limited contact. It may be to my advantage."

Sister? Maia felt her eyes start from her head. The golden eyes flashed once.

"Bear witness to my decree! Your father has paid for his crime and I have taken into account the punishment that has already been meted out to your mother. I could not have devised a worse one."

Aquila's features stretched into another smile, merciless and without pity. "You will be useful to your King and Country, Maia

228

Valeria. Be comforted in the fact that you are not without supporters, but I would urge caution. Success or failure will depend on your actions but this matter must remain private. Those who flaunt my laws will suffer!"

Maia could only stare, transfixed in the God's grip, until gradually the gold in the Priest's eyes became mere flecks and the Presence departed.

Aquila's gasps woke her from her trance-like state. Maia felt like she did when returning to her body after being with *Blossom*, but this time, instead of the smooth transition, it was as if she had been pulled out of herself then thrust back again any old how. She wriggled to get her blood moving again, but her head ached and her insides still felt weak after the Divine encounter.

It was no wonder that people went mad. Aquila and Vibia must be stronger than they appeared to suffer this contact on a regular basis. She wondered whether all Gods were the same or whether some might be easier to tolerate, perhaps the ones that had only one Divine parent. Like her, she thought with a shock. Still, Aura, Goddess of the breeze, wasn't one of the Twelve but a lesser, older deity, held especially dear by Ships and sailors. There had to be a difference. Then there was the question of her other family. An aunt and a sister?

Aquila had come to his senses and started in on the wine again. Vibia poured one for Raven, who accepted it gratefully and two more, one for herself and another for Maia.

"So," Aquila said finally. "Jupiter has spoken." Maia had thought his voice rich, but that was before the God had possessed him. "Are you content with his judgement?"

A strange thing to ask, she thought. It was definitely preferable to being blasted out of existence.

"Yes, sir, I am," she replied, realising with a sudden spurt of relief that she could return to her training and everything she had come to love. Captain Plinius and *Blossom* would be so pleased and her damaged body wouldn't be able to hold her back.

"I had a Sending from the Goddess as well," Vibia said quietly. "She is somewhat subtler than her spouse when she chooses to be."

Every ear pricked up. Juno, Queen of the Gods, Hera to the Greeks, was a mighty deity in her own right.

"She favours your cause, Maia. As the Goddess of marriage, she has some sympathy for your mother, though of course she could not condone the breaking of her husband's decree. She told me that your parents were married and that you are legitimate in the eyes of the Gods, so, for that reason, she could plead with Jupiter on your behalf. She also urges you to be cautious and not to reveal your inheritance, lest those you love be put in danger."

"But why did the *Livia* claim me as her daughter?" Maia asked. There were still so many missing pieces. Vibia concentrated for a moment.

"She was driven to madness, wanting what she could never have. She became obsessed with Valerius, but his heart was already elsewhere. The Goddess was watching as your mother and father married in the Temple at Portus, which set off the subsequent tragic events. It was done in secret but the truth leaked straight to his Ship."

"The *Livia* killed her Captain," Maia said, beginning to grasp the truth.

"Yes. The seed of insanity was planted within her already. It was nurtured and used to murder. Captain Valerius had to die for his transgression, even if he wasn't aware that he had married a Goddess. I sense the hand of another." She approached Maia, leaning in close to whisper.

"Beware the Huntress. She is easily angered and never relinquishes her prey." Louder she said, "Be thankful that you have been given a chance to show loyalty. All praise to the Gods, who in their wisdom have permitted you to serve them."

"All praise!" the others answered. Aquila still looked stunned as he rose to leave, hauling himself to his feet with a visible effort.

"I will rest now. Good luck, Maia. I look forward to hearing of your naval exploits. May Jupiter grant you strength and Minerva, wisdom."

"Thank you," Maia replied and meant it. The Priest paid the price for his privilege and authority every day and now she was beginning to appreciate that she would too. Nothing of worth came without cost.

Now was the time for her to repay her friends for the faith they had in her and to justify Jupiter's leniency.

She would have to become a Ship or die trying.

Epilogue

Silence, cold and loneliness. She lay in the deep darkness of her cave, only waking when her lair was disturbed by some unwary creature that stumbled into her underground home.

Constant hunger spurred her to feed, savouring the warmth and vitality that gave her the energy she craved. Only then could she patrol her boundaries, every inch of the surface a familiar path worn smooth through countless centuries by the movement of her body across the slowly yielding rock.

But it was never enough.

She slept once more, only the faintest rise of her breast showing that she was living and not some nightmare carving brought forth by an insane mind.

Suddenly, her senses flared to life. Something was approaching. At its core was a fire that called to her, waking her instincts and alerting her to the prey. Her eyes opened and she stirred, ready to stalk and strike, aching for the kill and the long, slow ecstasy of feeding.

"Hold!"

The voice compelled her and she writhed, frustrated. This was no ordinary meal. The fire grew brighter and she reared away from the sudden glare.

"I come to strike a bargain with you."

She squinted to see through the light. A female voice, a female shape, tall and slim. Human? No. The fire at its core was no mortal spirit, though she tasted a brief sweetness that spoke of human flesh before it vanished into a blaze that burned like the sun.

"What do you want with me?"

Her rasping voice, unheard for aeons, echoed off the rocky walls.

"We can help each other. You do something for me and I shall return the favour."

She drew a little closer, her heavy body scraping across her sandy bed.

"Nobody comes here anymore. My lovers are dust and my children have forgotten me. My beautiful children!"

"I haven't forgotten you."

"I know you," she spat. *"Spawn of Olympus! What can you do for me?"*

"You hunger."

"I always hunger. I am hunger."

"And I will help you assuage it. Kill for me. A mortal female."

"One human?" She was disgusted. *"I have devoured thousands! Is that all you can offer?"*

"No. After you do my bidding, I promise that I will not confine you again. Think of it! New lovers. More children, perhaps?"

She felt her hopes rise at the thought. No more crawling in the dark, hiding and existing on scraps. She would feed and feed and be replete at last, ready to give birth once again.

"I agree."

"So, Mother of Monsters, we have a bargain. I shall return for you soon."

The light faded and she settled down to wait, anticipating the feast to come.

Maia, Milo and Raven will return in 'Prey of the Huntress'

coming spring 2021

Hail, O Mighty Reader!
Don't worry, I'm not going to sacrifice a goat or anything, but I'd like to thank you very much for choosing this book. If you enjoyed it, I would be eternally grateful if you could **leave a review on Amazon**. *It doesn't have to be long – a couple of lines would be enough and really give me a boost as an independent author. It will also help me to reach more readers and keep the Ships sailing onward!*

Please check out my website **emkkoulla.com** *and my page on* **Facebook**, *where you can sign up to my mailing list to receive an* **exclusive novella, 'Son of the Sea', monthly newsletters** *and advance warning of future publications. I also warmly welcome any comments or feedback.*

About the Author

E. M. Kkoulla lives with her husband and two feline overlords in the Calder Valley, West Yorkshire. After many years of teaching very small children, she decided to finally put her degree in Classical Studies, along with decades of re-enacting 16th and 17th century life, to constructive use. Her hobbies include singing in various choirs, walking in the hills and watching anything with gods, superheroes and monsters trashing the landscape.

This is her first published novel.

Acknowledgements

I would like to thank all those who encouraged me along the way, especially my friend, Jane Powell. She was the first to encounter Maia, Milo and the rest and gave me the impetus to do something with them by demanding that I write more chapters immediately. Natalia Richards, whose books *'The Falcon's Rise'* and *'The Falcon's Flight'* are wonderful historical novels about Anne Boleyn's early life. Your advice and support are warmly appreciated, Natalia and I can't wait for *'The Falcon's Fall.'*

L. M. Affrossman, author of *'Simon's Wife'* and *'Herod'* who kindly lent me some of her beta readers. It was a good job, too, as their suggestions made me re-write my draft immediately, several times. You saved me, good people!

My friends Bob and Madeleine, up in Glasgow. David Gaughran for all his free online self-publishing resources and for answering my plaintive queries quickly and courteously.

Claire Rushbrook, my copy editor and all the helpful people at Reedsy, as well as David Morrison and Tracy Clark of Publish Nation, who turned this dream into reality.

Neil Barney, my eagle-eyed proofreader – thank you for your invaluable comments and feedback.

Thea Nicolescu, my amazing cover designer, who brought me face-to-face with Maia for the first time.

My husband, Stephen, who's been wondering what I've been doing closeted away for months on end.

And, last of all, to the magnificent Ray Harryhausen, who brought the mythology to life. I still have a thing about skeletons.